MOUNTING THE WHALE

by Colleen McCarty

ACT I

CHAPTER ONE

Carlyle felt the phone buzzing at her side, but her gaze was focused on the digital image inside the framed box on the back of the large panning camera. Even though Cybil was standing on the stage only fifteen feet away, Carlyle was more concerned with how her image was being displayed than with what was actually occurring in front of her.

"The most important thing to remember is that you've got to go all in," Cybil was saying. "When I was sitting at the table at the World Series of Poker, I suddenly saw how all the parts of the game relate to business. If you're on the fence about starting your own company, or you're on the fence about hiring people, or even if you're on the fence about falling in love, remember these three words: Go. All. In." *Good one, Mom,* Carlyle thought. Her mother certainly knew just when to insert emphatic pauses so the audience hung on her every word.

Cybil was trim and professional and her voice was sure. She had been on stage for years promoting Naturebar, so she was a pro at public speaking. When she decided to launch her personal brand of entrepreneurial self-help, she used her platform as a successful female CEO to springboard herself into the market. Though there had been repeated national marketing efforts, her books really only took off in and around Omaha, where a healthy hometown hero complex made her feel as if her success was global.

The same old catchphrases were being thrown around—"You are your own shareholder" and "Don't lose sight of the end goal—soulful

sales!"—peppered with snippets from the new book: "If you don't believe you have a winning hand, you've already lost" and "Your poker
face is only as good as your bluff."

The crowd erupted in applause as the host of the show, a bubbly wom-
an with hair the texture of cotton candy, beamed a smile back at them.
The set gleamed with staged precision. The green screen read, "Good
Morning, Omaha."

"Isn't she wonderful? We're so lucky to have the CEO of Naturebar
right here in our little nook of the world. We're going to take a break
now, but when we come back we'll find out what wonderful surprises
Cybil has in store for our studio audience!"

The cameraman counted down and the image on his screen revealed the now overly-ordinary looking couch in front of a green
screen. Carlyle looked down at her phone for the first time. What felt
like a balloon inflating in her stomach was what she vaguely recognized as hope. She had hoped that the gentle buzzing was Ethan, and
said hope was blooming rapidly.

Her little hope-balloon popped violently when she saw the message.
Cartel got me. Tell mom

She read it again to make sure this wasn't a stress-induced hal-
lucination. There had been an awful lot going on in recent weeks—
launching two new flavors, prepping for the new book release, Ethan
moving out—all of these things combined could have finally pushed
her over the edge. *Cartel got me. Tell mom*

Her eyes searched the crowd for her sister Valerie. It wasn't hard to
find her; Valerie had been screaming the loudest, and clapping the most
furiously. Carlyle thought it apt that she'd been tasked with the role of
hype-woman today, as she served this general purpose in their mother's life regardless of the presence of a studio audience. "Isn't Mom's
Thanksgiving dinner the best?" "Aren't her mashed potatoes to die
for?" "Didn't Mom do a great job on that presentation?" "Mom's the
best!" Her enthusiasm could be exhausting.

When their eyes met, Valerie's expression turned to one of panic,
as she gestured frantically toward her phone. She'd gotten the message too.

Carlyle looked down at her phone and opened up the message. The unknown number was in the 6-1-5 area code—San Jose, California. She didn't need to google it to know. This was the area code her other sister, Janine, had been floating around in recently. She distinctly remembered that Janine's phone number—the one she'd deleted from her phone months before—had begun with 6-1-5.

People were beginning to take their places again and the cameraman resumed his silent counting. The show was coming back, and for a moment Carlyle hesitated. She wasn't sure if she should interrupt the broadcast to let her mother know what she'd just received.

"Well, in honor of my new book," she heard Cybil saying, "I've given each member of the audience a copy of *Go All In: How Your Life and Business is a Poker Game, and How You Can Walk Away With All the Chips*. Also, as an added bonus I'm giving everyone a sample of our newest Naturebar—White Chocolate Walnut Crisp!"

Anyone watching could see that her mother genuinely cared for the people in the audience, as she generously shared her knowledge. And Carlyle saw the people of Omaha eating up every bit of it, crisp and all. No one had to know that Cybil Millicent Pierce had paid $250,000 just for a seat at the table at the World Series of Poker, or that she was the first one out of the tournament.

Carlyle looked at the clock on her cell phone. The show was wrapping up, and there was no sense causing a panic in the studio. She needed to wait until her mother was alone to tell her about the text she'd just received. *The company could suffer from any negative exposure*, she thought. She immediately hated herself for having to be the person who thought of such things.

People were beginning to herd towards the book-signing table. She saw her mother being ushered backstage and headed in that direction. She felt a firm but familiar hand on her shoulder.

"I'm assuming you saw this?" Valerie said breathlessly.

"Yeah, I guess we both got the same message. Do you think that means Tom got it too?"

"I think he probably did. If we don't tell Mom soon, then he will call her all frantic. We need to get to her before she checks her phone. If

Tom gets through to her first then he'll get her all worked up. We can soften the blow." Valerie was right. Their younger brother had a less-than-calming effect on their mother. But this was also true to Valerie's mission in life—being the supreme giver of information in a way that protected and propped their mother up.

"Let me call Marius and see if there's any more information he can find before we tell her." Marius was Cybil and Carlyle's effervescent personal assistant. They shared him equally, and if anyone had gotten any other forms of communication from Janine—or her supposed captors—it would've been him.

Carlyle saw her mother emerge and head to the book-signing table. Her "fans" clutched their free copies and waited in turn to get personalized advice from Omaha's only self-help guru and female CEO. "Go help her," Carlyle said to Valerie. "And keep her off of her phone."

Valerie scurried away as Carlyle hit the first number under her speed dial.

"Hey boss," Marius' high voice sang.

"Hey, we've got a situation," Carlyle said.

"Oh no, what happened? Did Bessie charge the stage again?" Marius was partly kidding. The mascot of Good Morning Omaha, a lovable dairy cow named Bessie, had been known to lose her shit if she wasn't given her Prozac milkshake.

"No, we're good there, the show went great. Mom's signing books now."

"Oh good. So what's up?"

"About ten minutes ago I got a text. It's from a 6-1-5 number and it says, 'Cartel got me. Tell mom.' Have you heard anything about this? I'm starting to get freaked out."

"Oh shit." Marius' normally cheerful voice fell five octaves.

"What is it?"

"I thought it was spam. I swear it just seemed like one of those crazy spam emails. *Mr. Chang wants you to know there is a million dollars in your bank account tomorrow if you help him get out of Shanghai… You have inherited a large sum of money from an African prince…* I always open them, because I think they're hilarious, but then I just sent it to the trash."

"Marius, slow down. What are you talking about?"

"It even had typos and everything. I just marked it as spam."

"You marked what as spam? What are you talking about?"

Marius began to sob. "Oh god. I'm so fired, aren't I? Ok, yesterday I got an email in Cybil's inbox. You know I flag everything that's important for her to read, the same way I do for you." Carlyle thought about her mother's email inbox. It was a scary and overgrown forest, the kind of place one would go to disappear. If it didn't have to do with urgent meetings, new Naturebar flavors, off-the-rack sales at Ann Taylor, or disgruntled employees who felt they might have a case against the company, it was likely not getting a glance.

"Well, this email came through from a strange mymail account. Here, let me pull it up..."

Carlyle's head felt fuzzy. *Could this be real?*

"Here it is," Marius began to read. *"We have her. Bring 500k to Progreso, Mehico. No Cops."* I mean, Mexico is spelled m-e-h-i-c-o. Who doesn't know how to spell Mexico? I trashed it thinking it was nothing. Do you really think some scary cartel has Janine?"

"Well, it's starting to look that way. It does sound a bit suspicious doesn't it? I mean, they didn't even use her name."

"Shoddy work, for a kidnapper." Marius had stopped crying and she could almost hear the humor in his voice. She couldn't help but smile, but quickly wiped it away.

"Please let me know if you get any more communication. And do some digging on the email address and also on Progreso. Where is that, anyway?"

"I'm looking at a map now, it's on the very eastern-most tip of the Yucatan. The nearest city is Merida." He pronounced Merida with a perfect Spanish accent. Somehow this annoyed her more than his previous negligence.

"That seems like a weird place for a cartel to be headquartered," Carlyle mused.

She looked toward the book-signing table and saw that the line was dwindling. She also noticed that Valerie had taken her mother's phone and was holding on to it until she finished signing books.

Carlyle made her way to the table and began to pack up everything.

"Hi honey, you're looking very intense. Tell me, does Ethan know yet?" Cybil shot her an intuitive glance.

Startled by the question, Carlyle blushed. "Know what?"

"That you're pregnant?"

Chapter Two

Just that morning, Carlyle had awoken to familiar monthly cramps. She'd sobbed over the whirring of her electric toothbrush. Toothpaste dribbled out of her mouth and down her chin, where it mixed with her tears and splattered all over the counter.

After consulting four different *Trying to Conceive* forums, Carlyle had checked her phone again. There was still no call or text from her husband, whom she hadn't seen since last week. Part of her knew it was better that she wasn't pregnant, but she'd wanted it so badly. She knew that a baby was the answer to all their problems.

Carlyle thought about her insides. She was furious that they refused to do what she required of them. Didn't they understand that her life, her happiness were on the line?

The constant stream of vibrations emanating from her phone shook her from her inner diatribe. It seemed that her job as the Director of Health and Wellness for Naturebar—and the never-ending list of duties that came with it—was both the cause and the effect of her fertility campaign.

Now, staring at her mother's expectant, proud face, it broke her heart to have to tell her that she wasn't pregnant. For a moment she forgot all about the text message and stammered through her own self-pity. "I—I—I'm not," was all she could squeak out.

"How do you know?" Her mother pressed.

Carlyle felt awkward about sharing intimate details of her cycle with her mother. "Ummm... cramps, I guess?"

"Oh, that's nothing. They're implantation cramps. I had them with all four of you." Carlyle was taken aback, both by her mother's frankness and by the very mention of her and her siblings as embryos. It was so rare that her mother spoke about things like her pregnancies or what her children were like as infants that it seemed the four of them must've sprung forth from her head like grey-eyed Athena. "I can see it on your skin. This is the one!"

Carlyle was a little creeped-out by her mother's prediction, and yet it made her strangely hopeful. Her phone buzzed and when she looked down it was Marius. "I'm taking my own car to El Bandito. Meet you there in fifteen?" Carlyle said to her mother and sister. She looked at Valerie and mouthed inconspicuously, *Make sure she's alone.*

"Hello," Carlyle answered the phone as she walked out of the television studio.

"Me again. Found something." Marius was curt and Carlyle could picture him reading from a lit computer screen. "I found this undercover blog—Blog Del Narco, it's amazing. It's written by someone inside a cartel that operates out of Progreso. They've been putting up journal entries every few days about what it's like to work in the cartel, and the writer even names people—big important people—in the ring. This person says Diego Malecón is the Don—er, the boss. They call him El Toro. He—El Toro—is pretty bad news. It looks like he is the main source for most of the cocaine and heroin in the Miami area. He's actually a Cuban, but he runs drugs by boat which is why he likes to be in Progreso—easy access to water."

"So you think this guy is connected to all of this somehow?" Carlyle's heart was blocking her esophagus.

"I don't know. Most cartels run out of border towns like Laredo or Juarez. Even Tijuana. He's the only one I can find who has any connection to the Progreso area. It's pretty smart, really, he's bypassing a lot of bloodshed by taking everything to the water."

"But he has to go a hell of a long way out of the way." Carlyle knew from managing some of the Naturebar distribution channels that the goal was to get the product to its destination in the fewest amount of steps. The Yucatan was a long way from Miami.

They paused and Marius wasn't sure if he should continue. "Here's the strange thing. This blog—it's gone dark for the last three days." He was silent, waiting for his words to sink in.

"Three days ago... but you said you got the email yesterday."

"Yeah, but let's say she's the leak—or the blogger, or whatever—they find out and they are going to kill her. She barters with them and tells them she has a rich family, yada yada yada, they settle on asking for a ransom in return for her swift exit of the organization. That could take a few days—getting the plan together and all that."

"Maybe. I don't know if Janine is the 'undercover blogger' type. Last time I saw her, her hands were shaking so much I doubt they could rest on a keyboard."

"You could be right. I just wanted you to have all the facts."

Carlyle wanted to believe her sister had a higher purpose in mind, but it would've been the first time she could remember Janine thinking about anyone but herself.

"Okay, I'm at El Bandito. Keep digging on this Toro person. See if he has any connection with Janine. Check her bank records and transfers over the last few years. You have all the passwords—"

"Honey—you all couldn't get your socks cleaned without me. I'll make it work." And with that he was gone. *He's taking on this private investigator role a little too easily,* Carlyle thought. But then, she had too.

Once she was seated at the table, she got out her phone and opened the web-browsing app that still had all her windows open from the day before. Her foot was jiggling nervously beneath the table and she told herself she needed a distraction from this insanity. She cycled back through the *Trying to Conceive* forums, looking for something she had missed. She read and reread all the comments, hoping to find some kinship with a woman who might be suffering as she was. She thought about her mother's confident pronouncement. *Implantation cramps.*

"I've been TTC for 3 years. My DH and I were about ready to give up. We did the BD when I was 1 DPO and 2 DPO. I've had cramps on and off since

then, and was sure it was AF but today I took a test and got a BFP! Hang in there ladies! GL!"– bibibaby

All the posts were some variation of the same. Cryptic and quippy paragraphs filled with abbreviations that you'd need Little Orphan Annie's decoder pen to decipher. Carlyle was almost fluent in TTC-ese by now, and she translated the easy ones in her head; DH meant Dear Husband, BD meant Baby Dance, AF meant Aunt Flo, and BFP meant Big Fat Positive. She had never commented or posted on one of these forums before. Commenting and posting on these forums was for losers—tragic women whose entire lives were lived by their ovulation cycles, women plagued by infertility and barrenness. To comment was to admit defeat.

Even so, Carlyle was tempted. This woman was in the exact same situation as her, and even now the dull cramps in her abdomen began to feel like a seed implanting in the ground, laying roots. "Bibibaby— Hi," Carlyle typed, "your post made me think I shouldn't give up hope. I felt cramps yesterday and was sure it was my period. Do you think I should take a test to be sure?" She clicked the button to post it and felt like those people who call into NPR for the first time, "long time listener, first time caller." She was a long time lurker, first time commenter.

Within seconds her phone buzzed. Bibibaby had sent her a response. "Test! You never know! GL!" GL… *Good Luck*, Carlyle reasoned. She thought about all these abbreviations and secret codes. It made her feel in-the-know and empowered to understand this secret language—the exact opposite of how she felt any time she thought about trying to get pregnant. She reasoned that if she and these women could not hold within them the ultimate secret of creation, then they could create and perpetuate the code of the barren and under-fertilized. She felt a sea of women's voices behind her, urging her to take a pregnancy test. She was sure, they were sure, it would be positive.

Maybe she should run across the street to the drug store and grab a pregnancy test—at least that way she would know, right? It made her sick that she couldn't stop thinking about a baby even when her sister was in the clutches of an evil drug ring. *If I can get an answer, then I'll be better prepared to deal with this situation,* she thought.

Her mother and sister walked in and made their way to her table. She placed her phone face down, embarrassed that one of them would see what she'd been doing.

"I had to shake some hangers-on, but we got here—just a mother-daughter lunch," Valerie said a little too enthusiastically. She looked at Carlyle for approval, and Carlyle smiled, knowing how hard it was for her sister and mother to say no to anyone who wanted to follow along.

"You really should just take a test, honey. Then you'll know," Cybil said calmly. Carlyle looked at her, stunned, unable to understand how her mind had just been read. "You're just like me. When I thought I might be pregnant it was all I could think about."

Carlyle felt a burst of shame. "I'll just run across the street and take one. It'll only be a minute," she said. She turned to say one last thing, "Get me an enchilada platter."

She wondered what Ethan was doing at that very moment. She needed that BFP. The BFP would make him come back, they would repair what was broken and they would be whole again. *Whole plus one.* She smiled at the thought.

She began to feel flushed and sweaty at the thought of taking the test. What if it *was* positive? She would be so ecstatic to tell her mother and Valerie, and Ethan too, of course.

She waited with the stick turned face down in the bathroom of the drug store. She'd locked the multi-person restroom because she couldn't bear the thought of sharing this treasured moment with strangers.

She counted down the seconds until it was okay to turn over the little plastic stick and see what her future held.

"These are like modern-day crystal balls, but way more accurate... and with more pee," she said out loud to herself. It did not sound as funny as she thought it would, and her voice echoed in the empty bathroom. "Stupid," she said, this time more quietly. She became acutely aware that there was no one around to perform for, no one to be funny for, no one to put on a show for. It was her and the stick. A scary and empty thought radiated through her, *Even this won't keep me from being alone.* An unexpected sob slipped out. She swallowed hard and fought back the weight of a thousand pinpricks along her arms.

She looked pointedly at the stick and turned it over. One vertical line, one horizontal line. If you put the two together they would make a plus sign. Despite the hundreds of tests she'd taken over the last year—it must be in the hundreds now, surely—she still hadn't memorized the particular implications of the one-line, two-line hieroglyphs. Fumbling with the box, she found the diagram. One vertical line and one horizontal line: not pregnant.

CHAPTER THREE

Carlyle exhaled what felt like a sea of breath. With the air, her hope and her aching insides left too. What she felt was numbness, both deafening and resolute. She was completely deflated and couldn't stand the idea of lunch, or of telling her mother about the text message. What made it worse was knowing she shouldn't have been surprised.

When Carlyle got back to the table, Cybil and Valerie were ordering their food. The world kept moving, people kept eating, all as if nothing had changed. Something—duty, perhaps—propelled her forward to find her seat at the table.

"Oh, Bunny! What did it say?" Cybil asked. Valerie looked on with hints of excitement and jealousy in her eyes.

Hearing her mother use the saccharine-sweet nickname she'd struggled to shrug off since toddlerhood, Carlyle was suddenly transported back to one of her first memories. It was the first day of school. Her mother drove her to the bus stop, where they both waited in the car. "Now, Bunny, you know what you've got to do, right?"

"Learn." Carlyle had been briefed.

"That's right. Learn. You learn the rules, because you can't break the rules until you know them." On her first day of kindergarten, Carlyle didn't quite understand why breaking the rules was the ultimate goal.

"Mommy, if I break the rules, I get in trouble. Janine told me so."

"Oh, Bunny, you know what I mean. The rules of life."

The bus pulled up and Carlyle hugged her mother goodbye. She grabbed her lunch pail, complete with matching thermos, and turned back three times to make sure her mother was still there. She waved on, and as the bus pulled away she watched her mother drive towards the office. Her private school was on the other side of town, and driving her there would have taken too much of her mother's time. But she made a compromise—on the first day of school every year, she would drive her daughter to the bus stop just down the street.

"It was negative," Carlyle said robotically, wafting back to the present.

"Oh." Cybil could not hide the disappointment in her voice. "Well, we'll get it next time." It was as if pregnancy was a sales goal or an award simply waiting to be attained.

"Mom, we have to tell you something." Carlyle knew she would have to be the one to deliver the news; Valerie being unable to disappoint their mother in any capacity.

On the table, Carlyle's phone buzzed again. Cybil turned it over and looked at the screen, her curiosity piqued as both a mother and a boss. She saw that it was her youngest—and no doubt favorite—child, her only son, Tom.

"Mom, don't—" Carlyle reached for the phone just as her mother answered the call.

"Tommy! How are you my lo—" her warm greeting was interrupted by what sounded like a combination of grunting, sobbing, and animal sounds.

"Janine's been kidnapped!" Tom screamed into the phone. "She texted me. Why hasn't anyone been answering my calls? This is an emergency!" He drew in a series of breaths, each deeper than the last. All three of them could hear him at the table even though the phone was not on speaker.

"Oh my god. What is he talking about, Carlyle?"

"Calm down. That's what we wanted to tell you. We wanted to wait till we were alone," Carlyle lowered her voice and looked around the restaurant. "Just stay calm. We received a text while you were on the show and it's possible that Janine has been kidnapped. There was an email that said they are demanding $500,000 delivered to Progreso, Mexico. They also said 'no cops.'"

Her mother sat back in her chair, flinging the napkin that had been in her lap onto the table. She was taking in the information, but could not hide her distress. Carlyle had seen this posture in disappointing board meetings and after the delivery of less-than-optimal quarter earnings.

Waiters arrived with hot plates of food and set them down in front of the three women. Not one of them reached for a fork. Carlyle realized that her brother was still on the phone, now sitting on the table.

"Tommy, are you still there?" Carlyle said in her most kind, sisterly voice. "We'll meet you at Mom's house in a little bit, okay? We're going to try to get a handle on this." She hung up, even though he was still trying to form words. "What are we going to do?" She directed her attention towards her mother. Even though she made a thousand decisions per day, she left the really hard ones to the woman in charge, and this was no different.

"Simple. Find out if it's real. If it's real, pay them. If it's not, then clearly Janine needs to go back to rehab."

Carlyle fought the urge to laugh. How ridiculous it all sounded when her mother broke it down like that. The problem was that figuring out if it was real wouldn't be all that easy.

"Well, I've had Marius playing detective. He was able to find one man who is connected to a cartel in Progreso. His name is El Toro—er, Diego Malecón." Carlyle told Valerie and Cybil about Malecón and with each word their eyes got bigger. She left out the part about the mystery blogger.

"So you mean this could really be… well… real?" Valerie questioned.

"It looks like it might be. We can't get any information off the email address. They probably created it just to send this email. I have Marius looking for a connection between Janine and El Toro. If we find anything there, we can assume she works—or worked—for him. That either means it's fake—they're in collusion—or she worked for him until she pissed him off and now he's keeping her against her will. It probably wouldn't have been too hard to find out that her family has money."

"Wow—looks like you've made some good headway." Cybil was clearly impressed with her daughter's P.I. alter ego.

"Are we just going to overlook the obvious here?" Valerie said. Cybil and Carlyle stared back at her, bracing themselves for a reality check. "Janine is an addict. There's no way to really know if this is real or not. Both scenarios are equally likely." One of Valerie's degrees was in statistics, so she'd likely already done the math in her head. "We either have to take a leap of blind faith—or not."

The three of them finished their food in silence, each lost in thought about Janine; who she was and how things had come to this.

Carlyle's mind wandered to one of her favorite memories of Janine. She flashed back to herself at twelve years old. She'd had a friend over—June, a rail-thin girl with bright eyes and nails painted every color of the rainbow. The two tweens were alone in the house, fantasizing about what it would be like when they were older. They began putting on Cybil's makeup, sequined dresses, and high heels. When they were all dolled-up they noticed the vacuous space in the clothing where breasts should go. Suddenly dressing up wasn't enough. Both girls had powerful urges to understand what it would be like to have boobs.

Carlyle had a brilliant idea. She took June upstairs and loaned her a bathing suit top. She donned one herself and gleamed.

"What are we doing, Carlyle?" June asked.

"You'll see," she answered mischievously.

She took her friend's hand and led her down to the game room, where her father's most prized possession stood proudly: the pool table. Carlyle reached into the corner pocket and withdrew two heavy billiard balls, the nine-ball and the seven. She tucked them strategically into her bathing suit top, where they perkily resembled two very hard, very round breasts.

June's face lit up. She began rummaging around in one of the pockets of the table and withdrew the thirteen-ball and the two-ball. She shoved them in the bikini top and did her best runway walk. The two girls exploded in laughter.

They were real women now. They possessed power and lust and the male gaze all within one moment. It was magical. The two girls flounced around waving their arms, doing the beauty pageant wave at no one in particular.

They were having so much fun accepting Oscars and posing for swimsuit spreads that they didn't hear Janine come in. Janine was seventeen, and had come into her breasts full force some time ago. Janine was womanly and lovely, and was already learning to play on this as her biggest asset in every relationship.

Janine couldn't stifle her laughter after watching the girls for a few minutes. "If you got it, flaunt it!" she called through her delirious cackling.

Carlyle felt her ears go hot and her neck and chest get splotchy, like they always did when she was embarrassed. She quickly removed her fake boobs and rolled them on the table, as if there was some chance that Janine hadn't seen them. June left them in, unabashed.

"Don't tell on us, Janine. Don't tell anyone, please," Carlyle pleaded. She could hear her sister recanting the tale over breakfast and she buried her face in her hands. "We just wanted to see what would happen, I mean, what it would look like when we get… I mean, when we grow our boobs." Carlyle looked hopelessly at her sister's perfectly formed chest. Could she even remember what it was like before she'd had her breasts? Probably not. It was hard to imagine Janine any differently than she was at that moment, effortlessly floating through time as a fully formed seventeen-year-old girl.

Janine's face slipped from laughter to soft understanding. She walked over to Carlyle and raked her fingers through her hair, moving it off her forehead and taking with it some of their mother's foundation.

"Little sister, you are perfect just the way you are. These things?" She unceremoniously squeezed her breasts. "You don't need them. You don't want them. They just create more problems than they're worth…" She drifted off. "But when you do get them, they'll be great and perfect, and… don't let just anybody touch them, you hear me?" She was suddenly angry and protective. "Boys will try to touch them; they'll take you to the movies, they'll buy your lunch, they'll drive you around in their cars, all so they can touch these dumb things. Don't just let them. Make them prove themselves, make sure they're worth it." Her eyes were sad. Carlyle knew in that moment that her sister had a whole other life than the one she knew about. And she knew that her other life was dark and full of things she might never understand.

Over the years, Carlyle thought a lot about her sister's words. They sunk deep, past her skin, past her muscle fibers—low, low, low into a buried place within her, a place where important things live. The things that make us happy, the things that define us, the building blocks of our lives, how we decide the difference between right and wrong. *Make sure he's worth it.* She had thought it so many times it had become a part of her. Like her tongue filling her mouth, so this tenet filled her being.

Carlyle snapped back to the present. "Tom will be in hysterics. We'd better get home to him. Let's all meet there and regroup." Within minutes they were headed for their cars; Valerie and Cybil traveling together, and Carlyle on her own.

CHAPTER FOUR

Carlyle drove straight to her mother's house. It was the house she'd grown up in, and yet it was completely unrecognizable to her now. The massive compound had taken on additions and remodels every year since her parents' divorce. It felt like her mother was determined to erase every trace of her father having lived there.

Since she had been sixteen when they'd divorced, Carlyle saw more of the truth about their parents' relationship. In the last few years of their marriage, Virgil and Cybil had been held together by a few paper clips and some chewing gum. That is to say, when the marriage crumbled, Carlyle hadn't been surprised. In fact, there was an element of relief that their sometimes-volatile and usually depressive father was no longer going to be living with them.

Her mind wandered to the impending stack of emails that was piling up in her absence, and she couldn't help but feel angry with Janine. She was always the one to throw a stick of dynamite into her family's attempts at normalcy.

When she arrived at the house, her brother Tom was curled up on the living room floor. He hugged a throw pillow to his stomach. His eyes were red-rimmed, yet glassy—evidence that even though he wasn't crying now, he had been. It was strange to see her nineteen-year-old brother—an avid football fan who listed "pumping iron" and "keggers" among his hobbies—in such a state.

"Tom, it will be alright," Carlyle said, going to him. She sat down cross-legged on the floor and patted his shoulder. She found herself completely perplexed at how to comfort him. "What is upsetting you so much? She hurt you so badly before she left, most people would say 'to hell with her.'"

"I got a call, I… I think she tried to call me. It was staticky." Tom could hardly get the words out. "I heard her in the background and some Spanish-speaking guys. Then more static, yelling, the guys kept saying 'El Toro, El Toro.'" He was frantic. Anxiety began to rise in Carlyle's chest.

"What number did it come from?" Her voice trembled. Cybil and Valerie walked through the door to see her clutching her brother around the shoulders.

"I don't know, the same number as the text, I think. It went quiet— no static, no nothing. Do you think they hurt her? I tried to call the number back and it was just some Spanish voice—it sounded like it was saying 'this number is no longer in service.'"

Carlyle sat back from her brother and up onto her knees. She stared into space. "I can't believe it. I can't believe this might actually be happening."

"She's our sister. I thought you, of all people, would understand. She could be killed. She could already be dead." His eyes widened as he contemplated what he had just said. "The phone going dead… that could've been her d-dying. She could've pissed them off for keeping her phone, for… for," he couldn't finish the thought. Tom had always taken family very seriously, even lately when they'd all scattered and the bonds that remained were hardly strong enough to resemble a family.

Tom immediately started crying again and ran to their mother, who suddenly looked frail and paper-thin. Carlyle watched her mother and brother mourn her misbegotten sister and wondered why she felt so alone, and so unaffected by recent events. She tried to imagine what it would be like to know her daughter was kidnapped—still, she failed to feel even a hint of empathy. There was a pain throbbing inside her ribcage, but she recognized it as something other than the pain her family must be feeling. She'd been feeling it for the last week, ever since her husband had packed his small overnight bag and left their home.

That must be it—I'm too selfish to understand anyone else's pain except my own. As she thought it, she understood both how true it was and how far she had to go to be the wife—and someday mother—she wanted to be.

"We should call the police," Valerie said under her breath. The rest of the family paused for a moment before going on about their passive courses of action. It was almost as if she had never said it.

"I know it was her. I know it. She's in real trouble, Mom!" The phone call that Tom had received had heightened the probability that she should alert the authorities, but her brother was not an entirely credible source. Janine had been his puppetmaster in a former life, and he would do anything to have that relationship with her again. *Could Tom be in on the plan too?* Carlyle wondered to herself before dismissing such a ridiculous idea.

"This is all my fault. I've failed her. I've never been a good mother to her. And now she's…" Cybil was collapsing under a lifetime of guilt.

Tom and Cybil were inconsolable. Their grief and sadness played off each other like light reflecting off of parallel mirrors. Valerie and Carlyle were able to wrangle them to their separate rooms, but any attempt at a rational conversation was hopeless. They all decided that they would pick up again in the morning, and come up with a game plan. "Time is of the essence here," Cybil said as she retired to her room. This confused Carlyle, being that time had been ticking since yesterday, when the original email had been received, and continued to tick into the night. Not knowing what would happen over the next few days, she took this night as a chance to organize her thoughts and perhaps find out more about the Narco Blog.

She pulled up the link Marius had emailed to her. She wanted to search the text for some hint that it could be Janine's voice on the other side of the screen. She read entry after entry. It seemed strange that the blog was written in English, educated English. Though it could be valuable to the writer to disguise it from the other members of the cartel. There were several news articles about the blog—lauding the writer as a hero, a patriot, a brave soldier in the war on drugs. Many highlighted the terrifying idea that the blogger would surely be killed, should they be found out.

Her eyes began to droop, and feeling as if she were no closer to a conclusion than when she started, she began to close her laptop screen. That's when she saw it. The line that changed everything. It was from an entry dating back a month, and the last line of the entry was: *You've got to make sure he's worth it.* The context was about a source—the blogger had been working as a mule, taking shipments back and forth from Progreso to Miami. The blogger had a source inside the DEA, a man denoted as Agent Bravo. The blogger talked about exchanging sensitive information with Agent Bravo, and not knowing who to trust. The entry ended on that line: *you've got to make sure he's worth it.* Carlyle's eyes scrolled over it again and again. Was it a coincidence? How could it be? Was Janine trying to send her a message?

She decided then that it was real. That her sister couldn't have been the hopeless, manipulating addict she remembered, but she had changed. She wanted to expose the exploitative drug trade and turn her life around. During this lofty pursuit, she'd gotten in too deep, and this was her cry for help. As soon as everyone was awake, she would tell her family, show them what Janine had written, and they would find a way to bring her back safely.

She began to put on her pajamas, pacing a trail between the closet and the door while donning each new piece of clothing. Should she wake everyone up? Should they go to the police immediately? She took a deep breath. This might be the last night of peaceful sleep any of her family members would get for a long while. The kidnappers knew there was money at the end of this—they would keep her alive, they *had* to. She would settle in, get her thoughts straight, and wait for morning.

She looked around her old room. Her mother had turned it into a guest room, and any remnants of her high school self had been removed. In the adjoining bathroom there were small, multicolored balls of hand soap, and a lotion dispenser monogrammed with the letter 'P.' She slathered on the fragrant hand cream in an attempt to slow her rapidly beating heart. "Don't make emotional decisions," she repeated to herself again and again. As she did, she began to calm. She shot-putted the panic out of her mind, purposefully and intentionally focusing on her own localized feelings.

CHAPTER FIVE

Coating her hands in thick, sticky cream was not something she did regularly, but it was something she thought she *should* do regularly. It made her feel motherly — not like any mother she'd ever known, of course, but more like a "royal mother," a collective cultural image of what a mother should be. Someone who wears aprons and sleeps in rollers and puts band-aids on scrapes. It felt good to rub her hands together, to "be proactive" when it came to wrinkles at the ripe old age of twenty-eight. For a brief moment, it made her feel as if she cared about herself. "No matter how much plastic surgery a woman has, you can always tell her age from her hands," Cybil had once said.

She knew there was something she had to do before settling in. She knew it was time. Time to call him. She picked up her phone; it was as if it weighed a thousand pounds. She bounced it, smoothed it, rubbed away the fingerprints from the screen. She felt similar to when she was waiting for the almighty stick to reveal its will. "Not Pregnant" had been its decree and like a blazoned standard following its king, her period flowed proudly, showing itself as a final gauntlet thrown down on all her dreams. "Ha!" it seemed to say. "Take that!"

She dialed and waited as the ringing grew deafening.

"Hello?" he sounded breathless.

"Ethan? Hi, it's me…" They were like strangers. It was as if they'd just had their first date and this was a contest to see who could go the longest without calling the other. She'd lost. "What are you up to?"

"Oh, I was just on the tread-climber." There was a long, empty pause. Was he supposed to ask how she was? Was he supposed to wait for her to tell him why she'd called? He was never good at this part.

"I, uh, I just wanted to call and let you know that I'm not pregnant. Again." She sounded cynical and deflated even to herself.

"Oh… well, that's probably for the best. At least, considering…" he trailed off. He wasn't sure what he should be considering.

"But I thought that's why you left. I thought… I don't know what I thought. Look, I know we're working through some stuff right now, so I haven't been bugging you. I haven't asked where you're staying. I'm giving you space."

"Carlyle…" he let out a deep breath. She could almost feel his heart rate slowing in his chest. It might even be working in direct inverse proportion to her own thumping heart. "It was never about the pregnancy. I didn't want space from you because you're not pregnant. I wanted space from you because *we're* not working. You're not seeing me. You thinking this is about you being pregnant or not being pregnant just proves my point."

She remained silent.

"I'm at Derrick's, by the way. I'm going to stay here for a while. I think I just need some time."

Derrick had been her friend first. They'd met in college. He was an art major and made good money now doing murals for businesses and festivals. When she'd med Ethan, Derrick had questioned her incessantly about her new mystery man. "He's a musician. There's no way he's gay," Carlyle had argued. "You think there aren't gay musicians?" Derrick had countered. Carlyle had been right—definitely not gay. But that hadn't stopped Derrick from hitting on him just to razz her. Now she found herself on the verge of a dry heave thinking about Ethan sleeping in the same vicinity as her dear old friend.

"I really think you should come home. We can work on things here. Besides, in about two weeks we can try again. I really think you'll be over everything by then." She sounded hopeful and aloof, and Ethan felt a pang of pity for how far she was from the girl he'd met and fallen in love with.

"Do you hear yourself, Carlyle? I don't want to try again. Not right now and not with your schedule the way it is. Do you remember the last time we had sex? You had the fertility book out with all your tabs marking the pages that outline the right positions. You were commanding me where to be and what to do and how to do it. I know I'm the guy, but I need a little more romance than that. I want to feel like you actually want to do it. I want to feel electricity. We've... lost that somewhere. You need to ask yourself why you even want to have a kid with me. Is it about us co-creating a life, or is it about the fact that every day you become more obsessed with your job and more like Cybil? Do you think having a kid will stop you from becoming your mother?"

He felt lighter. These were things he'd wanted to say since she'd started this fertility tirade eighteen months ago. He'd never felt okay telling her what he thought about it, because then he'd figured, how bad could it be? They would try for a few months, and then they would have a baby and she would finally be happy. But the baby never came. And she moved further and further away, delving into work, dinners, and meetings to avoid the reality that their marriage wasn't working. He realized he'd never been more relieved about anything than he was about the fact that she hadn't gotten pregnant. The thought made him feel like an asshole, but a moment later he ameliorated his guilt by reasoning that at least he was an honest asshole.

Carlyle was speechless. One of the things she'd always loved about Ethan was that he called her on her bullshit. He worked hard and made his own money. The string of boyfriends prior to him had been happy to bend to her will—whatever it was—because they saw dollar signs at the end of the road. They knew who her mother was, who her family was, and they had wanted a piece.

Ethan hadn't known who her mother was until he'd already said, "I love you." He'd said it after three dates, a fact Carlyle was still proud of. The fastest anyone had ever said that to her before was after four dates. This was a new record. He must be the one.

"I don't know what to say. Of course I love you." She sounded unsure and felt even more so. She was still regaining her breath after his comments about becoming her mother. Now that they were separated, she saw herself hurtling even further towards a certain future: alone, surrounded by yes-men, and unable to be close to anyone. If she was really honest, she'd been hurt very deeply by his comments about their lovemaking—babymaking?—so she decided to renounce him for the night. "I guess you're right. It's probably best we're apart right now. I'll talk to you sometime in the next few days."

There were so many things she wanted to say. She started to tell him about the text, about the kidnapping, the blogger, but she somehow wanted him to suffer—to push him even further away. She felt like a guest on a daytime talk show, so angry she could wield a chair. The feeling welled up inside her and it was a welcome rainstorm on the dry gulch of disappointment and self-hatred she'd felt all day.

"Okay, then," Ethan replied. He sounded stunned and maybe a little hurt. Carlyle allowed herself to feel satisfied, though she had to squelch a wave of sadness cresting upward from her guts. "I just want us to be like we used to be. I mean, I want you to be who you were... I mean, I know that girl is still in there." He felt clearer than he had in months, even though his words were stumbling.

"Well, goodnight." She hung up. It was the first time they'd gotten off the phone without saying, "I love you," in four years.

CHAPTER SIX

Carlyle settled into her bed — what used to be her bed — and opened her laptop. The words on the screen melted together as she could not stop thinking about what Ethan had said about the sex. Who was he kidding? Guys would take it any way they could get it. Think of all the sad losers masturbating to computer screens. He was lucky to be getting real live action, fertility book or not. At least, that's what she'd thought then.

It had made her feel utilitarian to use sex for its intended purpose — empowered even. She knew what to do, when to do it, and why they were doing it. It was much easier than wondering if the angle was good, if he was noticing her extra chins or even worse, seeing her body the way another person — not mounted on top of her — must. It was hard to enjoy herself while thinking about all her insecurities hanging out like laundry drying on a line. But sex with a purpose was another matter entirely.

A college boyfriend once told her: "Guys have a mental calendar of days in the week, and below the days are empty boxes. On days when they have sex, the box gets a check mark. The check mark means all is good and right in the world. An empty box means... not that." The message was clear enough. If you want to make a guy happy, check his box. She didn't think the way in which the box was checked mattered, just that it was checked.

Apparently it mattered. It mattered so much that Ethan had moved out for a now indefinite period of time, to sleep on the sofa in Derrick's immaculately decorated house. It mattered enough that he was fine with putting their whole history—their whole future—on hold. Her mind buzzed. She latched on to the sex as the problem, she wanted to close up shop, lock the doors and simply say, "You don't know what you've got 'til it's gone, I suppose."

She knew, though, that the roles were reversed this time, whatever the motives. She wanted it and he didn't. And nothing was more infuriating than that. She would have to sweat him out—he would grow lonely, he would miss her—and when he came back, she would be waiting with open arms.

She lay down and closed her eyes but couldn't stop thinking about their first date. They'd gone to the racetrack. It was smoky—something she hated—and she'd never been much of a gambler. They'd settled into the small bar inside that housed a few pool tables. Her father was a regular at the races, and maybe Ethan had thought the man had instilled in her a lifelong love of the place. What Ethan didn't know was that any money Carlyle's father won would be promptly lost the next day. Consistency had never been his strong suit.

The smoke landed on her clothes and mixed with her perfume and lip gloss. She saw Ethan shooting practice shots at one of the pool tables and he waved her over. They were both lit red by the beer neons hanging behind the bar. The betting window sat just outside the bar, and screens of the races—happening just outside—lined the walls.

They both waited tables at the same restaurant, Liberty's. When Carlyle had started there, Ethan would not stop asking her on dates. "Hey, you want to check out a movie?" he'd ask on Wednesday. "How about a picnic in the park tomorrow?" he'd follow up on Friday. She continued to rebuff him—partly because she liked to be chased, and partly because she had always heard you should never date someone you work with. "I can't, I'm seeing someone," she would respond, which only seemed to strengthen his resolve. One day, as she was layering three different kinds of mustard on someone's double chili-cheese Coney, she heard someone coming up behind her. She turned around with a smirk, prepared to deliver another rejection. It was her boss counting the inventory.

She was utterly crestfallen. She expected Ethan to be there with another date planned. She realized that saying no to Ethan was more fun than saying yes to anyone else.

So here she was at the track. *Why couldn't I have said yes to the movie or the picnic?* she thought to herself. *That's what I get for being stubborn, I guess. A face full of smoke and a room full of my father.*

Ethan was boyishly cute and had qualities no other man she'd been around had—persistence and stamina. He showed up on time to work. He made a point of being "the organized one" in his band. He said he was going to do something, and he did it. Carlyle realized even then what a rare quality that was. She'd been intrigued.

They swapped stories and played a few games of pool.

"So you're a musician?" Carlyle asked him.

"Yeah, I play bass in an experimental jazz band—it's like a cross between prog-rock and math-core."

Carlyle nodded along and didn't disabuse him of the idea that she was one of those cool girls who listened to experimental anything.

"Nice," she added. "And you play pool, too? And you like movies and picnics?" She liked joking with him about his multiple date ideas.

"Good thing you said yes to the track," he said. "The next thing on my list was to ask you to go swimming with me in the wave pool at Watermania." Watermania was Omaha's aging water park, replete with rickety old rides, partially deflated inner tubes, and the notorious wave pool. The wave pool was where the old ladies in swim caps floated on hot days as the only relief from the Omaha sun. The water would lie stagnant until a park worker turned on the wave machine every fifteen minutes. The pool would erupt in high, tumultuous waves. It was the closest thing to the sea they had. It was also a staggeringly disgusting experience, as the pool was rarely cleaned. Emerging from the water adorned with clumps of hair or a stray band-aid wasn't unusual.

She erupted in laughter as he stacked the balls in the rack. "This is the last time I'm going to be racking, because losers always rack," he said. She wondered if he would apply the same competitive streak to billiards as he had to getting her there in the first place.

"Are we not placing any bets?" she asked coyly.

"I already lost all my money to that guy, I bet him you wouldn't show up." She laughed. She found his self-deprecation refreshing and sweet. The sounds of the bell ringing to start the race, the announcer's fast nasal voice delivering second-to-second updates, everything faded into the background as they talked and laughed.

They played about four games of pool, all of which she lost except the last one—Ethan had missed the eight ball and she knocked it in by chance.

They headed to the parking lot and both of them knew it was time to say goodbye, but they weren't ready for the night to be over. It was so rare that Carlyle found someone she could talk to.

She was sitting sideways in the driver's seat of her car, her legs hanging out the side. He held her hands and leaned into her knees. They shared a sweet but short kiss—one where the lips overlap, like in the movies. She'd come far enough in life to realize that if you kiss someone straight on the mouth, you're a kissing amateur at best. The great kisses have just a bit of overlap—one top lip just above the other.

"Hey, are you hungry?" she asked him. It was probably not what most people would have said at that point in a date, but she didn't care about protocol. "I could go for some pancakes."

"Pancakes? You sure are a strange one," Ethan said, kissing her again. "I love strangeness, though." They proceeded to the nearest twenty-four hour diner, where they ate pancakes and drank coffee until four in the morning. Carlyle shared things that she'd never told anyone. She was strategic about what she shared, though, never telling him who her Mom was or where she lived. She tried to be herself, strangeness and all—minus a few key details, of course. And Ethan liked it. And she felt seen for the first time since she could remember.

Now she lay in her old bed alone, looking over the life they'd made together like a picture book. It suddenly felt as if she was starting over in a race that she hadn't known she was running. For the first time that day, she missed him. Really, fully and powerfully missed him— missed what they had together and missed how he made her feel. She saw the chasm she had created and had no idea how to bring the earth back together again.

CHAPTER SEVEN

Carlyle hadn't been able to sleep. Of course, given the circumstances, who would? Apparently her whole family could, because their faint snores echoed through the hallways of the enormous house. She'd gone down to the kitchen to find a snack what felt like five minutes ago. Now, she looked at the oven clock to see that it was 2:45 in the morning. She'd raided her mother's wine fridge, emptying an already open bottle of Moscato into a large plastic tumbler.

She was now exerting a powerful effort to push her fear away. Her mind was a beach and the waves of panic lapped away at any sense of security she could momentarily lull herself into. She thought of Ethan—he would be getting off work, managing the chain restaurant Mahoney's just a few miles from her mother's house.

"A proper wine pour is five ounces. You should pour strongly for three full seconds," she could hear him saying. Her glass was about seven seconds full. "Wine has to breathe, that's why wine glasses are bell shaped, to force the air into the glass and let it aerate." Ethan had honed his knowledge of beer and fine wine over his years of working in restaurants, and he'd taken his current management position with the promise that he could manage the bar at Omaha's newest steakhouse within a few years. The Cut—the newest venture of the Mahoney's franchise—featured a world class wine menu hand chosen by one lucky bar manager and sommelier. Ethan dutifully managed Mahoney's, a cheap Americana-fueled dining experience, hoping his dream job would pan out.

She looked at the common tumbler she'd chosen. It was hot pink and bore the emblem of a biker bar in town. She wondered how it had come to be here in her mother's cabinet, and couldn't help but notice it was the furthest thing from a traditional wine glass that she could have chosen. That was her, always having to break the rules, and Ethan was always trying to put them back together. He knew the science behind even the most common things. She liked that about him; it gave him a sense of purpose, like everything he did had a reason and a science behind it.

But that thought bothered her now, because a purposeful man does not haphazardly leave his wife for a week. His absence was premeditated, possibly irreversible. She knew he would not take leaving lightly—that once he'd done it, he would have a hard time reversing his action.

It was only now, sitting with what amounted to a small bucket of sweet white wine, that she realized how serious Ethan's leaving was, how unhappy he must have been to go. Carlyle was an impulsive person. If she had left him, he would have known it wouldn't have been real—it would just have been a test. She would want to see if he would chase her, or how often he would call, or if he would even miss her. But his leaving… his leaving was a different thing altogether.

She suddenly felt a sharp and knowing pain that she had lost something, like the feeling that you've left the house and forgotten something crucial in your daily routine. Only this wasn't just that she'd forgotten to turn off the stove or lock the door. This was something she had forgotten to do every morning for months in a row.

Carlyle had forgotten to love her husband. She had forgotten to realize that there was another person—a whole person with wants, needs, and experiences all his own—living in her house. It had appeared to her that he came and went solely because she was there, and they were married. He had been paused until she walked into the room. If she was not around, he ceased to exist.

She had forgotten to check in on him, to test the waters of their relationship, to make sure he still felt the same way. It was something she did frequently when they'd first gotten together, but she took it for granted now—that they were in love, that he loved her back. Early on in their coupledom, taking stock wasn't a big show; she would inquire with a look, with a light brush of the hand across the back of his neck, with a flinty laugh after a few beers. She would do these things and she would know from his reaction that he was still smitten with her, still preferred her to any other girl. He would watch her—take her in as if she were a scenic view or a melodic chorus. Over time, she stopped wondering if he felt the same way. It was a given that he'd settled on her, he'd decided on her. He thought she was beautiful and strange. She began to take solace in this as an infallible truth. She'd gotten comfortable and she'd forgotten to check.

Sick. She was going to be sick. She pushed the sickness down and forced the rest of the wine down with it. It made her neck tense up to one side, as if she'd just taken a shot of whiskey. She winced and let the alcohol shudder through her. Anything to push away this realization.

A shadow passed across the upstairs hallway and she was instinctively on her feet. *Great, here I am drowning my sorrows like a pathetic loser, when there's literally a kidnapper in the house,* she thought. *So self-absorbed,* she berated herself as she searched the kitchen for something she could use for protection. *Carlyle Pierce is done going down without a fight.* She wondered if Janine had said the same thing to herself.

She drew a butcher knife out of the block on the counter and waited in the stillness for the shadow to come again. She waited just long enough to begin questioning whether she had even seen anything. Had it been there, or was it just the wine playing tricks on her? Could one of her siblings simply have gotten up to use the bathroom?

There it was again. Shuffling, this time closer, just across the hallway that led to the kitchen. "Shit, there really is someone here..." she whispered. She wished desperately that Ethan was there with her, that he and his rational mind would tell her that everything was okay.

She didn't have time to reach out to him—or anyone for that matter. The intruder was in the kitchen with her now, his dark shadow darting for the door.

Chapter Eight

She flipped on the light and gripped the knife in both hands, hoisting it overhead, slasher-movie style. In the light, the darkly dressed man turned to her. His face was covered... all but the eyes. He did not come toward her as she expected he would, and once her eyes adjusted to the light she knew those eyes behind the mask were unmistakably her brother's.

"What are you doing?" his voice echoed loudly in the room, his eyes not leaving the knife.

"Really, dude? We're all staying here tonight because of a kidnapping, and you're running around dressed like a makeshift ninja? You scared the shit out of me! What are *you* doing?" Carlyle said.

Tom raised the ski mask. His face was grave. "I'm going to get her. I can't just let her die. I heard her on the phone. She is really scared. You guys are going to let her die!" His nostrils flared and Carlyle could see he'd given this a lot of thought, and thinking wasn't something he was prone to long bouts of.

"Tom..." She was overcome with appreciation for his earnestness in that moment. "I think...it's possible you're right." She looked at her brother, nineteen now and nearly a man. She didn't want to let him in on her blogger theory just yet, or show him how scared she was. She could not play down to him as she once could—was their sister really in danger? Maybe.

"She wouldn't fake this. I know her better than all of you. This is my chance to be the hero, to actually save someone. It's not up to us to

decide if she's worth saving. You won't stop me." His conviction impressed her. It seemed as though he had been practicing this speech
in the bathroom mirror. Tom had long felt inadequate in the shadow
of so many educated and important women: their mother; Carlyle,
now second-in-command at Naturebar; and Valerie, who had more
degrees than any of them actually knew. Everyone in the company
took Tom for the "less fortunate" Pierce child—he could make jokes
and attend cocktail parties, but no one expected him to succeed. He
could coast, take what was given to him, and live a simple—if not easy
and enjoyable—life. Up until this moment, that had seemed enough
for him.

"Well, how are you going to do it?" she asked, with real interest now.
A voice inside her head scoffed at the idea that she was actually about
to entertain Tom's plan, but she turned her attention toward him.

In a hushed voice he detailed his plan. "I'm going down to Big Pine
Key to convince one of Mom's captains to take me to Progreso. I'll
figure out the rest when I get there." Carlyle had forgotten about her
mother's home in the Florida Keys. About four years ago, Cybil had
participated in a deep-sea fishing tournament held by one of her larg-
est customers. It was supposed to be a fun retreat for CEOs and man-
agers to escape and let loose while participating in a mildly competitive tourney. Cybil had been devastated when she'd come in last, the
ladies' team delivering a single fish as their catch for the entire three-
day ordeal. The other teams were throwing ten, twenty, even thirty
shiny, glassy-eyed tarpon onto the docks. She'd left Big Pine Key in
shame, and had vowed that she would never come in last again.

She'd begun going down to the Keys every three weeks, hiring out
the same boat and the same captain, since it and he were the best.
C.J.—short for Captain Joe—hadn't hesitated when she'd offered to
buy a few boats and hire him and his crew as her full-time charter
team. The boats were available for hire, but mostly Cybil used them
to improve and hone her craft. She'd bargained a deal on a large house
not far from the beach, whose builder had filed for bankruptcy. By
the time the next fishing tournament came around, she was a professional angler in all but name. She took first place in her customer's

tournament, and began placing in local tournaments sponsored by large sporting goods companies. Carlyle always suspected that the fishing was Cybil's way of dealing with what most women would call an empty nest, although Tom still lived in her pool-house in Omaha.

Carlyle was surprised that Tom's plan actually had legs. If Progreso was just at the tip of the Yucatan Peninsula, as Marius had said, then she knew it would be a long journey by sea—but sea was the only way to go undetected. "I have frequent flier miles saved up. I could probably get us on the next flight out," she said. She'd applied for a mileage-earning credit card a year ago with the intention of traveling the world with Ethan. Though she knew her mother would fly them anywhere she asked, Ethan hated to ask his mother-in-law for money. They'd intended to make plans for a trip but she'd always been too busy or he made an excuse. She'd invited him to come on a few business trips, but he declined, saying he "didn't want to be her escort." Now she wondered if it was just the thought of being alone with her that drove him to put off taking a trip. They hadn't taken any trips together since she'd gotten the card, and her miles sat gathering dust.

"Really, you would do that?" Tom knew how much Carlyle valued her frequent flyer miles.

"Yeah, I don't know when we'll ever get to use them," she said hopelessly. "Plus, you're right, she needs us—we've got to get to her." Her brother's intensity and the warm fuzziness of the alcohol had allowed her to become enchanted by the idea of an adventure. If Tom believed so firmly in the story, then it must be true. He had been the one most wounded by their sister, and she admired his ability to look past his own pain in order to see the bigger picture. She suddenly saw her brother as more than a sports-obsessed, protein-pounding party boy. He was a person capable of forgiveness and compassion, two qualities she suddenly realized she could use an infusion of.

"What about Mom? Should we tell her?" Carlyle asked.

"No. This is something I have to do. I have to do it on my own—or with you, if you're willing to come." He was electric in the low light. Carlyle knew the feeling of wanting to accomplish something on her own, without the safety net of her mother's money or legal team. She seemed a long way from that now, with her easily-won corner office and expense account.

"Well, let me grab a few things. I can call the Marius from the car." They were going to do this. They were going to break away from the family unit and strike out on their own. If the whole thing was a fake, at least she would be there to expose Janine for what she really was. And if it was real... well, if it was real, they would have to figure out how to save her. "Oh, and you might want to lose the ninja get-up—I don't think they'll take kindly to that at airport security." Tom looked down at his clothes as if he'd forgotten what he was wearing. He looked up at her with a shrug and removed the ski mask, cramming it in the duffel bag at his side.

She ran upstairs to her room and looked across the contents of the overnight bag she'd brought with her. There was nothing to suit the beach—no bathing suit, no sunscreen, no long flowing maxi dresses that she suspected women wore on boats. It was early October, and easterly winds had already begun to chill Omaha. She'd packed a few pairs of the slim-cut, inexpensive jeans that were comfortable yet fit well. There were two tank tops, for layering under the sweaters and long-sleeved, ornate tops that made her feel bookish and artistic—yet still professional. She'd brought toiletry basics, plus some lip and cheek stain, a black eyeliner pencil and a minty chapstick. She hadn't anticipated any cause to look pretty in front of her family during what was meant to be a grief-stricken time. She threw all the clothes, both dirty and clean, into the bag, along with her cosmetics and toiletries. She felt devastatingly underprepared for a sea-bound adventure. There was no time to stop by her house, and instinctively she knew Tom wouldn't tolerate any delay.

A moment of doubt bloomed as she zipped the bag. The voice inside that had been whispering to her, telling her this was a bad idea and that Tom was the last person to trust in a reconnaissance mission, was screaming in her head. What was she doing? She was the rational one. Tom was the one who flew on blind luck. Valerie was fluid and unsettled. Janine would be the one to pack a bag that would magically contain all the things necessary for an impromptu beach vacation—the one to drop everything at a moment's notice to join their brother in his quest to find independence. Would Carlyle be the one to step into her place, and was it necessary that she do so in order to save her sister?

Was her sister even in danger? The question rang in her mind. A screaming voice inside said no. But the arms that grabbed the bag, the hands that swept her hair back into an intentionally effortless-looking bun, and the eyes that stared back in the mirror all said yes.

CHAPTER NINE

They caught a flight to Key West at 6:12 a.m. Marius' groggy voice was less than pleased when she woke him up to book the flight. "I am so coming in late tomorrow," he'd snarked.

As they settled into their seats, inserting the metal end into the buckle, Carlyle realized this was the first time she had been alone with her brother since they were kids. They were mostly quiet during the flight and she thought it strange that someone could be raised in the same house by the same people and still seem such a stranger to her.

"Have you heard anything from Dad?" Tom asked. Carlyle was startled both by the question's suddenness and its subject.

"You mean, does he know? About Janine?"

"Yeah. Do you think Mom told him?"

"I don't think so. They haven't talked in years. I'm not sure, though. Maybe." She waited for more questions from Tom, but they did not come. Carlyle thought about her father. The last time she had seen him, a few years ago, he was leaning over the railing, watching the horse he'd just spent his rent on come in dead last. He ambled inside to buy a beer with the few dollars he had left. The bar inside the racetrack was like any other hole-in-the-wall dive bar that boasted a few pool tables in the back room. The place was always brimming with smoke and the smell of stale spilled beer. It was the same place where she and Ethan had had their first date.

Her father had asked her to come down and watch the races. He had asked each of his children every Wednesday night for ten years after his divorce from Cybil had been finalized. This was the one and only time she'd obliged. She'd gone to watch, but also to tell him she'd gotten engaged. As far as she knew, none of her siblings had taken him up on his weekly ritual either.

For a few years after he'd moved out, her father repeatedly called and texted all of them, trying to organize dinners and Sunday picnics. None of these plans ever came together. The one time Carlyle had urged her siblings to go, she packed a picnic lunch and planned to meet everyone in the park. She carefully laid out the blanket and opened the oversized picnic basket she'd bought just for the occasion. She peeked in at the cucumber and cream cheese sandwiches she'd cut into small triangles. She wasn't usually one to cook, but she'd gotten so excited about the afternoon out with their father that she'd taken the initiative to organize everything. She sat on her smoothed blanket, perfectly placed to see the pond and the children playing on the playground. Minutes passed, then hours. Carlyle ate three of the triangles and fed the rest to the geese and ducks that hovered about. They honked their gratitude but promptly moved on.

When she'd asked what became of everyone, only her dad and Valerie had even bothered to make excuses. Her father had gotten stuck in an "all or nothing" bet—walking away was not an option. Valerie, who was finishing her Art History Masters at Nebraska State, had forgotten about the picnic in a rush to complete an assignment.

For the last two years her father had given up contacting them or trying to see them at all. Thinking about it now, it seemed strange that he was so absent, and even stranger that she hadn't particularly noticed. His absence was less like an explosion and more like a hearth fire dying out. It was there until it wasn't. Carlyle realized that her family had literally fallen apart—more than one member was missing—and she'd been too involved with her own, now-insignificant problems to notice. What kind of daughter was she? The kind of daughter who let her father's multiple attempts to reach out fall on deaf ears. The further she got from home and her safe, warm, ignorant nest, the more she began to dislike who she was.

There was no doubt her father would want to know his favorite daughter was in trouble, wherever he was. She thought to call him, but realized that she had no contact information for him.

For a moment Carlyle missed her father. He had always preferred Janine to the rest of them—openly so. It was hard now to even imagine her mother and father together, they were so painfully different. She had never understood them together. They had been married until the year Tom was eight, and then, as if their work together was done, Cybil and Virgil had parted. Cybil had just taken Naturebar national, landing a huge organic grocery chain. The money and the status had begun to go to Virgil's head, though he'd had no part in producing it. He began betting cars and expensive watches in his late-night poker games. The grisly regulars at the track were lining up to get their antes in. Some walked away with Rolexes, and a female jockey passing through Omaha actually won a car. It was a Black Audi, and since the rider's nickname was "the Black Widow," she took to the vehicle nicely.

The loss of the car was the final straw for Cybil. Virgil had quoted Wordsworth, saying, "Life is divided into three terms—that which was, which is, and which will be. Let us learn from the past to profit by the present, and from the present to live better in the future." Cybil saw that the only way she would ever profit from the present was to end her twenty-six-year marriage.

Carlyle could never tell if Virgil was a true stoic and existential intellectual or just a gambling addict. She knew her father had been active in lots of protests in the '60s, when he was just a teen himself. He'd even spent time on the Haight-Ashbury with Ken Keesey. The boys at the track loved him, and allowed him a dry erase board where he could write up his "stanza of the day," a tradition she wasn't sure was still upheld. Carlyle owed her name to her father, who insisted she be named after Thomas Carlyle—an obscure Scottish philosopher whom her father idolized.

Carlyle had told her father she was engaged to Ethan. His divorce had happened years before but he still half-heartedly tried to warn her off marriage, quoting another of his favorite luminaries, Ambrose Bierce: "Love is a condition only curable by marriage." It was hard for her to believe that either of her parents had ever loved each other. For the last few years of their relationship—the ones Carlyle could remember best—they floated in and out of rooms, orchestrating a delicate dance of avoidance. Her mother was an ever-growing power, devouring books and workshops on management, communication, and leadership theories; she was constantly trying to improve herself and her company. She had strict control of every aspect of her life, except her husband. By contrast, Virgil seemed to shrink into himself. He was prone to long bouts of depression in which he wouldn't leave their bed until three in the afternoon, and even then it was only to go place a bet.

Carlyle looked at her parents' relationship as a cautionary tale, and had been particularly persnickety when choosing a mate. She wanted children, of course, but not badly enough to put them through what she and her siblings had been through. When she chose Ethan, she chose him for the long haul. He had come from a divorced family too, and he agreed that divorce was not an option. "Marriage is something you work at," they'd both agreed.

Remembering their promises to each other and her father's harsh philosophical remarks was like rubbing course salt into a fresh wound. She felt claustrophobic inside the plane cabin and looked over to see her brother snoring and drooling onto his gauzy pillow. Glad she had taken the window seat, Carlyle lifted the partition to reveal the vast blue of the ocean bleeding into the new morning sky. The *Fasten Seatbelt* sign clicked on and the captain announced they were making their descent into the Florida Keys.

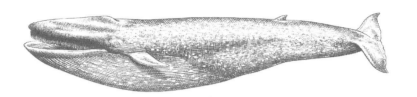

ACT II

CHAPTER ONE

Carlyle and Tom landed in Key West, which was about a thirty-minute drive from their mother's house in Big Pine Key. Their layover in Atlanta had put them into Key West at 2:30 p.m. After turning her phone off on the first flight, she'd left it off, trying to conserve battery power. As they headed to the rental car desk, she flicked on her phone. She suddenly became aware of herself and a sharp hunger in her stomach; she was starving. She wondered how much of a hurry they should be in.

She found seven text messages waiting: four from Valerie, two from her mother, and one from Ethan.

Where are you? - Mom, 5:18 a.m.

We are really worried, where are you? - Valerie, 5:31 a.m.

Are you kidnapped?! - Mom, 6:20 a.m.

Hope you're ok, we have no idea where you are. - Valerie, 6:42 a.m.

We've called Ethan, he has no idea about any of this. Thanks for making me have to have that conversation. Are you okay? Is Tom with you? Plz txt back. - Valerie, 7:06 a.m.

Are you okay? - Ethan, 7:11 a.m.

We just talked to Marius. He spilled it about your little rescue plan. We're getting on the jet and heading to Big Pine Key. I'll keep trying you, but meet us at Valhalla. - Valerie, 7:26 a.m.

Valhalla was what they disaffectionately called their mother's summer home. It was ridiculously large and obnoxious, according to Valerie's reports. "Very Nouveau Riche," Valerie had said with a tip of her nose in the air. Carlyle had wanted to explain to her sister that their family was the very definition of Nouveau Riche, but it seemed beyond the point.

Carlyle realized how stupid and selfish they had been leaving her mother's house without telling anyone where they were going. The wine had worn off and she was seeing things more clearly. Now she and her brother were considered missing too. She immediately called Valerie, who picked up on the first ring.

"Where the fuck have you been?"

"We just got off the plane. We're in Key West. We're renting a car to drive to Big Pine."

"Oh my god. What the hell were you thinking?"

"We weren't. It was Tom's idea. He wants to rescue Janine. We'll be there within the hour and we can all decide what to do." Carlyle cut the conversation short. She was exhausted and not in the mood for a long lecture. She already felt terrible about making them worry. She clicked the phone off and turned to her brother. "They thought we were kidnapped too, until Marius told them where we were." She finished signing the rental car agreements.

The woman behind the counter gave her a strange look as she tabulated the total for the car and the gas. Carlyle could feel the warm, delicate breeze and smell the sea in the distance every time the door to the car park opened.

"Your total deposit comes to $152.37," the clerk said.

Carlyle looked at Tom, who had pulled out his velcro wallet and was staring blankly at its contents: an ATM receipt and a limp piece of spearmint gum. It was clear she would be bank-rolling the rest of their adventure together.

"So, Mom's in Big Pine," she said to him as they walked to the car.

"What? No! She can't be here! This was my idea!" Tom seethed.

"Yeah, they're at Valhalla. We're going to meet them now." Carlyle could tell her brother was a little relieved that they really wouldn't have to pull off this rescue mission without their mother. Carlyle thought about what it must be like for a typical nineteen-year-old striking out on his own. "I think it rarely involves an Indiana-Jones-style cruise to Mexico," she concluded to herself. For all his nineteen-year-old hubris,

Tom breathed a large sigh, thankful that he would not be without his mother's backup. Carlyle could see now that the wine had informed too much of her late-night decision to run away, and she was comforted knowing that they'd fallen into the safety net that was their mother.

"Come on, what did you think would happen when they realized we weren't there? They were going ape-shit thinking we'd been kidnapped. They talked to Marius, and then they got on the jet. If we hadn't gotten stuck in Atlanta we would've beaten them here. Now I have to call Ethan and explain everything, which is something I really didn't want to do."

She and Ethan had the only pseudo-functional relationship in her family right now, and she did not want to draw attention to the fact that they were having problems. Valerie hadn't had a real boyfriend since college, and Tom had a revolving door of girls at his beck and call, but he would call none of them his girlfriend. To her knowledge, her mother hadn't even been on a date since the divorce. The Pierce family considered themselves unlucky in love. When Carlyle married Ethan, and they continued to be happy and in love for more than eight years, it seemed the curse had been broken. Or so they had thought.

She knew she should have told Ethan she was leaving. But she hadn't. She wanted him to miss her. She wanted him to wait by the phone. She wanted him to want to come home. She was sure she would be back by the time that happened, and he would never even need to know she was gone. Though their relationship had been happy until recently, her family had always been a sticking point between them. Janine left a wake that affected even her most distant acquaintances, and Ethan disapproved of the way her mother handled problems. "She just shoves money at things, as if that makes it all go away," he'd said once before, when they were talking about her mother's response to Tom's expulsion from school. She'd bribed everyone but the bishop at the small Catholic school to just let Tom graduate.

"There are few things that money won't fix," Carlyle remembered saying.

"But those are the things worth fixing the right way. Sometimes you need to spend time; you need to listen. There's no replacement for just loving someone anyway—despite what they've done." It was frustrating to Carlyle that she remembered how amazing her husband was only after she'd let him slip away.

As they drove, she dialed him. She was embarrassed to have this conversation in front of Tom, but there was no way around it.

"Hi," she said, too loudly into the phone.

"Hey, are you okay? Your Mom and sister were freaking out this morning." He wasn't sure whether he should be really concerned, or if this was just another Pierce family episode.

"I'm in Florida, driving towards Big Pine Key," she answered, dodging the question.

"Oh, I bet it's nice down there. I know you always wanted us to go," he said.

"The weather's pretty. Everyone's tan. We're going to have to take one of Mom's boats to Mexico and try to find Janine." She threw it in with the pleasantries, hoping this would make it sound less crazy. It didn't.

"There aren't cabins in those boats. Where will you sleep?" Ethan was always the practical one. When her mother had bought the boats, he'd researched them to see what they looked like and how fast they could go. It wasn't the boats themselves that captivated him; rather, his interest was an extension of his ongoing fascination with how Cybil spent her money. "These are the nicest fishing boats on the market," he'd told Carlyle. From the research he was doing, she thought he might be interested in going down to fish. She'd invited him to go several times, but they never made it. She always had to work, or he wasn't feeling up to so much family time in close quarters.

"That's the question you ask? Not, 'What happened to Janine?' or 'Why do you have to go get her?' You ask about the boat? For your information, she's been kidnapped. We think it's a cartel. Who knows what she was getting into. They're trying to get Mom to pay a ransom. We still haven't really talked about how we're going to handle it, since Tom and I just kind of..." she trailed off. Carlyle was breathless with anger. She was angry at her family's absurdity; angry at herself for participating; and angry that Ethan wouldn't get tangled up in it so easily. He didn't even seem to care about her or the fact that she was gone—all he cared about was the boat.

"Well, I just figured she'd gotten herself into trouble somehow—I mean, that's what she does. Are you in danger? Like, real danger? You don't actually think this is real, do you?"

"I don't know. No one does. I think that's why we're here, because we don't know. If we knew it was real, I'm sure Mom would have called the police." She was quiet for a minute. "I miss you," she said. She knew it was against their current code of conduct to confess such a thing, but it escaped her body like a loose strand of hair; quietly and without a struggle.

He sat for a moment thinking about how only his wife would tack on such a trivial phrase to the end of a diatribe that included words like *police, kidnapping,* and *cartel.* She could go from macro to micro just like that. Do people still love and miss each other in the midst of a kidnapping caper? Do people pine for each other in the middle of a machine gun shoot-out? It all seemed too surreal for him. Yet when she said it, he became aware of a well of sorrow within himself. He was pierced with regret about the fact that she was in Big Pine Key—the center of the beautiful Florida Keys—without him. She'd needled him for months about a vacation, to get away, to relax. She'd even taken a night off and blown up a pool floaty with a cup holder and placed it in the living room, tucking his favorite beer in the coozie. *Finding Nemo* played on their flat-screen— the only semi-tropical themed movie in their collection.

He came home and they'd tried to sit in the pool floaty together on the hardwood floor, but it kept falling over. With it they would tumble and laugh and kiss each other. "I just wanted us to have a moment of vacation right here at home," she'd said. In this moment he could not remember all the excuses he'd given her to put off a trip, but none of them seemed good enough now. He pictured her and Tom cruising along Overseas Highway, the wind in their hair, and he realized he would do anything to be there with her now.

"I miss you, too. Wish I was there," he said earnestly.

"Me too," she replied. She felt giddy that he'd returned her affection.

Maybe there was hope after all. "I'll let you know how it all goes."

"Okay. Well, be careful. And good luck, I guess." His sign-off felt weak. "What do sailors say for good luck?" he asked.

"Umm, don't fall overboard?" she bantered back.

And just like that, they were their old selves again.

CHAPTER TWO

When Carlyle pulled up to the house, she was shocked. This was her first time here, though she'd been invited many times and even canceled a few trips at the last minute. Though she'd heard tales of Valhalla, she'd had no idea about the house and she was markedly surprised by its size, location, and beauty. The house sat on almost two acres stippled with the big pines that gave the Key its name. The back of the house abutted a mangrove creek—the shallow water and brush that led out to the ocean. On the large branches of the mangroves she could see iguanas sunning themselves and white herons perched, waiting for fish.

The house itself had a Tuscan-tiled roof and statuesque columns that transported Carlyle to a European piazza. Among the big pines were dozens of local plants—hibiscus, palm trees, irises, belladonna, and cacti. The property jutted out into the creek, splitting it into a fork that made room for two boat docks, one on the west and one on the east. From the driveway she could see a pool and hot tub sparkling in the back yard. She was taken aback by the visual evidence of the level of wealth her mother had achieved on her own.

Before they could get their bags out of the trunk, Cybil came charging out of the house. She grabbed Tom around the neck and dragged him along as she walked toward Carlyle. She grabbed Carlyle into a hug with her brother. She held on to her two youngest children. Carlyle could see tears welling up in her mother's already-puffy eyes. Within seconds, tears were streaming down Cybil's face and she made no motion to wipe them away. When Carlyle or Tom would try to move away, she would grasp on tighter, still not ready to let go.

"How did you beat us here?" Carlyle asked, her face still pressed against her mother's. She hoped that starting a conversation would bring Cybil back to reality.

Without loosing her embrace, her mother replied, "We took the jet. I'm assuming you stopped over in Atlanta?" Cybil knew flight schedules like most people knew their neighborhood roads. Her tone of voice was all logistics, but she still held them close to her. Tom had begun to walk the cluster toward the door.

Cybil finally released her grasp. Her tear-streaked face was angry. "How could you two leave like that? What were you thinking? We thought you were dead. Machete-ed to pieces on some Mexican road." Their mother had a penchant for drama, often asking disturbing questions about violent movies that she swore she could not stomach. *Oh, but does he get shot or stabbed? Stabbed? Where, in the chest or in the gut? Don't tell me! The gut? It was the gut wasn't it?* It was as if she was trying to ward off the macabre by delving into its details.

"Tom wanted to save the day," Carlyle answered, gesturing toward her brother.

"Oh, honey, you always save the day in my book," Cybil said, grabbing her son's cheek. He groaned and pushed her away, shooting Carlyle an exasperated look. She could see why he wanted to accomplish something—anything—on his own. "C.J.'s inside. We need to talk about options. You two left before... well, let's just discuss it as a family."

Carlyle's phone buzzed, and she looked down to see it was Marius calling. "Hold on guys, I may have some more info. I'll be there in a sec." The family went inside and left Carlyle on the driveway to take the call.

"Thanks for ratting me out! What have you got?" Carlyle said, picking up the phone.

"Thanks for waking me up at 3 a.m. And, anyway, it's funny you should ask. I've got a boardroom full of Senior VPs all wondering why neither you nor Cybil are here for the Strategic Planning meeting. I've also got about four reporters on hold waiting for a comment from you on the new research that's just come out about gluten—"

Carlyle interrupted him. "We've had a family emergency. That is all you are allowed to say. I don't want anyone getting any ideas or any one digging deeper into this. We need to protect Janine, so this story can't get out, okay?"

"So what should I tell the VPs?"

"Barry can lead the meeting, the slide deck is on my shared drive. As for the reporters, just tell them: 'All of Naturebar's products are gluten-free because we believe that gluten causes negative long-term health effects.' Now—what do you have on the blog and El Toro?"

"I couldn't find any financial link between Janine and El Toro. She has been dealing a lot in cash, and the last three days she's taken out a withdrawal from an ATM in Progreso. The blog is still dark."

"Wow, so at least we know she's really there. But we don't know if she was forced to make the withdrawal or just walked casually up to the ATM and took the money out? Is there any way we can get some camera footage from the ATM?"

"I'm a step ahead of you, boss. I called the bank and asked them about it. Told them I was with the local PD." He paused as if waiting for an affirmation of his dishonesty. Carlyle said nothing and he continued. "They said that usually they have footage for domestic ATMs, but foreign ATMs are a different story. Most of them are outdated and don't have cameras. They told me they'd look into it, but not to hold my breath."

"Shit," Carlyle said definitively. "Well, keep monitoring her account. Maybe we'll get lucky. At least we know the whole thing's not total bullshit. She *is* in Progreso."

"Right."

"Listen, Marius. We're in Big Pine Key now. We haven't talked it over yet, but it looks like we might be going down there to try and get her. Consider me and Cybil out for at least the next week." She'd gotten used to referring to her mother by her first name. "If anyone asks, make up something—a retreat, a monastery where talking is forbidden—whatever. Make it work."

"Make it work," was their code for saying, "I know what I'm asking you to do is impossible, but pull it off anyway." Marius was the king of making it work. She ended the call abruptly as Marius began to speak again. If it was important, he would text her. She turned to head inside the gargantuan house, and tried to prepare herself for what the next few hours might bring.

CHAPTER THREE

Inside, Carlyle found her mother, Valerie, Tom, and C.J. sitting on barstools around the open kitchen counter.

C.J. was the captain of Cybil's deep-sea fishing fleet. When she'd started coming to Big Pine Key, she began a campaign to suss out the best fishing boat captain in the Keys. TThe towns in the Keys were small, and mostly populated by seasonal residents. Among the townies, there was fierce competition on the water. It was universal, though, in her inquiries, that C.J. was the most hated captain around. C.J. took out only the most fastidious fishermen. There was no horseplay or slacking on his daily fishing charters. He was serious and to-the-point. Whether this was why he was hated by all the other fishermen, or if it was because he really was the best, Cybil wasn't sure. After twenty years in management, she'd decided that if people hate you, there's a fifty percent chance you're good at your job, and a fifty percent chance you're just an asshole. In C.J.'s case, he was an asshole who was good at his job. He could captain anything from a dingy with an onboard motor to a decked-out houseboat.

Cybil trusted C.J. implicitly with all things sea-related. In the past two years, she'd come down for every tournament in the area. Her goal was to become *Female Angler of the Year*, an honor bestowed upon only the most deserving professional anglers, women who hauled in hundred-pound tarpon and Sailfish without breaking a sweat. C.J. had been frank with Cybil when she'd told him her goal. "You'll never make it," he'd said. "It'll take five years to get you to where those women were in high school. They were born on the water. You're at a natural disadvantage. And then there's your age to consider..."

She'd stopped him cold. "No matter my age. Just take me to where the fish are and I'll reel 'em in. Think you can do that?" Since that conversation, C.J. never brought up her age again. In fact, it was a matter that her children had been instructed never to broach. Cybil had forced Valerie to lie to C.J. and tell him she and Cybil were sisters. "I just don't want to be treated any differently on the boat," Cybil had explained. Carlyle knew the truth, that her mother wanted to retain her youth and beauty, and that keeping the captain and his crew in the dark about her age was just another way of staying young.

C.J. sat inordinately close to her sister, and Carlyle picked up a light blush coming from Valerie's face. "A beautiful sister, and a beautiful daughter. How come you never told me, Cyb?" C.J. was attempting to compliment Valerie, but Carlyle saw her face fall.

"We're her daughters. Both of us," Carlyle said. She wasn't in the mood for her mother's lies, and couldn't imagine keeping up that charade, what with all the other moving pieces in this situation. Her mother shot her an angry glance. "There's the two of us, and we have another sister. In fact, that's why we're here."

"Well... this is interesting." When C.J. looked at Cybil—a woman he thought he knew well—she avoided his eyes and her face grew red to match her already-mortified daughter's.

"C.J., I think that's the first time I've heard you use a word with more than four letters," Cybil lashed back. C.J. was tough on her on the water, which was one of the reasons she chose him to be her teacher. She could find a lax yes-man anywhere back on land, but C.J. would not bullshit her, and that service came at a dear price. Since she let him reprimand her so often while they were fishing, it was nice to remind him once in awhile that she was the boss.

"Can we move on, please?" Valerie said. She seemed genuinely hurt.

"What are we going to do?" Carlyle asked the group.

"Shouldn't we call the police?" Valerie asked again. Eyes darted around the circle.

"That's one of the specifications of the kidnappers—not to involve the police," Cybil pointed out. Carlyle thought about the word "spec-ifications." It sounded funny here, that kidnappers would have spec-ifications. Wouldn't they be more likely to have demands? A contract has specifications; a kidnapper has "do this or I'll fucking kill this bitch." Still, that was pretty specific.

"I really want to avoid contacting the police. We have a public company. If it comes out that two of the chief officers are off hunting some kidnappers, that will seriously affect our brand and ultimately our stock price. I don't want to risk it unless we absolutely have to." Carlyle heard the words coming out of her mouth, but it felt like they were coming from someone else. Was she really so cold?

"I'm sorry, can I just suggest something here?" Valerie interjected. Carlyle waited with bated breath to hear what her sister was going to say. "Has anyone thought that she might be faking this whole thing? She's been dirt poor since her last stint in rehab. Tom, just think about what she did to you. Do you think she would hesitate to take Mom for half a million bucks? She could be trying to get enough money to coast in a beach house on the ocean for the rest of her life…" Valerie's voice faded away for a moment, as though the thought of a beach house life was such a faraway dream that it shook her to the core. She could almost taste the salt on her lips and feel her feet making erasable foot-prints in the sand, her toes being kissed by the tide. She snapped back to reality. "I mean, $500,000 is not a lot of money. Why not a million? Two million? I mean, Mom? Have you thought about this? Should we all uproot our lives for this hoax?"

"Well, I thought that too, Valerie," Carlyle interjected. "I've had Marius do some digging for us. Remember, we know that there is a drug cartel that operates out of Progreso. We've also found out that Janine has visited an ATM in Progreso in the last three days. So we know that she is, in fact, there. We don't know if she was forced to take out the money, or if she's just living it up until we get there."

"Oh, god," Tom muttered. His face was pale and he'd begun to break out in a light sweat.

"I had thought it was fake, too," Cybil admitted. They all knew Janine. They had seen what she was capable of over the past two years. "The amount is odd. But, it seems an amount that I would be able to get relatively easily. Maybe they're professionals and they're playing this very smartly."

For the first time the focus shifted to Tom. He sat staring wide-eyed with his arms crossed over his barrel chest. He was a perfect physical specimen, with dark brooding eyes and a baseball tee that stretched over his frequently flexed arms and pecs. He looked at his family as if they were a pack of wolves. "I can't believe you all are even my family," he said with the quiet angst of a stilted teen, which he still technically was. "She's our sister. She's your daughter, Mom, and you would just leave her in the hands of those... those animals?!" He got angrier as he spoke.

"Tom, this is the woman, yes, our sister, who single-handedly got you expelled from high school in the middle of your senior year." Valerie didn't pull any punches. Though everyone at the table knew what had happened, Valerie was the first to string together this particular element of cause and effect.

Bits and pieces of the story had been told, of course, about how Tom had become the kingpin weed dealer in his small Christian private school. He relied on Janine and her townhouse as the hub of his weed empire, which they really built together. In the space of just a few months, every high school kid in Omaha knew where to find the best quality weed, and they knew Tom was the contact person. His chest puffed with pride every time someone recognized him. Janine knew how to keep him on her side—a steady diet of compliments. When his school finally found the root of the marijuana problem, they had no choice but to expel him. Cybil was the last to know, and when she came home to find her only son in tears and handcuffs, she knew she had to separate Tom from his beloved older sister. He was still young, she reasoned; he could still be saved.

"That doesn't change anything. We've all made mistakes. We have to save her. We're all she has," Tom answered simply. Carlyle tut-tutted at him for his naiveté. *Everything is so black and white when you're young,* she thought. Good, bad. Right, wrong. Save her, or leave her to those animals. If only it was that simple.

CHAPTER FOUR

"**M**om," Valerie continued to focus her attention on convincing their mother to forget about this charade, "have you tracked down the diamond-encrusted hummingbird yet?" Carlyle and Tom's ears perked. They didn't know anything about their mother's favorite brooch, or that it was missing. Cybil's favorite animal was the hummingbird. Any time she gotten dressed up for a charity function when they were children, she had always put on the hummingbird brooch. It had sapphire wings and an emerald tail, and was so light it looked like it might flit away at any moment—which, Carlyle had considered on many occasions, was the same feeling you got from Cybil. Her children wondered if that was why she liked hummingbirds so much, because as soon as you caught a glimpse of them, they were gone. This was how Cybil liked to be in the world, too—untouchable.

Cybil looked at the counter. Carlyle could see the exhaustion beginning to tug at the delicate skin around her mother's eyes. Cybil took a deep breath before telling her children what had happened.

Cybil had met Lucille, her best friend, at 225 Chophouse—one of Omaha's nicest restaurants. To Cybil and Lucille, being best friends meant seeing their names on the letterheads of charity events they co-chaired, getting invites to girls' weekends in Tahoe and Oahu, and sharing the latest gossip about their country club members' salacious affairs with caddies and tennis pros. Over brunch quiche a few weeks ago, Cybil noticed her one-of-a-kind hummingbird brooch nestled in the folds of Lucille's silk patterned scarf.

"Why are you wearing my brooch, Lucille?" Cybil asked, immediately halting the conversation. "That's not funny."

"Whatever do you mean, dear?" Lucille blushed and looked down at the intricate ornament. "I saw this in DeBeers when I was in New York last weekend and thought of you, since it so resembles yours. I thought we could be hummingbird sisters!" She laughed lightly, trying to thaw Cybil's cold stare.

"Lucille, my brooch is one-of-a-kind. I seriously doubt that DeBeers would make anything that close to it, not to mention that mine has been missing for months. May I see it?" She knew how and when to turn on the bulldog-like ferocity she generally kept hidden under a docile exterior.

Lucille wrestled the pin out from her scarf and reluctantly handed it over. Cybil flipped the pin clasp up and found the black scribble she knew marked her already one-of-a-kind piece of jewelry. When Carlyle and Tom were small, they had conspired to make Cybil stay home with them instead of going to yet another weekend soiree. Carlyle snuck the brooch out of Cybil's closet and passed it off to Tom, who was ready and waiting with a black permanent marker. They both knew that if they could black out the hummingbird, their mother would be unable to attend an event without it. Luckily, Tom had started his scribbling on the back of the pendant. When Cybil caught him, she couldn't help but be a little flattered that her children wanted her home so badly. No real damage had been done to the bejeweled side of the brooch; sitting around the counter now, she couldn't recall if she'd gone out that night or stayed in.

"You went out," Carlyle said. Cybil started to question the truth of it, but the decisiveness in Carlyle's voice encouraged her to abandon any efforts at rewriting history.

"So anyway," Cybil continued, "I said, 'Lucille, look. See this black scribble? That's the mark that Tom made the night he tried to get me to stay home. I guess that was about twelve years ago now. My, how time goes by quickly.'" Cybil had a way of delivering clichés that made them seem entirely novel.

"Oh my god. I am so humiliated. It *is* yours after all." Lucille put her

head in her hands, too embarrassed to look her friend in the eyes. "I...
I didn't get it at DeBeers. I did go to DeBeers, that part wasn't a lie. But
I didn't get this there. I found this at Diamond Jim's—the pawnshop
on Fourteenth Street. I find a lot of good stuff there, and it's pretty
cheap. I saw this and thought that it so resembled yours, it would be
something to bond us. Now I'm just horrified."

Lucille's husband was an oilman who'd inherited his company
from his grandfather. Lucille could just as well have her face embla-
zoned on the side of their private plane, so the thought of her shop-
ping at pawnshops was both humorous and unimaginable to Cybil.
Lucille's admission was akin to exposing a sick sexual perversion, or
a long-standing heroin addiction—at least by Omaha high society's
standards.

"I told her the secret was safe with me," Cybil said with a mischie-
vous glance around the counter. "But I didn't bother bickering over
the bill when she offered to treat."

When the hummingbird had gone missing, Cybil had assumed
Janine had taken it somewhere to pawn for money, but she'd had no
idea where that might have been or how to track it down. Multitudes
of other goods had disappeared and she'd assumed they'd met the
same fate as the brooch. When she saw the hummingbird on Lucille,
she was both relieved and deeply saddened. She was so happy to be
reunited with her long lost favorite heirloom, but distressed to find
out the truth about what had happened to it. This confirmed her fears
about Janine. It angered her and made a sick hole in her stomach to
think that she could have created such a cold monster. Since then, she
wasn't sure to what depths her second daughter would sink, and the
possibilities frightened her.

"And to think, Lucille even tried to get me to pay her the three
hundred bucks it had cost her at Diamond Jim's. The nerve of that
woman," Cybil seethed.

Valerie had known that the hummingbird would be the final nail
in Janine's coffin. The whole family loved that pin as if it were a pet.
Now they all knew the truth, and how low their sister had sunk in the
months before her retreat back to California.

"Here's my two cents, not that anyone asked, but I think she's kid-napped herself," Carlyle said boldly. After putting together the infor-mation from Marius, this was the inference she had made.

"It's true that she's been very angry with me since I cut her off fi-nancially," Cybil said. "About a month ago she reached out to me and told me that she was homeless—moving in and out of shelters as beds were available..." Her voice began to quake. "I still refused to help unless she cleaned up her act for real this time. I haven't heard any-thing since." The other siblings knew very little about their mother and Janine's falling out. Carlyle only knew it would take an awful lot for Cybil to cut any of them off.

Carlyle and Valerie were on to the same logical conclusion, but the truth was, there were a few more powerful motivators for Janine to kidnap herself. First and foremost, she would be trying to get back at all of them. In Janine's narcissistic sense of justice, they would all be sorry they had treated her so poorly when they realized she was in danger.

It seemed that Janine was in dire straits—but had that led her to make dangerous decisions that could lead to being taken, or was she simply at the end of her rope and grasping at straws?

"So what are we going to do?" Carlyle asked the group again.

"Sounds like there are two options—number one, we ignore the note. Do nothing and hope she's all right. Number two, we go down to Mexico to get her ourselves, avoiding any nastiness with the press and the police," Valerie summarized the situation and made it clear by the tone of her voice which option she preferred. "If we go, and it's not real, then it will just be a nice family getaway."

Chapter Five

They all looked to Cybil for a decision. As usual, even though the girls had had their say, the final choice was up to their mother—the one who was ultimately responsible for the ransom if she wanted to pay it.

"What are we going to do about the boats?" Cybil asked. And like that, they all took it in that this was really happening. Without a definitive yes or no, Cybil had made her decision clear. "Is there any way we can take the fishing boats? We can just get some tarps at the FishMart and sleep under those, maybe?"

Carlyle saw no need to further alarm her family with her information about the mystery blogger. They were going to Mexico, and that was that. Giving them further reason to worry because of a hair-brained hunch seemed unnecessary. She would keep this one to herself, at least for now.

"It's a twenty-hour journey at least," answered C.J. "There's not enough room in the hull for all the supplies we would need, and we can't be makin' any stops, 'specially not if this is an under-the-radar rescue mission. We've got to get there as fast as we can and y'all have got to have room to sleep. You won't have that in the outboard boat. Cyb—I heard you know someone down here who's got a yacht. Think we could trade up for a few days?"

Carlyle watched her sister watch C.J. It was as if she'd developed a crush on him in just the last few minutes. She felt sorry for her sister, and wanted to tell her not to embarrass herself.

"I know you're not seriously asking me that question. Are you suggesting I go to Todd Novak—the best fisherman in the Keys and the only person who beat us last year in every sailfish and tarpon tournament—and request the use of his yacht for a few days?" Cybil was breathless. Todd Novak was her pseudo-arch-nemesis and arguably the reason she began fishing in the first place. Todd owned STRENGTHbar, a meal replacement and protein bar company he'd started in his garage in the early '90s. Todd was known for his Ghandi-like approach to business—he was a pacifist. He was the only man in the world that Cybil knew of who had grown a company as quickly as he had while using what he called the Peaceful Presence management style. This meant he did not believe in hostile takeovers, mergers, power plays, top down management, or any other traditional—what he would call "carnivorous"—styles of management. It was rumored that he threw back every fish he ever caught. Local lore told that Todd Novak had caught a 290-pound tarpon—two pounds heavier than the world record—and threw it back. Apparently the crew on his boat begged him to let one of them keep the fish. "It is not for us to disturb the delicate balance of nature," he had replied.

"I cannot do that. I can't. It's unheard of. Besides, I've only met Todd a couple of times. I doubt he'd even remember me…" Cybil drifted off. She thought of the health food conference they'd both been at a year earlier. Todd was at the bar surrounded by salesmen and other health food business owners. "Novak, you give new meaning to the term *granola*. You mean to say even if you could make millions, you still don't believe in mergers?"

"What if I let you buy my company for ten dollars, Todd?" one man said.

"You can have mine for five," another man said.

These men owned huge, profitable enterprises, but they were stunned at Todd's dedication to his pacifistic exterior. Even so, Todd's business was worth three times any of their companies' valuations.

"C'mon man, don't you want to make some money? I'll sign it over to you for free. And no dolphins were harmed in the making of this transaction!" The man burst into laughter and several others followed suit. Todd sat like a stoic sipping his Perrier, saying nothing. Cybil—at home in the company of men showing off—stepped into the circle and laid down a crisp twenty-dollar bill.

"I'll let you have this twenty and in exchange I'll take STRENGTHbar off your hands," she said with a smirk.

Todd Novak looked at her, stunned. It took him a moment to realize that she was only joking in an attempt to take the spotlight off of him. His brown eyes sported unusually long eyelashes for a man, but they were hidden under the small, rimless glasses he wore. She could see a sparkle in his eye as he picked up the twenty and loudly pronounced, "Done!"

The men that surrounded them went quiet, their jaws open to reveal the popcorn and bar peanuts they'd been shoveling into their mouths. Todd stood up and put his hand on the small of Cybil's back to lead her out of the crowd. "Let's go hammer out the details," he said, struggling to hide his smile.

Once they were away from the gawkers, Cybil and Todd laughed. "I'm sure I'll get a call later about my stock price taking a dive, but that was so worth it," Todd said.

"Wait, you mean you weren't serious?" Cybil said, half joking and half truly wishing she could own STRENGTHbar, the most successful protein bar company on the market. She'd followed Todd's rise to the top and thought of him as a new kind of corporate hero.

"Well, I'd be more willing to entertain your offer over drinks," he said. His face had turned serious and she suddenly realized how tall and imposing a figure he was. As they chatted, he stealthily led her to another one of the hotel's many bars, this one much less boisterous. A blazing fire roared in the hearth and two leather armchairs appeared to be waiting just for them. They sat down and he ordered a vodka soda, she a glass of Prosecco.

"Cybil Pierce. I have to confess that you are not at all how I thought you would be," he said.

She felt her face flush from the heat of the fire, but also from his gaze. She was nearing fifty-five, and could not once remember a man's gaze making her feel so girlish and unsure. "Todd Novak. How did you think I would be?" She mirrored his speech pattern, if only to reassure herself that she was, in fact, speaking with *the* Todd Novak.

"Well, word on the street is that you're a total hard-ass. I mean brutal. Is it true you once fired eighteen people because they took too long in the bathroom?" She looked at him sternly, as they both knew this was a breech of the non-disclosure agreements each of them had to sign every time they let someone go. "I know you can't really tell me, but what I meant to say was that you actually seem…" he paused, "pretty sweet to me. And funny." He bowed his head and placed his hands palm to palm. He whispered something in what she identified as Hindu. After this ritual, he spritzed the slice of lime perched on the rim of his glass and took a sip.

"To be fair, ten of those employees were doing blow in said bathroom. And… thanks." She suddenly felt underdressed even though she was wearing her typical corporate attire: a smart navy blue business suit with a colorful camisole peeking out at the waist and décolletage. "Well, is it true you won't fire anyone?" She'd heard this through the industry rumor mill and scoffed—how could anyone run a business without firing anyone? She'd dismissed him as a quack then, but now she wasn't so sure. His stare was intense and attuned. He was confident, yet not cocky. He took in everything that happened around them while at the same time focusing on her, making her feel as if she were the most important thing in his life.

"Yes, I suppose that technically is true. I just have my lackeys do it," he was deadpan, but couldn't help cracking a smile after seeing her stunned expression. "But seriously, I believe that firing is something of another time. It's a bit Paleolithic—kind of feudal, really—this idea of firing. Even the word—*firing*—it sounds dangerous, frightening, horrific. The last thing I want my team to think of when they think of me is terror. Fear makes people shrivel up. Stress makes them break down. I want my tribe to feel uplifted, comfortable, cradled. I want them to be free to be their most creative selves. But I didn't ask you here to talk about business, Cybil. I'm tired of talking about business."

Although she tried to remain rational, Cybil was mesmerized. She'd studied all traditional forms of business, leadership, and management.

She focused on being a "highly effective" person, and compared to most other people in her field, she was very successful. But looking at Todd, she felt she'd done it all wrong. She fired people. In fact, she rather enjoyed the desperate stares from her employees in the moment they realized their jobs were in her hands. She was a woman in a man's world. Throughout her career she'd put on her proverbial war paint—foundation, blush, and mascara—and gone into battle. She was sure there was no place for softness, vulnerability, or understanding at work. Work was where you went to get away from all of that. Work was black and white. She was able to keep everyone at arm's length, and with a gentle reminder of who held the purse strings, she was able to get the best out of people. Or so she'd thought.

All those years she'd felt guilty for enjoying the work, for not wanting to be home with her children. She knew most working women waited impatiently for five o'clock so they could rush home and see their families. She'd never felt that way. She'd never wanted to take the armor off. So she kept it on. She slept in it. She ate in it. It became a second skin.

Now looking at Todd, she felt the armor coming loose. She took a big swig of Prosecco and exhaled. "Okay, no business," she responded. "Is it true you threw back a 290-pound tarpon?"

His eyes were shocked but his mouth was smugly sure. "I never thought I would find a girl who's equal parts businesswoman and angler! Where'd you hear that story? Do you fish near Big Pine Key?"

"You can't fish anywhere in the Keys without hearing about the great Todd Novak and his Buddhist fishing practices," she said. "I have a house in Big Pine and I own a few boats. I fish with C.J., I'm sure you know him."

"I've heard of him. I think C.J.'s fishing practices would be considered the opposite of Buddhist, whatever that is," he said with a laugh. Even though they seemed to be polar opposites, he was deeply intrigued by Cybil. They continued their conversation into the night. Servers brought more drinks. She threw her head back, possessed by a laugh she thought she'd lost long ago. It wiggled free from a small, kind place inside her that grew steadily as the night marched on.

CHAPTER SIX

Eventually, fuzzy and buzzy from the drinks, they wobbled up to his room. She enjoyed his sure, confident touch leading her to the bed.

"Lay down flat on your back." He wasn't forceful, but something deep inside Cybil told her she didn't want to know what would happen if she disobeyed. She complied, and realized she was hungry to be told what to do. Every day she ordered people around; constantly, people looked to her for answers. It had hardened her. She wanted to be soft in this moment. "Cross your arms over your chest. Close your eyes." She was still fully clothed, but she felt on the brink of an orgasm as he gently ran the back of his hand across her cheek. His hand traveled down her side. She opened her mouth to let out a moan and he shushed her loudly. "Don't speak. Don't even move." Again, he wasn't forceful or mean, but she knew not to disobey. He stood over her, silent for a long time. Her tingling and desire began to fade, but she knew he was still near. She dare not move or open her eyes.

A low chant, almost a whisper began to escape from him. It sounded like the same foreign tongue in which he'd prayed over his drink, but this was somehow older—more removed. As she listened she felt herself relax completely. Even though she still had the spins from so much wine, she'd never felt so still. Her cells felt as if they'd stopped oscillating, and though she could still breathe, her lungs ceased to move. She was part of the bed, part of the world, at one with nature. Her mind was clear and free from worry, something she hadn't experienced since she was a small child. The chanting continued and she couldn't tell how long she had been lying there, but she still hadn't moved.

She heard the sound of fabric moving—it must be him walking. But in which direction? Toward her or away? She craved him with every inch of her body but tried to remain in her detached, statuesque state.

The chanting stopped abruptly. She felt a presence hovering above her. "Open your eyes," he whispered. She could feel his breath on her face and it smelled of crisp mint. Before her eyes were even fully open she found herself devouring him, kissing him forcefully on the mouth and pulling him on top of her, their bodies moving together as one.

The next moment all of their clothes were off. She couldn't remember the details of getting them off, but the important thing was that whatever had separated the two of them was now gone. She had never been a woman with a large sexual appetite—the years since her divorce would be considered celibate to most—but suddenly it seemed that if she and Todd could not have sex, she would die right there from wanting him.

Her eyes begged him for it, but he knew this moment well. He lay down next to her, placing his head in the crook of her arm. He took his fingertip and drew lazy designs across her skin, amused when she looked at him with panting desire.

She took control and climbed on top of him, and it felt to her like climbing Everest—this ascent to intimacy. But once there she was filled with what she craved. Todd lost his stoic demeanor and an urgent pleasure came over him. They melted together, the sweat and heat of their bodies moving in rapid progression toward their common goal. The stillness from before returned and yet this time, it was different. It was a slow-motion, pulsating calm—one blunt and too-short moment where infinity seemed to exist. And she and Todd were plunged into it together, writhing, desperately clinging to the feeling that was already gone.

She descended and returned to Earth. It all felt a dream, much too beautiful to exist in this world. They said nothing but drifted off together, feeling as though they had looked into each other's souls. Cybil remembered a brief, unforgettable moment just before falling asleep in his arms during which she was in love with him. It was all of a sudden, like she'd jumped into a puddle. Her feet had been dry, and now they were soaked to the socks.

Morning came through the thin curtains of Todd Novak's hotel room. Cybil opened her eyes, her face so close to his neck that her lashes brushed his skin upon opening. Immediate horror overtook her as she slowly moved to the edge of the bed. She moved at a sloth's pace to avoid waking him. She gathered her things and dressed as she moved toward the door.

She held the latch for as long as she could to avoid the slam that came standard with most hotel room doors. She scampered down the hallway to the elevator.

Since that encounter, Todd had called her assistant on a daily basis. Luckily he had forgotten to ask for her cell phone number, so he'd had to try to reach her through other channels. Flowers came weekly for awhile. Soon his unreturned phone calls dwindled to a weekly nuisance. She breathed a sigh of relief. In the bright light of day she saw there was no place for someone like Todd in her life.

There was no way she could believe that he really liked her. He was certainly after Naturebar. No one could be completely against mergers, and her company was starting to get noticed by many of the large national retail chains. It was the perfect time to snatch it up. All of her adult life she'd been the breadwinner, supporting her husband, her children, her employees, even some of her friends. She knew that if the money was gone, her dependents would go too. She kept herself hidden, just in case that day came. Cybil had always known she was truly alone. To have a man who was her equal approach her was too good to be true, and she wouldn't let herself fall into that trap.

Besides, she was too much to handle even for herself sometimes, not to mention her baggage—four fully-grown but still tethered children. One of whom was unpredictable and unmanageable. How could she explain Janine to Todd? How would he understand? He had never been married and had no children. She was sure *her* children weren't the best introduction to parenthood. She pictured him saying, "Children, the idea of children is so prehistoric…" And think of the pre-nups! No—she was driven to remember their tryst for what it was: one fun, outrageously unsustainable night, never to be spoken of again.

CHAPTER SEVEN

"Mom," Valerie said. "Mom, did you hear C.J.? He contacted Todd Novak for you. He's willing to loan you the yacht."

"What?" Cybil exclaimed, too loudly.

"Yeah, well when you called this morning and said it was an emergency, I went ahead and called his ship captain. He told me Novak was here in the Keys and he gave me his number. Can you believe that?" C.J. said. "Anyway, I talked to him—told him you needed to borrow a yacht. It was weird, as soon as he heard I worked for you, he said yes to whatever I was askin'! But he said it was under one condition…"

"Oh, here we go. What is it?" Cybil's fingertips were on fire. She knew what he was going to ask, and she had not had time to prepare for it.

"He said he wanted you to go to his house and ask him to borrow the yacht in person. That's the only way he'll loan it to you," C.J. said. He looked skeptical.

"Well, that's really creepy," Carlyle said. "You said you've only met him a couple of times, right Mom? Why would he want to see you in person?"

"Um, well, I'm not sure. He's a Buddhist, for Christ's sake—I don't think he's dangerous…" she trailed off, flashing briefly to his breath on her body, his intense gaze. "I don't want to do this. There has to be some other way. Maybe we should just pay these fuckers," she said. Cybil rarely cussed, but when she did it was emphatic and hung in the air. Everyone wanted to comment on how vulgar she'd been, but they knew better.

"Pay who? Pay the kidnappers?" Valerie asked. It was the first time she had acknowledged the possibility that there might actually be kidnappers.

"Yes. Can you get the president of the bank on the phone? We're just going to do this and get it over with," Cybil had already fished out her checkbook while her family stared on in utter shock.

"I don't get it, Mom. You would rather pay some *kidnappers,*" Carlyle's fingers formed air quotes around the word, "than go see some guy who wants to loan you a yacht for free?"

"Just leave it, Carlyle, okay?" Her mother was yelling now and visibly on the edge of her sanity. "Do you have him?" she asked, her voice taut. She gestured to Carlyle's phone, wanting to know if she could speak to the president of Omaha National Bank. He was a friend who frequently joined Cybil's foursomes on the golf course.

"Uh, no, I don't have him…" Carlyle gave her mother a questioning look as if she were trying to convey something they both knew, but maybe she'd forgotten.

"Find a way to get the money. We're going to pay her, or them, the half-mil. This has gone on too long, we're not going to Mexico. It's over." She put her hand across her forehead so her thumb and forefinger were on her temples. She rubbed her fingers in a clockwise motion as she closed her eyes to the world. The thought of having to see Todd again made her feel physically ill. She couldn't look into those eyes again. She couldn't watch him sip vodka soda again. She couldn't let him get close again.

"Mom, can I talk to you in private?" Carlyle said.

"Whatever you need to say, you can say it here," she said, not removing her hand from her face.

Carlyle looked frantically around the room, from Valerie to Tom to C.J. They all stared back as if they were watching a movie. This was something she was hoping not to share with her siblings—especially not with C.J. there. It was something she hadn't even brought up to her mother, though it had been in the back of her mind since she'd checked the accounts a month before.

"Well…" she started, but paused to consider how she wanted to proceed. "I was just doing some routine number crunching—checking

our assets, in case we wanted to go ahead and expand that extra pro-
duction line, like we've talked about. I checked your accounts and
your liquid assets to see what we might be able to come up with for
collateral. Uh," she stopped and fidgeted with her shirt, displaying an
uncharacteristic lack of confidence. "So, the thing is, you don't have
half a million dollars of liquid assets... right now." She added the
"right now" part to soften the blow, but it was not effective.

"What? We grossed three hundred million dollars last year and
I don't have five hundred thousand dollars? How is that possible?"
Cybil looked truly shocked. Carlyle wondered how it was possible she
was so clueless about her own personal financial situation.

Valerie and Tom's jaws hung open. Carlyle gave her mother that
look again, the one that said, "Are you really going to make me say
it?" and "Don't you know the answer to that question?"

"Well?" Cybil asked again.

"Cybil." Carlyle paused, gathering the strength to spit out the
words. "The poker? Have you not been paying attention to the online
poker? Last I checked, you'd lost three hundred thousand dollars this
year with no signs of slowing." Carlyle had become very matter-of-
fact and annoyed about Cybil's lack of vigilance with her own money.
She'd worked so hard for it, and she didn't seem to notice that she was
pittering it away.

Cybil's face went dark. She cast her eyes down, unwilling to look
at anyone in the room. Her mother's embarrassment was palpable,
and Carlyle watched as she processed the information that now hung
in the air like a putrid smell. "How is it possible?" Cybil muttered
to herself after a long time. "I broke even, then went in with half..."
she seemed to be reviewing the events of the most memorable games
she'd played over the last few months.

Her children were under the impression that Cybil played poker
now and then at the local Pawnee casino, and then there was the time
she'd bought into the World Series of Poker tournament. Since her
most recent book was about poker, they'd just assumed it was the
newest in a long string of talents and hobbies that Cybil had taken
up and mastered in her life. Tennis, golf, sport fishing, badminton,

scuba diving… Cybil's competitive spirit was indomitable. When she became better than most people at a sport or activity, she moved on to the next thing; it was not about having fun or the love of the game, it was as if she needed to be constantly better than the average person. She followed a formula: buy all requisite equipment for said activity, find the best teacher in the field, become better-than-competent at each element that dictated success, repeat.

With the poker, though, she'd not followed the formula. After her encounter with Todd Novak, she began to feel a new kind of emptiness. Her daily activities no longer seemed challenging. She went about her life with a sense of removed indifference. Her children noticed the shift toward melancholy, but collectively attributed it to Cybil's age and, they supposed, impending menopause. One night, she'd made her way to the local casino, simply looking for something—anything—to fill the void. She'd laid $5000 down at the window and the woman changed it into chips. She headed to the only high-stakes poker table in the place and anted the single thousand-dollar chip that bought her into the game. She felt a rush; the blood flowed into her hands and face for the first time since Todd Novak had looked at her with his knowing stare.

She returned again and again to the window to change out chips, and the other players at the table looked at each other with a mix of surprise and knowing. "A scorned housewife spending her husband's money," they thought. She'd lost $50,000 that night. When she finally returned home, her clothes soaked with the scent of smoke, she set up an online poker account, determined not to lose that kind of money ever again. Never mind the nagging thoughts that told her to be careful, be more vigilant or look for tells—she just kept clicking bet, bet, bet. When she had an opportunity to go all in, which was almost every game, she did. She was obsessed with the romance of the gesture. "It's a wonderful metaphor," she thought one night. "It's a way of saying to the world, 'I can risk it all, I am ready to part with everything I have for the promise of something better.'" Yet while she risked it all at the table, she became more and more fearful of risking anything in her real life. Infrequently she would think of Todd. When she saw that STRENGTHbar made it into the Fortune 500—something she'd always wanted for Naturebar—she thought of calling to congratulate him. Just as a friend, a fellow warrior on the battlefield.

"Hi, Todd, just wanted to say congrats on the 500," she practiced in the mirror. But the more she played out the conversation, the more she heard herself rebuffing him again and again. She never called.

Sitting here now in her stately Florida home—Tuscan tiles above and below her, granite counters beneath her hands—she felt how cold her world had become. Her children stared at her, in their eyes a mix of fear, wanting, and uncertainty. She wanted to reach out to them, to hold them as she had when they were small, squishy newborns. They hadn't known then and they wouldn't remember, but she'd held each of them and cried over their soft, fuzzy heads, wishing them nothing but love and kindness in their lives. She thought of her second daughter, and felt the hole in her heart where Janine had once burrowed a quiet, soft place.

It appeared she was faced with a choice to go all in, but this time there were no chips, no tables, no cards; there was only the world in which she lived. The world in which she carefully fashioned intricate armor and heavy war paint around her elaborately construed defenses. Across the walls she could see her children, she could see Todd, she could see everything she helped to grow but could never touch. She knew that if she ever wanted to have a better life—to nurture her children or become close with Todd—she would have to lay the armor down. But although she'd so frequently pushed the chips across the table, ready to abandon all she knew for the illustrious unknown, she felt unable to do that now when it really mattered.

It occurred to her that they were still there. That even after learning that she didn't have enough to pay the ransom, they were still there. For all they knew she was going to have to file bankruptcy, sell everything, move into a trailer—and yet there they stood, by her side. This astonished her and yet also filled her with something akin to love—but different. It was the thought that they would be there no matter what, no matter how much money she had, they wouldn't leave her. She felt a tickle behind her eyes and knew tears weren't far away.

"Okay. Looks like I've really screwed the pooch this time," Cybil said. She tried to cover her emotion with humor. "I'll get dressed to go see Todd. C.J., get everything ready for the journey—I expect us to leave tonight." With that, she jumped up off the barstool and headed back to her bedroom.

CHAPTER EIGHT

Carlyle watched her mother scurry from the house. She could not tell if Cybil was in a hurry due to excitement or the necessity to get the errand over with. She had known about the money only for a few weeks. Marius had been the one who caught on first—he'd flagged Cybil's account to notify him of any transactions larger than ten thousand dollars. A month went by before he'd told Carlyle.

"Can we go *out* to lunch today?" he'd asked without trying to conceal his need for a private audience. Carlyle and Marius rarely went to lunch just the two of them unless there were a lot of papers to sign or one of them had a craving for something specific. Carlyle tried to be careful about becoming friends with people in the office. She and Ethan had friends from college, and a few people he knew from the various restaurants he'd worked at. It seemed every time she got close with someone from work, they simply wanted to know information about her mother—something to give them an edge, to help them get promoted. She liked Marius, though, and he'd shown no desire to be upwardly mobile. He seemed happy being a personal assistant and he was good—unexpectedly good—at anticipating the needs of others.

"I have to tell you something. I know it's not my business, it's her money and she can spend it as she likes… well, okay let me just say it." Carlyle sat in silence waiting for the bomb to drop. "I started paying closer attention to Cybil's spending habits these last few weeks because it seemed like money was just draining out of her account.

She's gambled away hundreds of thousands of dollars in the last year—sometimes she goes to the casino, but mostly it's been online. Poker, I think. When I saw the new book title, I thought she might be able to write it off, but that still doesn't solve the problem..." he trailed off, waiting for a tongue-lashing from his boss, who was the same age as he was.

Carlyle sat quietly for a few minutes, unsure how to respond. It was true, it *was* Cybil's money. She'd worked hard her entire life to support them, and for part of the time their father... now that she was older wasn't she entitled to have some fun? But she had a company to think about. They were considering another capital investment—Cybil had always been the one to put her money back into the company. Was she just going to gamble it away until there was nothing left? Did she have a gambling addiction?

Gambling addiction made her think of dim Las Vegas casinos, smoky old men with nothing more to lose, losers waiting for their next big score. Her mother didn't seem to fit that profile. It was true, she was lonely, but had it really come to this?

"I'll take care of it, Marius. I really appreciate you coming to me. If you see any other unusual behavior, please come to me first." They finished up their meal and headed back to the office. Carlyle had meant to bring the issue up with her mother, but there had been a lot of traveling and she'd lost track of the issue. Her personal matters with Ethan weren't helping things either. She could think of little else.

The more shocking piece of the puzzle was that Cybil had had no idea how much money she'd lost. This frightened Carlyle, who knew her mother to be a controlling, structured person who would not be likely to lose track of three hundred thousand dollars.

All this time she'd thought Cybil knew what she was doing; this level of negligence displayed a new level of her mother's deepening psychosis. She had noticed her mother's decline over recent years, but hadn't found the words to talk about it. They were more colleagues than mother and daughter now. When Carlyle had accepted the position at Naturebar, it was partially because she could see her mother was losing the edge that had always made her the competitive, straight-forward risk-taker that had launched the company to its success. Carlyle had hesitated even to take the job—she was the one who looked the most like Cybil, and everyone in the office began to whisper that she was the CIT: Cybil in Training. Since she had no intentions of taking over her mother's position, it irked her that she found herself spending more and more late nights at work and taking more and more business trips while Cybil herself took up gambling and fishing.

Ethan had seen it first, before she'd been willing to admit it to herself. "You're becoming her," he stated matter-of-factly. He hadn't known it, but his saying this was the impetus for her fertility crusade. She'd had a plan: she would get pregnant, and leave the company to be a stay-at-home mom. Nothing would infuriate Cybil more. They could make the finances work somehow, she'd thought. But something deep down inside made Carlyle question her ability to follow through. And her body refused to cooperate. So she felt there was nothing wrong with enjoying the work, and doing a good job, until that little plus sign came.

Sitting here in Florida, surrounded by her mother's opulence, she could see how easy it had been to get sucked in—how easy it continued to be. She stared down at her phone, aching to call Ethan, to tell him about Cybil's gambling, about losing the money, about chasing kidnappers. She wanted to let him in, but something stopped her.

"You won't stay home," she heard him saying. It was one of their big fights—she replayed it again and again in her mind. "You'll have the baby and go right back there, back to work. You'll travel and you'll win awards and you'll retreat from us, just like she did from you. You didn't have to take that job, you had other options."

"What other options did I have? You'll never be able to support us on a bartender's salary!" She knew this had wounded him. He saw his chosen career as so much more than a bartender, and they had talked about opening their own restaurant someday. "You get to chase your dreams because I took this job. It's not forever, but we can save money and live life on our own terms." She'd tried to convince him, but as the words came out she realized she was trying to convince herself.

"Having a baby isn't going to fundamentally change who you are. You won't suddenly be the kind of person who could stay home with kids. I don't want that for you. You're too driven. You'd end up resenting all of us—yourself included. I don't see why it's Naturebar or stay home. Isn't there another option that could make you happy?"

She went quiet then, not knowing how to answer, or what happy even looked like. They never finished the conversation, though she often wondered what she should've said next.

Now she looked around at the proverbial pieces of her life as if they lay scattered around her. One missing sister. One detached, neurotic mother. One estranged husband. One job she simultaneously liked and feared. Two siblings she felt she hardly knew. Tears streamed down her face as she picked up her phone and began to type a text message.

I just want to find my way back to you. You once asked me what would make me happy, and I don't know the answer, but I know happiness begins with you.

CHAPTER NINE

Cybil thought for a moment there must've been be an ashram of monks just beyond his door, but realized after the second time she pushed the button that it was merely Todd's doorbell. It was calibrated to play a Tibetan meditation chant. She chuckled a bit at how much Todd resembled the stereotype of himself.

It took almost no time for him to come to the door, which told her he was waiting for her.

"Cybil!" he said. "Let me tell you, you are a hard woman to get ahold of." She knew he was trying to make her more comfortable about the fact that she'd been fiercely ducking him.

"Yeah," she said, looking away. His face, his glorious face, had not changed in the year since she'd seen him. It seemed even her memory couldn't bear to deliver the full extent of his beauty to her consciousness; this was the only explanation she could think of for having forgotten the way his visage made her feel. "We're going to have to make this quick. I've got to race off to Mexico for a tournament—you know how brutal the circuit can be..." she trailed off, seeing that he didn't believe a word she was saying.

"Cyb, I talked to C.J. Not to mention I own a Fortune 500 company." *He just had to rub it in*, she thought. "I have the wherewithal to find things out. I know Janine's in trouble and I want to help any way I can. Let me just talk to you for a minute, is that okay?" he asked, but did not stop to wait for an answer. "After I couldn't reach you, I started to think there might be some reason why you would want to pull away from me. I know you're scared. I know you feel like you've got bag-gage. I followed up with some of my people. I know you, Cyb. I don't know what you need the yacht for, but I don't need to know. I don't care why you need it. I'll give it to you, you can have it. I just want to be able to talk to you now and then. And if you like it, then maybe we could even see each other." In his rehearsed speech, he'd been much cooler, but he couldn't play down his affection for her when she stood so breathtakingly close.

This was it. Go all in, or play it close to the chest. She had to make a decision. Her mind was rattling. The last man who had talked to her like this was her ex-husband, and even then it had been thirty years before. She'd never admitted to Virgil that she only took a husband because that's what women did. Further still, in all their years togeth-er she'd never told him that she hadn't wanted children—she'd only felt a subdued but prominent feminine obligation to produce children for him. When she looked back now, it occurred to her that she had never loved Virgil, and that Todd Novak was, quite possibly, the great love of her life.

She checked herself. She was nearing sixty. She was slender and though most people thought she was around forty-five, she felt herself way past her prime. And it wasn't particularly that she'd never loved Virgil, it was more specifically that she'd never believed in love at all. While other women around her swooned and swelled, she calculated. While they baked, she built. Virgil and the kids had been accessories, like a nice tennis shoe or a favorite golf club (hers was the nine iron). She remembered the intense relief she'd felt on the day her divorce had been finalized. She'd relished being single, but in more recent years—as her children got older and progressively further away—she'd felt a kind of aloneness that was foreign to her. She supposed most women would label it loneliness, but was this—loneliness—was it enough reason to give up her independence? She settled on it, just then. She decided to keep the chips close.

"Todd, we had one wonderful night together. Anything more than that and I would just disappoint you."

"You've exceeded every expectation I've had of you so far, and I don't see any end to that pattern," he said. "Besides, we need to release ourselves from expectations. Expectations are our own beliefs about ourselves cast out onto others."

"That, right there. That's why this won't work," she felt herself snapping and breaking like a dry twig. "I have expectations. I have goals. I fire people. I kill fish. I keep people at arm's length. I use money to control people, to cripple them, so that I will never be alone. But that's all I ever am—alone." She hung her head. The words had burst out of her, more honest than she was willing to be with even herself. She wished she could collect them, like confetti scattered on the floor. Even now she knew she should be crying, but the tears would not come. Her throat was dry and flinty. Todd reached for her shoulder but she pulled away.

"I keep one foot out the door in every area of my life. I disappoint. It's what I do. And even though you're above it all and your suffering exists outside of you and all that bullshit, I will still find a way to fuck it up." Still standing in his too-echoey foyer, she was matter-of-fact, honest, and unwavering. These were things she had known about herself for a long time, and it was refreshing that now someone else knew them too.

He examined her. She did not falter under his gaze. In any other situation, these words and this presence would not match. Other women would cry, plead, whine, or howl at the realizations contained within her words. But not Cybil. She knew what she was, and she was not trying to hide it from him. She was more Buddhist than she knew. He whispered, "I want to show you something."

Todd took her hand and led her through the house. The minimalistic decor and artifacts from his travels to the East blurred by them as they passed. He stopped at a wood paneled wall scored with vertical lines; when he touched it, a lighted touch-screen keypad appeared. He typed in a code, and a piece of the wall jutted out mechanically, forming the shape of a door within the wall. He pulled it open and guided her inside.

The room lit up as they walked inside, the lights motion-sensored. Hundreds of mounted animals stared back at Cybil from shelves that lined the walls. A Kodiak bear stood tall next to a bald eagle, a caribou, and a moose. The room was huge, and nearly every inch was covered with the stuffed creatures that made up Todd's collection. Many of the animals were highly endangered—a Bengal Tiger and a huge African Elephant were among the most taboo of the menagerie.

Fear rose up in her, and she turned to run from the room. Todd's arm shot up and he grabbed her forearm—his grip was firm. His skin touching hers brought her back to their night together. She remembered the feeling of power he had over her, and her desire to obey him. She turned and faced him.

Chapter Ten

On the far wall she saw it — its silvery tail and spiny dorsal fin turned concave to give the illusion of movement against its dark wooden mount. The tarpon was massive and glorious, and she could almost feel the pull of the rod as the monster fought against the end of its life. She remembered from the story that it was 290 pounds, but it looked bigger.

Todd took in the sight too, as if it were his first time seeing it. Though she could see a sense of pride puff up in his chest, she could also sense his shame. They walked along the shelves and he told stories about how he'd procured each animal. "When I was younger, more set to prove myself, I had a hunger that was insatiable. I started my company from nothing, putting ingredients together in my parents' garage and forcing my athlete friends to try different variations until I settled on the very first STRENGTHbar recipe. Success came to me fairly easily. There was really no competition and we grew fast. I was on the warpath. The bigger we got, the bigger I thought I needed to be—the more powerful, the scarier, whatever. So I started going on safaris, hunts, quests to prove myself. All over the world, I killed, maimed, and hunted the biggest and most beautiful animals. I started with regulation game animals, killing them only within the mandated seasons… but then that wasn't enough. I wanted to go outside the lines. I wanted what no one else was able to get." He looked around the room, and Cybil watched as a clouded sorrow overtook him. Tears came to his eyes.

"I can't undo all the pain I've caused, Cyb. I can't give back the lives I've taken." Tears streamed down his face, but he made no attempt to wipe them away. She reached over and rested her hand between his shoulder blades. "I got out of control. The tarpon was the last time. I spent three hours reeling him in. I felt like Ernest Hemingway." It was token among anglers that Ernest Hemingway was one of the greatest fishermen who ever lived. Hemingway had asked one of his crew members to fashion an El Salvadorian birthing chair into a deep-sea fishing chair, so that he could put his feet up into the stirrups and gain leverage against the fish who pulled with all their might against the rod and reel. Hemingway would fight huge Marlin and tuna for hours, having his crew pour food and water into his mouth. "I finally got him up and… I felt superhuman. I had bested one of nature's most magnificent animals. We drew him up into the boat and I watched as his massive body flopped and struggled for air. His flat eyes seemed to look right at me. I knelt down, watching him flounder. The crew on the boat were back-slapping me and high-fiving. It was supposed to be one of the most exciting moments of my life. Most people will never see a fish this big, let alone catch one.

"But as his light started to go out, I felt mine going out too. I cried out to the captain to throw him back, to please throw him back, but they wouldn't. There was no way they were going to throw back the biggest tarpon any of them had ever seen. I watched him die there, like I had with hundreds of fish before, but this one was different. Something had changed. I couldn't do it anymore. I told them to take me back to shore and I wept over the fish, stroking his scaly body. Perez, the first mate, forced me to mount it. He said I was just having a hard day, that I would be thankful after some time had gone by. That was five years ago. I haven't killed anything since then.

"Do you see why I wanted to show you this, Cyb? We are not the people that we have always been; we are the people we decide to be today. I'm ashamed of what I've done in the past, but I recognize that what I have been is not what I am."

Cybil's mind was reeling. She wasn't sure if it was because of all the dead animals staring at her, or if it was Todd's narrative, but she was off-balance. She looked into the glassy eyes of the fish and then back to Todd.

"My daughter," she began, "I haven't done right by her. I haven't protected her like a mother should. Janine was always the sweetest girl. She wanted to be a photographer and an interior designer. She's very creative. But I..." she hesitated, unable to say everything. "I just couldn't stop life from coming at her. She was so young," Cybil metered herself, wondering how much information was too much. Even a Buddhist stoic couldn't be expected to forgive everything. Here Todd had just shared the darkest depths of his soul, and still she was having trouble being completely transparent.

"Anyway, she's in trouble now. Well, we think." She looked at Todd's confused face and decided to continue. "She's been kidnapped. It all sounds very dramatic, but the truth is—and my other daughters agree—that she might have made up the whole thing. The last we heard of her, she had no money and was cycling onto whatever prescriptions she could get hold of. That's why we haven't told the police. I don't want to subject Naturebar to the press nightmare if an international man-hunt turns out to be a hoax." She sighed hard. It was the first time she'd told the story to anyone other than her family and C.J. and she realized how crazy it sounded. "They've told us to meet them in a small fishing town on the tip of the Yucatan with $500,000. To be perfectly honest, I don't have $500,000 freed up right now. I've become a little too fond of online poker. I wasn't aware until recently that it's eaten up almost all my liquid assets.

"Back to the point, you were saying that we don't have to be who we have been. I agree with that. I need to take this trip. Janine is lost— one way or another—she's gotten this way because of me, because of things I did or didn't do. I'm out of money. If the circumstances were different I suppose I could just pay the ransom and go on about my life, continuing to touch things but not feel them, but I can't do that anymore. I've been closed, shut down, on autopilot for many years. When you and I had our night together," she blushed, "I caught a glimpse of how things could be different. I don't know how to get there from here, but I do know I have to get Janine. I have to try to right some wrongs, and maybe discover what I've been running from all these years," she said. They were quiet in his menagerie for a long time. She wanted to break the silence, but his eyes told her that he was contemplating her words. She felt exposed but also illuminated.

"Cybil, I've decided on you. I've decided we make sense. I am used to getting the things I want," he looked around regretfully. He took a seat on the hard, plastic lighted floor. He crossed his legs lotus style and kept talking, "but there was one factor that I didn't consider when I decided on you, and that was—you. I have been everywhere, I have succeeded and I am proud of what I have accomplished, but I have done it alone. I have no one close to me, I have no one to share anything with. When you and I were… together, I saw you as the to-tal package. You have kids, you're a family person, and yet you also run a successful business. I thought you could teach me how to be close to people. I thought we could be yin and yang for each other. But now, after hearing your story, I realize that you are just as alone as me." He stared into the void, a thousand eyes on him but only two that mattered.

Cybil realized why his courting attempts had been so intense. She wanted to shrivel up and turn to dust. "So, you thought I was the corporate June Cleaver," she said. He laughed loudly, and it was all at once as if they both remembered that happiness existed. She sat down on the floor across from him and attempted to mimic his lotus. Finding herself not quite flexible enough, she settled for crossing her legs in front of her. "To be honest, this is the first time I have ever want-ed to be close to someone," she said. "And I have never wanted any-thing so badly." She looked up at him intently. "I have to ask you. The last time—the first time—we were together, what were you chanting?"

He looked around again, wanting to avoid the question. He'd hoped it could stay an unspoken thing between them, like most particulars about making love to someone. Embarrassed, he answered, "It's from the Tibetan Book of the Dead…" She looked frightened. "No, no, it's not that weird. It's from the section on rebirth. The Tibetans believe in reincarnation. They believe that when you die, you come back as someone else. They believe you get another chance. I guess I feel like I've taken so much life that during sex, the epitome of life… I want to be reborn, to regenerate, to help my partner begin again as well. It's a strange thing, I know. Some guys like whips and chains, I like chanting. Is it a deal-breaker?" He looked like a child who'd just revealed his favorite hiding place, vulnerable and hopeful.

She thought back to that night and realized that since then, there had been something different in her, something new. She'd been unable to continue with business as usual after that—she had been acutely aware of what was missing.

He leaned forward and kissed her, putting his hand to the side of her face. His hand searched until it found her earlobe and he tugged it gently. This was her favorite part about making love to him, and she frequently found herself tugging on her earlobe over the past year trying to replicate the effect. She began to crave him again, as she had the last time. "Do it now, do the chanting now," she ordered. She lay on her back flat as a plank and closed her eyes. She crossed her arms across her chest. She could feel the tingling of anticipation shudder through her.

He began his low whispery call to the gods, but this time as he did it he began to undress her. She surrendered to him, letting him reveal as much of her as he wanted, as slowly as he wanted. She fell deeply into his trance.

They joined together there on the floor of the taxidermy room. Their bodies were both strong and healthy, weathered and experienced. Their lovemaking possessed the quiet desperation of those who know it might be the last time they would be together like this. In the future, one of them might come to their senses. A pulsing fear was ever present, the idea that they were too damaged to be anything more than the contents of that room: hollow shells once capable of connection, but no more.

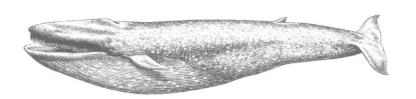

ACT III

CHAPTER ONE

"**W**ho did she have to fuck?" Carlyle whispered under her breath cynically as soon as she set foot on the yacht.

"I know, right?" Valerie replied, though Carlyle had not meant to be heard. Their eyes darted up to the mirrored ceilings, then to the deck, which housed a twelve-person hot tub and as many sun chairs.

Carlyle walked over to a large tufted armchair in what would've been considered a living room, had they been on land. She lifted her arms and glided into a chair, an exaggerated gesture to make her sister laugh. She mimicked sipping tea with her pinky out. With each movement her sister had to suppress more laughter. She stomped a foot, bit her lips and winced her eyes.

"What's so funny?" Cybil asked, walking in behind them. She looked around at the expertly-designed room. A glass bar had been folded out of the wall, complete with every kind of cocktail glass and top-shelf spirits and liqueurs from around the world. Cybil walked to the bar and selected a small, low-standing fluted glass. She ran a finger across the liqueur selection until she landed on what she searched for: St. Germain. She glazed over what would have been her normal selection; Bailey's would not accent her light and flirty mood. This must be what love felt like. She pulled out the intricate bottle and poured a shot's worth into the glass. Her daughters watched intently. Their mother rarely drank, and they weren't sure what it meant when she did. They felt they'd spent their lives trying to decode her actions, never quite landing on the answers they sought.

"Carlyle's just impressed... by the boat. It's... nice." Valerie was still suppressing laughter, but her voice had a hint of suspicion in it.

"It's not a boat. It's a yacht. Todd was very nice to let us borrow it. Did you all have any trouble getting supplies?" Cybil did not wait for an answer. "Since we're keeping a low profile I told Todd to keep the crew to a minimum."

"We took care of the groceries and everything. I guess we just weren't expecting the boat... I mean yacht, to be this nice," Valerie said. Again she was trying to goad her mother into divulging more information about her relationship with the yacht's owner.

"Hot damn!" C.J. burst into the room. "This shit is off the chain!" Tom followed closely behind him. The two had been running from extravagant room to more extravagant room on the ship, hooting and hollering like a pair of gorillas released on an open jungle.

"Did you know there's a sauna? A fucking sauna? And he even has a disco. It's like a club down there! Stripper poles, two bars and even a whale! I don't know who this guy is, but I want to be him." Tom gleamed. He was the youngest and had been raised in the shadow of Cybil's success more than her other children had. He was used to a life of luxury and he had come to expect it.

"Did you say a whale?" Cybil asked, feeling the heat of her skin from under her collar.

"Yeah. The ballroom stretches probably a hundred and fifty feet on the lower level—I think he also uses it as a garage for the tender boat. That's what the crew guy called it. It's literally a smaller boat they park *inside* this boat, and we ride it to shore. How awesome is that? Anyway, in the middle of the room suspended from the ceiling is a fucking whale. It's probably fake or whatever, but still it's so cool. Mom, can we get a yacht?" Carlyle laughed and silently congratulated herself for anticipating her brother's next question.

"Tommy, let's just enjoy this trip and we'll see what happens."

"Didn't you hear? Mom lost all her money playing poker. That probably means there won't be any yachts for awhile." Valerie could not hide her disapproval. Cybil winced at the attack, although she'd anticipated it.

"You'll all be more than fine," Cybil replied, her tone thick with resentment. She'd provided for each of them since their first flickers of life. She felt she'd done more than right by her children, who lived in nice houses in safe neighborhoods, and who would never have to worry about money in their lives. *Janine is the exception*, Cybil thought. All Cybil expected of her children was that they find some passion in life and follow it through to its fulfillment.

"You can do whatever you want with your money, Mom. It is yours after all," Tom replied, trying to ease the tension. He shot a look at Valerie that said, *Now is not the time.*

"Well, I don't want you all to worry. We're doing great. Last quarter's numbers were healthy and our research shows a lot of growth in the snacking and meal replacement categories. We'll make it back in no time," Cybil effortlessly switched into business mode. She expected her children to maintain a general understanding of business and a specific understanding of Naturebar. "Carlyle can fill you in with more details if you have interest."

"Well, that's not going to matter if you're a *gambling addict,* is it, Mom?" Valerie said. Carlyle was surprised that her sister would not let the issue lie. She wanted to bring her hands to her face to cover her eyes, but she knew she would peek through the cracks in her hands, unable to block out the carnage.

"Do these questions serve a purpose other than to make me feel guilty? I'm taking steps to remedy the situation. Guilt will only weigh me down," Cybil replied gracefully. She could feel Todd's ease wearing off on her. Carlyle could see that Cybil was hurt, but she never faltered. "Now, I'm going to take a look at that whale." She did not invite anyone to come along, and no one asked to join her.

They had been at sea for seven hours, and for five of them Carlyle's head had been hanging over the side of the boat. Nothing she'd experienced before could compare to the continuous and unyielding motion of rapid sea travel. The water was perpetually turbulent, giving her no relief from the discomfort of seasickness.

Rather than stay in her room, Carlyle preferred the sea air on her face. She did not care that she had turned the same sickly shade of algae green that stained the once-white buoy ropes around the boat.

Tom approached her cautiously, making sure to avoid any possible backsplash of puke. When he was sure he would not get doused, he leaned against the side of the boat next to his sister and took something small out of his pocket. He rolled the small white cluster between his thumb and fingers, and brought it to his lips. He licked the edge of the rolling paper slightly, patching a hole on what he thought was an otherwise perfect joint. He lit the fat, lumpy cigarette and held the smoke in for a long time. When he breathed out, the smell almost made Carlyle wretch again.

"You should have some. It'll calm your nerves. Make you feel better," he said.

Carlyle wasn't sure if he was genuinely concerned, or if he just wanted someone to get high with.

Seeing her doubt and potential disapproval, he added, "Works for cancer patients, right?"

"At this point, I'll try anything," she said. She turned her back to the sea and slid to a seated position, using the side of the ship as a backrest. Tom slid down next to her. He handed her the joint. She grabbed it as close to the tip as she could—she remembered this part from the few times she'd smoked pot in high school. She brought the joint to her lips and inhaled deeply. She momentarily abandoned the irrational fear that she would not ever be able to breathe again, which is what had kept her from becoming a heavy user of the stuff.

She attempted to hold in the smoke, but it burned all the way up her windpipe and out to the edges of her nostrils. She let the smoke out with a chesty cough and handed the joint back to Tom. "How do you smoke that stuff all the time?" she asked in a raspy voice that was part genuinely labored and part embellished. He brought the joint back to his lips and drew in a deep drag, bringing the joint down to a nub.

"I just do, I guess," he said. He handed her what was left of the roach. Even though the thought of taking another hit pained her, she had to admit she felt better than she had since they'd left the dock.

She inhaled the burning embers, coughing again as she breathed out. Tom's face had already been taken over by that familiar slack-jawed look. He brought his hands to his face and rubbed up and down, as if to erase the events of the day.

Chapter Two

Carlyle began to feel a warmth beneath her clothing, even though the October night was chilly. Her face felt as though it was radiating light. She smiled and then suddenly laughed brightly in a way that startled her, causing her to laugh again. Tom laughed too, and through the fog and skunky smell, she realized this was the first time she had laughed since Ethan had decided to leave home. There had been small guffaws, choice smirks and closeted sighs that resembled laughter, but no actual laughter had escaped her until now. She thought about what she would have done had Tom offered her the joint at home. She would have leapt up in judgment of him and turned her head in disgust. She had been trying to create a hospitable environment for a baby to grow, after all.

Of course, the baby. Or lack thereof. Her life's obsession had all but disappeared in the face of Janine's turmoil. She partly hated her sister for that, but also partly wanted to thank her.

She awkwardly stood up, unable to find her footing. When she looked at Tom self-consciously, it seemed he was still laughing to himself and had not seen her stumble. She turned to face the sea and the vast expanse of sky. The stars seemed to have appeared since she'd turned her back. The light blue pools of light sparkled in the sky, their reflections winking back at her in the waves.

She felt the distinct urge to dance—to lose control and not know exactly what was going to happen next. She began to sway with the rhythm of the sea, coming close to tumbling across the broad expanse of the deck, but maintaining just enough balance to keep from falling. She swayed down the deck toward the back of the boat.

Tom's laughter exploded behind her like a pile of wood suddenly catching fire. She looked at her phone and realized that she'd been stampeding around the deck for the better part of an hour. She still felt fuzzy, but was beginning to realize what her stumbling-earth-mother dance must've looked like to an onlooker. Carlyle was swept up in his laughter and allowed a few minutes of hilarity at her own expense.

She came to sit next to him in the deck chair. The only sounds they could hear were the loud brushing of the sea against the boat as they trudged forward to their destination. Tom took a drag on the cigarette he was smoking, holding it between his index finger and thumb, as James Dean would. Silence settled in, and a strange fear overtook her that she had no idea who this person was sitting in front of her, or what she had to say to him.

"So what really happened, Tom? What really happened when you got expelled?" She had been wanting to ask the question, but Cybil or Valerie would always offer their opinions before Tom was able to answer for himself.

He looked at his cigarette from the side, as if attempting to gauge how many drags he had left. He leaned back in the lounge chair. "Well, I just got all wrapped up in it, I guess. Did you know there were scouts? Scouts had come to some of my football games. I got a few emails, some of the schools were looking at me. I could've played college football. But then Janine happened, you know?"

"When did it all start?"

"Well, when Janine got back from Mexico, I guess. Like, March 2011?"

"Wait, when was she in Mexico?"

"You know, she was there for a month. Mom took her to that rehab place and she skipped out after, like, two days or something. She went to Mexico. She came back all tan, don't you remember?"

"Uh, no. She told me she'd been in rehab. I didn't know she left early!" She shook her head. Even though she knew Janine, she was still surprised. "Does Mom know this?"

"If you don't, she probably doesn't. She came back with a couple of huge trash bags full of weed. It was good stuff too. Kush. She called me to help her move some furniture into her new condo." Carlyle remembered scathingly that Janine's reward for completing rehab had been a new, fully furnished condo. "She smoked me out, and asked if I wanted in—I mean, if I wanted to help her with a business opportunity. Football season was over and I was pretty bored at school. I didn't think much about it. I just said I would. I think I would have done anything for more of that stuff…" he trailed off. Carlyle thought she saw him salivating.

"Did you think there was anything strange about your 31-year-old sister asking her 18-year-old brother to sell weed?" She was being patronizing and she knew it, but she was suddenly so angry at both of them.

"No. I mean, I guess. There was just so much of it, and with her being newly back in town, she didn't know anyone to sell it to." His tongue was slack and she knew he was still high. "She needed someone who knew the town. That's me. People love me. I'm a natural salesman." She could hear Janine's words funneled through Tom's mouth. This must've been how she exploited him to do her bidding. She tried to place her hand on the chair to sturdy herself, but it fell through the slats and she had to correct herself to keep from falling off the chair. She realized she was still high, too.

"Well, where did all that weed come from?" Carlyle asked, hoping he hadn't noticed her almost-face-plant.

"I don't know." He continued acting as if he hadn't seen it. "She was always on the phone. You know, I didn't think much about it then, but she was on the phone with Dad a lot. She would talk to him for hours on end in her bedroom with the door closed. I would be weighing the bags or counting the money, and she would be on the phone. I could never hear what they were talking about but she would always come out and say 'Dad says hi,' or 'Dad told me to tell you to study harder,' or something like that."

"This is all so strange. We hardly ever talk to Dad. He texts me randomly from different numbers but I haven't seen him in a few years.

Why would she want to talk to Dad so much?"

"I don't know, maybe she missed him?" Tom answered. "She was always his favorite."

"True," she said, her vision becoming cloudy. Suddenly her head felt as if it weighed more than the entire ship.

"After she recruited me I sold drugs to pretty much every kid at my school, and then some kids from other schools. I had to get another cell phone. Looking back now, it was only a matter of time before they found me out. I was so stupid, I wasn't even really trying to hide it. The principal found a circle of freshman girls on the football field after school passing a joint. One of them turned over my second cell number so her parents wouldn't send her to boarding school. They weren't sure who the phone number belonged to, so they had the girl set up a meet, you know, she texts and asks me to bring the pot. I brought it and they had the cops there and everything. They brought me home in hand-cuffs. They tried calling Mom, but I guess she was on a flight. These two officers waited there with me for six hours until she finally came home. I was blubbering like a baby when she saw me."

Carlyle suddenly felt immense pity for Tom. He had become involved in something much deeper than he understood. Perhaps they all had.

"I still don't see where Dad fits into all this," she said finally, after a long pause. Tom looked at her blankly and she consented that she was in no shape to solve a mystery. "I'm starving." This time when she spoke, she knew Tom would be interested.

"I bet there's some killer food down there. Is your stomach up to it?" She'd momentarily forgotten about her stomach doing flips just a few hours before. She did a mental check, thinking about food and waiting for her stomach to lurch. It didn't react.

"Yes. Let's see what we've got." The two headed off to the kitchen, and for a moment Carlyle understood why her siblings—Janine and Tom—liked to do drugs. She felt close to Tom in a way she never had before. They'd been through the same thing—something no one else had experienced. The moments of awkwardness melted away and she wondered why it took smoking something to feel connected to her own brother.

CHAPTER THREE

Valerie ventured up to the cockpit. There she found C.J. surrounded by backlit electronics displaying their location, their route, the engine calibrations and even an underwater camera. She fixated on the shadows of fish looming below the boat on the screen.

"Do you really know how all this stuff works?" she asked shyly.

C.J. jumped, startled to find her right behind him. "Oh hey, girly. To be honest, I only know about half. Hopefully it's the important half!" His southern drawl could be mistaken for that of someone from Alabama or Mississippi. Valerie never thought of Florida as a southern state and was always surprised by the accents and the number of confederate flags she saw each time she visited.

Valerie had been in college since she was nineteen. She was now forty. She had a degree in just about everything from philosophy to electrical engineering. She'd followed through to get her doctorate in sociology and now she taught three classes a week. Even though she was a professor now, she still didn't want to give up learning new things. Cybil was just glad that professors and their families got half-off tuition, because she'd paid the school a large fortune over so many years.

Valerie had never been good at flirting, or dating, or anything related to relationships. Research, papers, assignments—this was where she felt comfortable. But she liked C.J. and they had done this before.

She moved in closer to him, though his back was still facing her. She could smell the sea on him and it reminded her of the last time they were together like this. She'd come down for a routine fishing trip with her mother. She was accompanying the board of directors, and Carlyle had pulled out at the last minute—something about Ethan. The board was a stuffy lot, even for her, and she enjoyed doing her taxes. She must've been fifty pounds heavier then and though she never felt fat—the weight she'd put on was in all the right places—she was acutely aware of how much space she took up. There had been a gentle curve between her bust and hip that she sometimes missed, particularly when one of her bedraggled girlfriends dragged her out to a dance club. Dancing was much more fun with curves.

Her mother had just hired C.J. and Valerie had found him instantly magnetic. It didn't matter to her that he had no formal education; she liked the way his muscles flexed when he began to reel the lure in, and how boyishly excited he got when he called out to the crew, "Fish on!" They were out in the shallows catching bait her first morning on the boat and his arm had brushed hers. "Look out there, see where the water gets nervous? That's where we'll find the mullet." He was pointing to a discoloration in the sea, a place where the ocean's bottom changed from sand to murky grass.

After that, she'd gone out of her way to covertly touch him, and stood near the back of the boat with him even though the board members stood on the bow drinking beers and smoking cigars. When they pulled the boat back into the marina after a long day, C.J. had asked her if she would meet him at the bar up the street. Giddy, she ran back to her mother's house to wash the smell of fish and cigar smoke from her skin. C.J. was not the type of man she normally dated—not that she really dated enough to have a type. She liked the idea of a fling with C.J. because it would stay in the Keys. She'd never intended to develop feelings for him.

Being in his presence now, she breathed in the scent of fish and salt that always seemed to linger on him. To her it smelled like escape. She brought her hands to his shoulders and began to massage his thick, ropey muscles. "You're tense," she concluded.

"Yeah, it's all this fancy equipment. Give me a compass and a paper map, that's my kind of sailin.' All these computers make me nervous, 'specially since this ain't my chariot," he said. She could see he was hesitating over the thousands of buttons and levers before him. For a brief moment, she wondered why her mother hadn't asked Todd Novak to supply the captain too, but she knew the answer before she could ask the question. Her mother wouldn't want to explain to another captain why they wouldn't be alerting the Coast Guard, or any other regulatory body, about their undocumented journey. C.J. was indebted to Cybil and he knew not to ask questions.

"With all these fancy do-hickeys, you'd think there was an auto-pilot button?" she asked slyly.

"Well, I hope so, I'm startin' to get hungry," he said. C.J. was not picking up her hints, but she didn't need him to. She stepped around him and began to examine the panel of electronics. C.J. never bothered to ask any personal information about her, so he didn't know that she probably knew more about this ship than anyone else on it. Had they been on his boat, he would have been much more protective of the equipment, but not knowing his way around, he gladly stepped aside to let her tinker around. She consulted the digital map that broadcast their position via satellite. After massaging a few of the controls, the ship took over. She made sure the course was set towards Progreso and flipped a few switches.

"That should do it," she said. "But we shouldn't leave it unattended. Are there any crew members who can keep a look out until you get back?"

"You sure are somethin,'" C.J. replied, turning to face her for the first time. "I'll send someone up," he said as he looked into her face. He put his hand to her neck and caressed her lips with his thumb. He looked as if he was trying to decide something. "Gah, I'm sorry Valerie, I just can't do it," he said finally.

"What? What's the problem? Last time I was here… I just thought you liked me. We spent those four nights together," she reminded him. The rejection fell hard, leaving her confused.

"I do like you, I just…" he hesitated again. "I like bigger girls. It's what gets me goin.' Now that you're so little, I just—I'm not feelin' it."

She looked down at her flat chest and stomach. The hot yoga classes she'd been going to three times weekly had given her stomach a slight hardness accompanied by shallow lines that could be considered a four-pack. She'd become so proud of her new body that it was hard for her to imagine anyone not liking the way she looked.

Had it been Carlyle or Janine he'd been talking to, there was no doubt tears would have followed, and Valerie felt herself choking them down. After years of learning everything she could, devouring information, she still could not learn this. "What can I do for you then? To make it how you want it?" she asked, hopefully.

C.J. crossed his arms and sat quietly for a moment. Valerie placed her hand on the zipper of his jeans and pressed the fabric into him. She rubbed up and down. He looked at the floor. After half a minute of what she thought was sensuously heavy petting, she was surprised not to feel an erection growing beneath her hand. Inwardly she was even more crestfallen, but she remained optimistic. She withdrew her hand and looked to him for an answer. His face brightened and she could see that he had an idea.

"Let's go to the kitchen," he said, grabbing her hand and leading her down the stairs to the first level.

Chapter Four

When Cybil had finally found the extension ladder in the corner of the boiler room, her compulsion to climb onto the whale's back had become overwhelming.

When she first saw it, she'd been breathless. She remembered Todd's parting words. "There's a surprise for you on the boat," he'd called out to her. She looked back at him with a smirk, but did not ask what it was. She simply got into her car and drove away. In fact, she had forgotten all about it until she'd heard Tom's report of the whale in the ballroom.

Walking down the stairs to the lower level of the yacht, her heart pounded. Before her was an elaborate ballroom/dance club/strip club/boat garage hybrid. It spanned the entire lower level of the 250-foot yacht. At the far end of the expansive room was the tender boat, as Tom had said, and she could see the outline of the bay door that would open, allowing the smaller boat to be birthed in order to take the boat's occupants to shore. There were two bars, one against the wall and one near the middle of the dance floor that was flanked by two stripper poles. The glasses stocked behind the bars were nestled safely in their rattle-proof shelving.

Above it all hung the whale. Her belly was suspended about fifteen feet above the floor. Cybil pictured leggy blondes in bikinis posing the same question over and over to Todd: "Is that real?" they would all ask, astonished at their idiosyncratic host. He would assure them it was a replica. She could hear him saying that he loved and revered the animal as the queen of the sea. He would spout out something about how he wanted to remind everyone aboard the yacht about the majesty of the ocean.

She felt proud and privileged to be in the inner circle of those who knew the truth. She knew before laying eyes on the whale that it was real. Now standing in its presence, she supposed it was a Blue Whale. After seeing Todd's trophy room, she somehow loved him even more, though she knew it was reprehensible. With every endangered animal she took in, her admiration flourished. She pictured him on the African savannah, in Indian villages and in the cold frozen wilderness of the Yukon. She was giddy at the unearthing of Todd's flaw, and even more in awe of the fact that he had overcome it.

She knew there was no other place she could go to be close to him in that moment. No other place than on the back of that whale.

Once she gutted the ladder from its place among the tools and other practical equipment required for running a ship, she attempted to carry it the length of the ballroom. It made a hideous screeching and scratching sound as she dragged it across the floor. There was no doubt she would receive a bill for the refinishing of the hardwood. She had to take a break, as the ladder was heavier and the journey longer than she expected.

On her way past the bar, she laid down the ladder and went to check out the inventory. A standing bowl that reminded her of the receptacle that held holy water in church stood in her path. It was full of travel-size bottles of liquor like one would find in a hotel mini-bar. *Party favors*, she thought. She shoveled two handfuls of the tiny bottles into the pockets of her puffy vest. Now that she was fueled up, she grabbed the ladder again and lugged it the rest of the distance to the middle of the room.

Once there, she extended the ladder and rested it on the whale's side. On the slick wooden dance floor, the ladder's feet slid. It would never hold her weight. She looked around until she saw a rubber floor mat behind the bar. She placed it under the ladder's feet and tested her weight by climbing up a few rungs. It held fast.

Finally, now out of breath, she ascended. It felt as though she was climbing to heaven. Though she was not one to savor things—most of the time it seemed like she was racing to move from one thing to the next—she took each step purposefully and examined the animal from every angle as she gained more height.

The whale was magnificent. Her tiny eye—which seemed microscopic in comparison with its body but was actually the size of a cup of tea—seemed to see all the world. Her underbelly was lined with ridges, which Cybil touched as she traveled up her side. There were still remnants of algae and barnacles that had latched onto the whale while she had been alive. Her mouth had been fashioned into an open position, and where Cybil expected to see teeth, she saw thousands of bristles—like those on a broom.

Cybil reached the top of the whale. She realized she was about forty-five feet off the ground and only a foot or two from the cold metal ceiling. She carefully climbed from the ladder to the back of the whale and straddled it like a horse. She thought about the relationship Todd must have with his taxidermist; it was probably the most intimate relationship Todd had cultivated—until now. She fished a tiny bottle from her pocket and twisted off the lid. She tipped it up into her mouth quickly, emptying it. She threw the empty bottle off the edge of the whale and listened for the tiny shatter. She threw her arms up and giggled, feeling free.

How many people could say they'd ridden a Blue Whale? Not many. She knew as she sat there that she would remember this moment for the rest of her life. She pictured recounting the story to Todd, telling him that she knew no other way to understand him than to see what he had seen, and to mount his mounted whale. She thought about his chanting and what it had meant. Was she really reborn? Did she really have the chance to be another person, to live a different life? Sitting here now, she felt that Todd had brought her back from the dead.

She bent over gently, gliding her hands along the whale's skin. Her left hand came across a deep gash. She knew this must've been the place where Todd had gaffed the whale in order to catch her and—ultimately—mount her here. She'd forgotten for a moment that this creature had had to be killed, and that the object of her affection had done the killing. He'd sought it out. He'd relished it. Though part of her was repulsed, another part was excited. She took a bottle out and tipped up another swig.

A few more bottles shattered to the ground. The empty ballroom began to spin and Cybil knew she needed to find her way off the whale and get to a bed. But the thought of the long journey down exhausted her, and so she laid down on her stomach, her legs still splayed out, straddling the whale's back. Her eyes blinked slowly and in one final attempt to get comfortable, she moved her hand beneath her face.

Sleep hit her harder than the liquor, and in her last smidge of wakefulness, she heard the ladder clatter to the floor in a series of loud cracks.

CHAPTER FIVE

C.J. and Valerie stumbled into the kitchen. She went straight for the refrigerator and pulled out a can of whipped cream and a plastic carton of strawberries. When she turned back to C.J., he was shaking his head.

"Way too healthy," he smirked. He went to the pantry and pulled out a package of ho-ho's. Valerie swallowed hard. She hadn't eaten a ho-ho—or any bread-like product—in over six months. He opened the package and tore one of the small brown cakes in half. The white curlicue of frosting on top stretched as if it didn't want to let go. He dipped his finger into the center of the cake, scooping out the cream. She stared on, feeling a flush of heat come up from her hips.

"Take off your shirt," he said. She obeyed, removing the thick cable knit sweater. She took off her glasses and folded them neatly, placing them on the counter. His face fell a bit, taking in her naked flesh. She stepped closer to him and grabbed his hand, smearing the cream down her chest and between her breasts. Then she grabbed his other hand and crammed the brown cake into her mouth. As she chewed he began to lick the cream from her skin. She shivered with delight. She looked down to see the fabric of his pants tighten. *Victory,* she thought. He grabbed her by the waist and hoisted her up onto the counter. She was lighter than he expected, so she gained air too fast and he lost control, making her come down on the counter hard. A dense thud followed.

A rustling came from the floor to Valerie's left. She looked over and tensed in shock to find two bodies lying on the tiled kitchen floor. C.J.

jumped, then after a moment, giggled at the scene. Valerie calmed down when she realized that one of them was her sister, Carlyle, using a sack of potato chips as a pillow.

Leaning over further, she could see that the other body was Tom. His arms crossed beneath his head and he slept in the fetal position. On his face was the residue of what looked like a combination of ice-cream, cheezy poofs, and maybe even cheez whiz.

Valerie looked at C.J. She knew this might be her only chance to convince him that she could still satisfy him, even as a skinny girl. She gathered all the junk food in her arms and whispered,"Let's get while the gettin's good. Knowing my brother, there won't be a single cheezy poof left by morning!" Tom's propensity for the munchies was legendary throughout the family. Unforgettable was the Thanksgiving morning they had awoken to find all the groceries—those reserved for the preparation of their mother's hallowed dinner—were eaten. He had passed out on the table surrounded by empty cans of cranberry sauce.

Valerie shook her head at Carlyle, a confused combination of shame and amusement crossing her face. Her younger sister by ten years had been offered the job she thought was meant for her. She'd jumped the line, so to speak. And here she was, high and probably drunk, passed out on the floor. She took her phone out and snapped a photo of her siblings—you never know when something like that might be useful.

"I hooked Tom up with a dealer before we left Big Pine," C.J. whispered as they left the kitchen. "I told him to be careful what he bought. That guy does not fuck around. He's kind of like a mad scientist. Who knows what they smoked!" C.J. laughed and they slunk away into their private foodgasm.

Carlyle stood suddenly, putting her hand to her mouth. Her stomach retreated into her spine and she realized she was going to be sick. Her hand remained clasped tight over her mouth. She ran to the bathroom, barely making it to the toilet before the vomit began to escape from beneath her fingers. After running a hand towel under cool water, she pressed it to her face and behind her neck. *Seasickness, followed by smoking pot, followed by a junk-food binge,* Carlyle thought. *Brilliant. Less than a day with these people and I don't even recognize myself.*

She emerged from the bathroom to find Tom still cuddled up on the floor. She resolved to leave him there as a pseudo-prank and also because the thought of bending over to rouse him upset the delicate digestive balance she had just achieved.

She ambled her way back up to the fourth level. Her room was next to Cybil's, and she felt it strange—after a glimpse at the clock next to her bed, which read 1:52 a.m.—that the light was on and the door to her mother's room was open. Although the bed was calling to her, she decided to peek in and make sure she was all right.

Her mother was not there, sleeping or otherwise. This concerned Carlyle. Cybil's black, compact, hard-shelled suitcase was open on the suitcase rack. Her mother's cosmetic bags were evenly spaced and precisely placed on the bathroom vanity. But Cybil was nowhere to be found. There was no sign of her having lain in the bed, since it was still expertly made. She hadn't seen her mother since Cybil had decided to go look for the whale Tom had been talking about earlier.

The whale! At least it was a clue. Since it was the middle of the night and it had been so long since she had last seen Cybil, Carlyle felt compelled to check on her. Perhaps she too had fallen asleep somewhere unconventional.

Carlyle headed for the stairs and began to descend to the bottom level, where Tom had said he'd seen the whale. When she got to the garage, she heard glass crunch under her foot as she walked toward the center of the room. She looked underfoot to see the remnants of tiny liquor bottles littering her path. They looked to have been thrown and shattered all over the floor. There was a deep and jagged scratch in the floor that mirrored the two feet of the ladder that now lay on its back in the middle of the floor, just to the side of the hanging whale.

Carlyle could not imagine what kind of person found a whale to be a suitable item of decor. *How impractical,* she thought. *Wouldn't a hammerhead or a giant squid have the same effect without all the hullaballoo?*

Nonetheless, the whale was impressive. She looked around the massive room, and yet she still could not see her mother. It was obvious she had been here, but where could she be? The immense room was almost completely empty, devoid of good hiding places. She looked at the ladder, then to the whale. It was then that she saw her.

Carlyle spied her mother passed out on the back of the whale, a sparkle of drool escaping her lips. The laughter burst out of her like a bullet from a gun—loud and all at once. Though the laughter echoed off the faraway walls, her mother did not stir.

"Mom!" she called. Nothing. "Mom!" she called again, cupping her hands to her mouth. Her mother lifted her head and turned her face to the other side, laying down again.

Exasperated, she let out an enormous groan. Carlyle began to maneuver the ladder up to the side of the whale. She took each rung deliberately and carefully, pushing away the feelings of her earlier wobbliness. Her hand reached out to graze the side of the whale. She got a chill along her spine and suddenly she thought it was possible that this whale might not be a replica. There were pores, ridges, wrinkles, all too intricate to have been faked. She knew she was touching a dead thing—a thing that had once been living and was now dead at the hands of the person who hung it here. She recoiled her hand and felt the nausea return.

Her feet remaining sure where her stomach could not, she continued up the ladder until she came face-to-face with her sleeping mother. She realized, staring at her then, that she looked much older than Carlyle had ever noticed. When she looked at her mother she still saw the woman she'd been twenty years earlier. Her sleeping face lacked the hardness and pure will it possessed when she was awake. Carlyle saw wrinkles and a dimness that she hadn't noticed before, and wondered how long it had been since she'd looked at her mother from this close up.

Carlyle gingerly reached out a hand, being careful not to tip the delicate balance of the ladder. She took her mother's shoulder and shook it gently. Cybil startled awake, sitting up fast and nearly smashing her head on a nearby ceiling rafter.

"What? What is it?" she exclaimed.

"Mom, it's okay. I came up here to wake you up and help you down. The ladder fell. You could have been stuck up here for days!" Carlyle explained.

Cybil wiped her mouth on her sleeve and pushed her dark hair out of her face. The side of hair that had been pressed into the whale was matted and sweaty. Cybil looked around, dazed, not exactly sure how she came to be straddling a whale.

Carlyle, having little regard for her mother's mental state, thought this was a perfect time to ask a few questions. "Mom, is this whale real?"

"Yes," Cybil said without hesitation. "It's one of Todd's trophies," she slurred.

"Why did you feel the need to climb on top of it?"

"I… I'm not sure. I felt drawn to her. At least, I think it's a her." Cybil was looking around now, trying to figure out the best way to climb down. "You're going to have to climb down and hold the ladder for me," she said decisively.

Carlyle quickly climbed down and placed both hands on the sides of the ladder. "Okay, I'm ready," she called upwards. Her mother mounted the ladder and began to climb down. "So what's up with you and that Todd guy?" Carlyle asked as her mother's feet neared the belly of the whale.

"It's complicated, sweetie. Right now I just want to get some sleep," Cybil touched down on the floor and patted her daughter's head. "Thanks for helping me down."

"Well, there's something you should know," Carlyle said. Her mother stood impatiently, thinking of her bed and the pounding behind her eyes. Her expression belied her intense desire to be alone. "Never mind. We can talk about it tomorrow, when we're both more clear-headed."

"Sounds good, honey," Cybil said dismissively.

Carlyle walked up to the cabin level with her mother in silence and when they arrived at their respective bedrooms, each entered without saying goodnight.

CHAPTER SIX

Carlyle woke up before everyone else and went down to the dining room in search of a protein source and a way to connect to the internet. Although her memory of the night before was hazy, she was still shaken by two very strange things: one, the conversation with her brother in which she learned some new facts about Janine; two, her mother having passed out on the back of a real stuffed whale. Though she fell asleep as soon as she'd gotten into bed, her sleep had been fitful. She'd woken in the early morning, when the sky was a deep indigo indicative of the sun's impending appearance. Her eyes had snapped open to escape a scene in a dream that had shaken her to her core.

The events from just hours before were replaying exactly as they had—she saw her mother on top of the whale, she steadied the ladder to climb up to retrieve her, but once she got to the top she was horrified by what she saw. It wasn't her mother at all on top of the whale, it was herself. It was her own face that she stared into. It frightened her so much that she fell off the ladder and her eyes shot open just before she landed headfirst on the hardwood floor of the ballroom.

She turned over and over again in bed, yet each time she closed her eyes she saw her own face drooling and slack, pressed against the rough skin of the whale.

Now she sat in front of her computer monitor, thankful that she didn't need the services of a dream dictionary to decode this message from her subconscious. Her own issues would have to wait, because she had some more pressing concerns to clarify.

A cheery chubby-cheeked woman emerged with a plateful of pastries. "Can I make you some eggs? Or pancakes?" Judging from the apron, Carlyle assumed she worked with food, but none of them had met her or even known she was on the ship with them. "I'm Suzanne, the chef. Sorry I wasn't available to you last night. My seasickness was insurmountable," Suzanne had answered every question Carlyle's expression must've been asking.

"I wasn't myself last night either. Some eggs would be great," Carlyle said, taking a pastry off the tray.

"Coming up! Eh—" she began to say something but stopped. "There's a young man on the floor of the kitchen. He's asleep. I've left him there for now, but do you object to my waking him up? He's a bit in the way."

Carlyle smiled. "Please wake him up with something loud and clattery." With that Suzanne left with a chuckle and continued to chatter even as she left the room. Carlyle set her attention to booting up the satellite internet connection, and pulled a pen and paper from the writing desk that sat at the entrance between the dining room and the sitting room.

She began to mentally recount the timeline of what Tom had told her the night before. On the paper she wrote:

Caspirada – Christmas, 2010
Janine in rehab – Jan 4, 2011
Janine left rehab – presumed Jan 6, 2011
Janine moves back to Omaha, moves into condo – beginning of March, 2011
Tom expelled – May 1st? 2011
Today's date – Oct 4th 2012

She stared at the paper with intent before pulling up her email client and beginning an email to Marius.

Marius –
Find out anything you can about Janine's whereabouts between Jan 6(ish) 2011 and the end of February 2011. Any strange transactions, large cash infusions, strange emails etc.
Also, can you please find my dad? We should tell him that Janine is missing. Anything more on El Toro? Or ATM footage? I may have something soon.

Get back to me ASAP.

P.S. If you can't figure out her email password, Geoff in IT can probably hack it.

P.P.S. You didn't hear that from me. Make it work.

C

Carlyle sent the email and waited before pulling anything else up. Footsteps fell in the hallway and she looked up to see Suzanne with her eggs. "Thanks so much," she said and waited for the chef to chatter her way back down the hall.

She waited nervously to hear the *ping* which meant Marius had written her back. She stared down at her notepaper and the word *Caspirada* made her unable to ignore the flood of memory taking her back to that Christmas with her family. It was the last major holiday Janine had spent with them. Cybil had decided on a change of scenery since there were no young children to consider anymore; she thought it would be nice for everyone to get out of town for Christmas and head to her timeshare at Caspirada, a golf and residential club in Napa Valley.

Caspirada was other-wordly; the grapevine-lined hills rolled for miles around, and the air had just a hint of the sea, which was about 100 miles to the west. Caspirada's two golf courses were both ranked in the top ten golf courses in the world. It would not be uncommon to see Tiger Woods or Phil Mickelson taking practice swings on the driving range. The insides of Caspirada were just as impressive as the rolling landscape; the five-star restaurant had a new menu for every meal, rotating with the produce of the season and what was available at local markets. The spas—one for humans and one for dogs—were equally as highly rated as the golf courses, and fulfilled every whim of the golfers' wives who tired of waiting all day for their husbands to finish the course. When one did return from either the course or the spa, it would be to a private house—dubbed a casita—complete with one or two bedrooms, a full outdoor kitchen and fireplace, and a curated selection of wines chosen based on the guests' answers to a personal taste questionnaire.

Cybil usually reserved her time there for high-level management retreats or for the wooing of a large distributor. However, she thought the experience was an appropriate gift for her children, instead of adding to the litany of trinkets and electronics she generally gifted them year after year.

There was another reason Cybil had wanted everyone to go away together. She was planning a deep-dive rescue mission of her second daughter, and she knew that the best way to coax Janine back to her former self was a few weeks in wine country with people who loved her. Before the trip, she'd sat her other children down and told them that she wanted everyone to try their best to reach out to Janine. To make sure she felt loved, to make sure she felt connected to them. She'd made each of them name one way that they would try to bring Janine back. Cybil started.

"I've booked her a day at the spa—a seaweed body wrap to help detoxify her, a massage and a mani-pedi. Nothing's ever made me feel brand new like a spa day."

Valerie was up next. "I'll play Centipede with her at the arcade in the clubhouse. We used to play all the time as kids. I think it will bring back good memories for her."

Carlyle chimed in, "I'm going to bring my knitting needles and yarn. I'm still learning how, but I want to try to knit her a scarf to show her how much I miss her and how much she means to me."

Tom struggled. "I think I'll just try to talk to her, see where her head is at," he said finally. Tom was not known as a great conversationalist, but they praised him for his effort anyway.

Cybil added something else. "I also bought," she paused as she took something shiny from her purse, "this angel painting to protect her." As she spoke she scratched off a 99-cent tag from the thrift store on the corner. The painting was in a Renaissance style, but had luminous gold paint surrounding a beautiful, modern haloed angel. It was small, the size of a cigarette case, and had a lid on a hinge, so that it could be closed up and carried safely in a pocket at all times. Once opened, the icon could stand upright on a table, supported by the lid behind it. The outside was intricately painted with flowers and vines.

The siblings looked around at each other, unsure whether their meager offerings would please the goddess Janine.

CHAPTER SEVEN

Throughout the trip, Janine had cycled through a routine of marijuana, Ativan, Depakote, Paxil, and Pinot Noir. She'd been in and out of conversations and seemed unable to get comfortable. She would sit for thirty seconds fidgeting, try laying down, then pop up a few seconds later, convinced she needed a hot shower. When the shower wouldn't do it, smoking a joint would. But then that would bring her down too far—she would be too sleepy for her liking—so she would down an energy drink and a Paxil. There was no regard for the labels or instructions on the pill bottles, all of which cautioned against mixing them with alcohol and other medications.

It was as if being within her body itself was uncomfortable—intolerable. She always seemed to need another distraction from how she was feeling at any given moment, and whatever feeling it was consumed her. The family, especially Cybil, had been shocked at how far Janine's condition had declined in recent months. They were driving themselves mad with worry, wondering what she would do next, wondering if they would find her in a ditch somewhere if they left her unattended.

After a filling dinner of bacon-wrapped pork tenderloin and chanterelle mushrooms, Janine and Enrique, her tag-a-long boyfriend, took one of the golf carts for a spin around the grounds. The wheels screeched as the pair did doughnuts around the ninth hole. Other guests—clad in plaid pants and collared shirts—had to pick up their cigars from where they'd fallen out of their gaping mouths. The concierge desk no doubt had a line of enthusiastic complainers re-counting how their peace of mind had been ruined for the evening.

Janine and Enrique peeled around the corner and parked in the designated spot to meet Cybil and the rest of the family, unfazed by the reactions from the other patrons of the club.

"No, we're winning!" Tom exclaimed above the noise of a rousing family game night. The score was in dispute. Carlyle wished Ethan, the resident trivia master, could have come, but he'd had to venture to the other coast—South Carolina to be exact—to comfort his ailing father.

The family sat out on the veranda of the small casita where families stayed while on sabbatical from their lives. The northern California night was crisp and logs crackled in the fireplace. Janine slouched down on one of the outdoor couches, face-first.

"Napoleon!" she slurred, the correct answer to the question being posed to Cybil and Tom's team.

"Yes! We get that one! We get that point!" Tom called.

"Goddamnit, Janine! Now we're losing!" Carlyle snapped. Indifferent to the upset in the game, Janine buried her face in the weatherproof cushion. Thus hidden, she reached her arm down into her purse, which was never far away. The hand rummaged around like a mechanical arm in a claw machine, hopelessly grabbing and coming back empty.

Her head popped up as she dug further still. The hand moved fast-er, more frantically. "Shit, shit, shit," she muttered to herself. Enrique's face went pale, as if he knew what she was looking for, and knew what would happen if she didn't find it. "They're gone, it's all gone. I had it on the golf cart, it must've fallen out—" She was up now, grasp-ing at the air, at the furniture, at anything real, hoping her pill bag was somewhere within reach.

Instinctively, the family stood up and began looking on top of things, under things, in cabinets and suitcases. "It's got to be out in the driveway or the parking lot." Valerie looked at Carlyle. On an eight-een-hole golf course full of cart trails and hiking paths, the tiny pill bag could literally be anywhere. The weight of the fact that they might not find it pushed down on everyone. Cybil's eyes looked drawn. This family could barely handle Janine in her medicated state; how would they fare with her detoxing off all her meds? The words "powder keg" came to mind.

After everyone had scoured the casita and part of the driveway outside, a timid knock came at the door. Janine, Enrique, and Tom had told Cybil they were going to retrace the steps—or doughnuts, rather—that they had made earlier in the golf cart. Cybil stayed behind, and was the one who opened the door to find a paunchy, middle-aged security guard holding Janine's pink and silver-striped pill bag.

It was much larger than a typical pill bag would need to be. This was a large rectangular makeup bag, so full the zipper was puckering at the sides, straining to accomplish its one and only task.

"Evening, ma'am," the guard said. The bags under his eyes looked puffy, and his eyes were ringed in red.

"Oh, thank god you found it!" Cybil said, unable to hide her flood of relief. She reached for the bag only to have the guard step back from the doorway.

"I believe this belongs to your daughter, ma'am?" he questioned suspiciously.

"Yes, it's her medication. She needs it, so if you could return it, I'd be so grateful." Cybil's words had teeth, and they came out much more angrily than she'd intended. "I mean, thank you so much for finding it. We really owe you one."

"Ma'am, I'm sorry, but I just can't give this back to you in good conscience. It wouldn't be right. I am an instrument of the law. The medications contained in this bag, as well as the *illegal drugs*"—he whispered, even though there was no one else around to hear them— "should not be mixed. Not to mention, some of these prescriptions belong to people who are not your daughter. I may be stepping out of my bounds, but I needed to let you know that this is a lethal mixture here," he gestured to the bag. Lowering the bag by his side and stepping forward, the guard's face softened. It looked like he might be contemplating extending a comforting hand to Cybil's shoulder. He thought better of it. "You're her mother. I'm a parent, too, so I… I know you've got to do something," he said.

The guard was an employee of the country club, not an actual cop, which made it even more impressive that he was able to gather the courage it took to say these things. The employees of Caspirada were trained that no exception was too large, no request too outlandish—guests of the resort were meant to feel at home, which they technically were since they paid a yearly fee to have access to the retreat for thirty days out of the year. The employees regarded each guest like a beloved, aging parent who needed a guiding hand to choose a wine for the evening.

Cybil was surprised and taken aback by the guard's accusations. She hadn't known that some of the prescriptions bore the names of people who were not Janine. Though she supposed the reaction he expected from her was anger, she took him into the house and gingerly requested he take a seat.

"What is your name?" Cybil asked somberly.

"Lenny," he said as he found a seat on the couch. Grapes, wine bottles, and expensive-looking cheese wheels danced across the thick upholstery.

"Lenny," Cybil started, "it sounds like you know a lot about this type of thing. What do you mean when you say this is a lethal combination?"

Lenny looked down at the bag, which he now clutched as if it were his passport to leave a war-torn country. "My wife," he said, his eyes suddenly hollow. In the light he looked older, but Cybil could tell it was the kind of age one gets from experience rather than time.

Carlyle and Valerie entered the room quietly, and although they saw the object they had been searching for clutched in Lenny's hands, they said nothing, taking cues from their mother to hold steady. Lenny was undisturbed by the new people in the room, because he was somewhere else, with someone else.

"My wife, she was not well. Mentally, I mean. She went to lots of doctors, had lots of tests done, but she never felt quite right within herself. She couldn't be happy..." he began to trail off. "I should've been able to make her happy, but I couldn't. Anyway, she had a bag like this, full of pills. She kept it with her all the time, afraid to let it out of her sight.

Two years ago I came home and found her on the floor of the bathroom. She… she'd died. The doctors said it was cardiac arrest. That her liver and kidneys couldn't take the punishment of all those chemicals and pills she put inside her all the time. Maybe she did it on purpose, I don't know, but… I'm sorry, I shouldn't have told you all this," he said, suddenly realizing where he was, who he was with.

"No, Lenny, thank you for telling us," Cybil said gently.

"I just—I came across this bag when I was doing my nightly patrol. I thought I was hallucinating. I thought it was a nightmare, some bad omen. But I looked inside and saw your daughter's name. I remembered the complaints about her driving the golf cart and I thought I had a chance to do some real good, to save someone since I couldn't…" He took a deep breath, and for the first time looked around the room to see Valerie and Carlyle. Carlyle's face was streaked with tears and Valerie sat stunned. Neither said a word.

"I knew it might cost me my job to say something, but I couldn't help myself," he concluded.

Chapter Eight

Just then, Tom, Enrique and Janine entered through the door of the casita. With them came the skunky, putrid smell of marijuana smoke. Each of them looked dazed. Janine spotted her bag and the man holding it. An overly-thankful swoon of relief came over her face.

"Oh my god, you found it! Thank you so much, you're my hero!" She bent over the back of the couch where Lenny was sitting and draped her arms around him in a hug. He looked uncomfortable, straightening his back militaristically. Janine dropped one of her hands toward the bag in his lap and tried to pluck it from him. He held on tight, and Cybil reached over to grab Janine's hand, unfurling it.

"Honey, we were just talking with Lenny about what's in your bag. It seems like you might have some explaining to do." Cybil looked directly into her daughter's face for the first time since they had been at Caspirada. She held her wrist and tried to see the girl she once knew.

Janine ripped her hand away defensively. "What are you talking about, Mother?" Janine was the only one who called Cybil "Mother" rather than "Mom," and it was only when things were about to go very wrong.

"Well, for example, this Depakote is prescribed to Stanley Whitlatch. Mr. Whitlatch is only to take this medication once per day in the morning, or when he feels a seizure coming on." Cybil had taken one of the bottles from the bag, which still sat on Lenny's lap. She grabbed another. "This Paxil is prescribed to Louise Stemler. Would you like to tell us what's going on, Janine?"

Enrique looked at the floor and rubbed the back of his neck, exposing a wet armpit stain on his orange t-shirt. Janine crossed her arms in front of her. She glared angrily at Lenny. "It's none of any of your business," she slurred. "These are my… well, now they're mine, anyway… I need them. They help me. I don't see why it's any of your business," she said again.

"Because it's against the law to steal other people's medication," Lenny said.

"You're not the law, you're a rent-a-cop. You can't do anything. You're not even allowed to have a gun. So you should mind your own damn business," she snarled.

"Janine, Lenny is trying to help you. We're all trying to help you," Cybil said.

"*Lenny?* Oh, *Lenny* is trying to help? Seriously, Mother, you're going to stand up for this stranger instead of your own daughter? You should have him fired. He has no business butting into our affairs."

"Where did you get the medicines, Janine?" Cybil asked, not falling into her traps. Thinking back now, Carlyle was proud of her mother. She'd expected her to bow and shuffle to Janine's marching orders, as her mother usually did. The normal power she held in everyday situations would fade, her shoulders would slump, her eyes would cast down, and she would give in. It was as if Cybil owed Janine something, something that she'd neglected to give her many, many years before.

Janine swallowed. She looked at Enrique, who shrugged. It was a might-as-well-come-clean shrug. "Enrique gets them for me from his job." She looked down pitifully, knowing that her power play had failed. She was moving on to another well-known maneuver, the Pity-Me-I'm-Weak defense.

Enrique was an orderly at a nursing home in San Jose. It took a few moments for the family to put together the pieces of what Janine was saying. "You mean he steals them from the residents at the nursing home?" Valerie asked, incredulous. The pair looked at the floor.

"They can just ask for more. The pharmacist there doles out medicine like bubblegum. She assumes they've lost them, or flushed them down the toilet in another 'they're trying to poison me' rampage. It happens all the time. They don't even miss it. But me, I'm sick, I need it." She cocked her head to one side and shrugged a shoulder to her ear, a childish pout coming over her mouth. She held out her hand in a final attempt for the bag. Neither Lenny nor Cybil made any move to give it to her. She sat for a moment with her hand extended and when it came back still empty, she clenched her fists. She let out a low-pitched, grunting scream and stomped a foot repeatedly. Since all other tactics had failed, Janine saw no other option but to take the bag by force.

She moved quickly around the couch and coffee table and lunged at Lenny. Valerie and Carlyle looked at each other, stunned. Cybil stood up quickly and grabbed the phone to call 9-1-1.

"Whoa, whoa!" Tom rushed to the middle of the scrum that threatened to become a brawl, trying to pry them apart.

"It's for your own good, you need to learn to live without these, Regina!" Lenny yelled. His eyes had regained a glossy, other-where look.

Janine screeched at him, high-pitched animal noises punctuated with phrases like "Mind your own business, Paunch-o!" Carlyle could only assume that Regina was Lenny's dead wife. This made her feel closer to and more protective of him than she did her own sister. Carlyle ran behind Janine and grabbed her waist, attempting to pull her off of Lenny, while Tom worked to separate them from the middle. Arms flailed and still Lenny steadfastly held onto the pink and silver bag.

The zipper of the bag was still open, and as Lenny squeezed the case tighter and tighter, trying to fight Janine off with his elbows and head, the pill bottles began to pop out of the bag and spill out onto the floor. They rolled in all directions, making clattering noises as they fell. Neither Janine nor Lenny realized that the objects they were fighting over were no longer in either one's possession.

One of the bottles rolled to Enrique's feet while he still stood motionless, watching the chaos ensue. Surely he had been witness to Janine's outbursts before, because he seemed unmoved and unwilling to jump into the fray to aid either side. He picked up the bottle near his feet, and after peering at the label, opened it and slid a few of the white ovals into his mouth. He put the bottle in his pocket and quietly exited the room.

When the police arrived, the family came out onto the black asphalt drive clutching sweaters around themselves, their faces blinking red from the reflection of the lights on the cop car. They watched as Janine was forced into handcuffs, still resisting every form of physical contact. The police in the sleepy town of Santa Rosa had certainly seen nothing like her before, and she behaved as if she'd watched one too many cop shows. She said nothing as they read her Miranda rights, her family looking on in confusion and pity.

A female police officer had gone inside the casita to collect the "evidence," all of the pill bottles that had been in Janine's bag as well as the rolled joints tucked in the side pockets. Only about half of the pill bottles belonged to Janine; the other half were lettered with the names of the residents of the Punta Vista Nursing Home. There were twelve bottles in all—Vicodin, Valium, and Hydracodone mostly, as well as the pills Janine had been prescribed for bi-polar disorder.

Lenny was asked if he wanted to press assault charges. If he did, Janine was sure to go to jail for a long time.

The casita was quiet once again. Though the altercation had only lasted about three minutes in all, the family felt as if they had been at a rock concert; everyone yelling still, even though the loudness was over, their heads foggy and their eyes bloodshot. The next day they would find bruises, but not know how they had been obtained. As much as they didn't want to admit it, the energy of the room was lighter now that everyone knew where Janine was, and that she was safe there—and that they were safe here.

Carlyle wasn't sure what deal Cybil had struck with Lenny, or with his bosses at Caspirada. Surely they would want to fire him for getting so involved in their guests' personal affairs. She assumed there was a trade-off, something to the tune of him keeping his job but not pressing assault charges.

It was two months before Carlyle saw her sister again. Cybil had gone down to the Napa County jail, which consisted of two holding cells, a kitchenette and a few offices. Carlyle liked to think there was a wine tasting room off to the side of the cells, complete with wooden barrel tables and floor-to-ceiling wine racks. She imagined the policemen and women standing around, swirling their red wines in the bottoms of their glasses, discussing the acidity and oakiness of the most recent cabernet.

Cybil spoke to Janine through the bars about her "condition" and told her she would only agree to bail her out if she went straight from jail to a rehab center in Tucson. She had been on the phone most of the night trying to secure a place for Janine—the center was exclusive, remote and impossible to get into. She'd managed to get her in, but only if she arrived the next night. The program was forty-five days, with an optional fifteen-day overstay. Cybil had had a tricky time explaining the situation to the intake nurse.

"What medications is the patient currently taking?" she asked. She was unable to answer the question as it should have been answered, and told the woman she would have to ask Janine that question when she arrived.

Janine agreed to go. She wept at the thought that she would not be able to say goodbye to Enrique before she left. "He's already gone," Cybil told her. No one had seen him since the first mention of calling the police the night before. Janine's eyes turned hard.

"He's gone?" she asked. Her mother nodded. "Bastard," she uttered.

Cybil accompanied Janine all the way to Tucson, completing all the necessary paperwork to ensure her daughter a first-rate rehab experience. She watched as the techs at the facility searched Janine, patting her down in rubber gloves. They went through her suitcase and found one solitary bottle of Valium housing three lonely pills. It went straight into a trashcan, the contents of which were trucked away to the dump the very moment the admission tech left the room, as if it contained hazardous waste, or Agent Orange.

Carlyle wondered now if Janine ever had any intention of staying in rehab and getting help. *Or is she just beyond all hope?* Carlyle thought.

CHAPTER NINE

Ping! came the sound from her computer, and though it was quiet it shook her from her memories like a foghorn on an open sea.

She opened the new message from Marius.

Boss,

Jan 6, refund of $34,400 from Silver Springs Rehabilitation Center direct deposited to Janine's account

Jan 8, cash withdrawal from six different ATMs in Juarez, Mexico totaling $30,000 (!!!).

Just little things for the rest of Jan and Feb. – most of the spending occurs in Mexico, various border towns.

Then back in Omaha she starts betting from $1500 to $5000/week on horses. It doesn't look like she ever won.

Everything else must've been in cash.

Re: Blog – a notice was posted that El Secreto (the writer's code name) has been compromised. Several news sources and authority figures are trying to find out what happened and free this person before they are killed.

Re: Toro – looks like he's in Miami right now. His wife is a big charity benefactor, ironically. She threw a benefit last night and he was there, the Miami Herald reported on it. If he's holding Janine, then his employees are doing the holding in Progreso, but he isn't there.

Re: Dad – I'm looking for him now. I'll get back to you.

M

"Are these eggs not the best you've ever had in your life?" Tom said, bursting through the door with a plate piled high. On his way to the table he grabbed two danishes and set them atop his breakfast mountain.

Carlyle looked at her plate of now-cold scrambled eggs. She'd forgotten to eat them. "Oh, uh, yeah they're great," she said, trying to act nonchalantly. She shoveled a few forkfuls into her mouth, but the food turned to sand. She watched her mother and Valerie come through the door as Tom began to eat.

Carlyle wondered if she should bring up what Marius had found. Would it make a difference now? They were already on their way. Perhaps it would ease her mother's mind a bit and keep her from climbing on top of other random bits of taxidermy that might be stashed around the yacht.

For the first time since they'd left, the family sat down to a meal together. They looked warily—and a little wearily—around the table at each other. They craved something else to talk about besides Janine; their minds and bodies had grown tired of the subject, but there was nothing much the four of them had in common. Carlyle decided that full disclosure was the best idea, and broke the awkward silence.

"I heard back from Marius about some things," she said. "And I want to get all of your thoughts about the facts." Her sister looked rabid—ready to grasp at anything that could prove Janine was not really in danger. Tom folded his arms and looked at the floor, not amped for another family meeting. Cybil set her jaw and plunked her coffee mug down on the table. She had their attention. "First, I want Tom to tell you what he told me last night."

Tom let out a big sigh, and with some added cajoling he told his mother about Janine's leaving rehab and going to Mexico. He had never talked to Cybil about his foray into salesmanship, and Carlyle could tell the thought of her only son—her baby—dealing drugs made Cybil squirm from the inside out. "She stayed in Mexico for like two months and then came to Omaha." He finished the story even more emotionally drained than he had been telling it the night before. Carlyle did not like making her brother relive his most shameful memories but she felt the story held more water coming from him.

"And what did she have with her?" Carlyle pressed.

Tom mumbled and the entire table craned their ears to hear his confession. "What?" Cybil said, visibly on the edge of patience.

"Trash bags full of weed!" Tom exploded. "Are we done?" He turned to Carlyle, upset that she had betrayed their confidence from the night before. Whatever fraternal bond the two had forged under the influence of Tom's drugs was now broken.

"Tom, you're not on trial here." Cybil tried to quiet him. "You've been punished enough for what happened. This is new information to me. I never wanted to press you for the details because you were so upset. But the more we know about the situation we're going into, the better."

Tom looked at the ceiling and the well of rage began to dry up. The tension from his shoulders released and he rested his arms on the table. A hand came up to cradle his face.

Carlyle took a deep breath and continued. "Okay, now that you know that—here's what Marius found. Silver Springs—the rehab place—refunded Janine $34,400 into her account. Two days later she withdraws the equivalent of $30,000 cash in and around Juarez.

"Marius also told me that El Toro—the drug guy we thought might have kidnapped Janine—is in Miami. His wife threw a huge charity event last night and he was there, the Miami Herald snapped a picture of the two of them. From what I've read about El Toro, he's not really a 'hands-off' type of guy. One of the anonymous blogs I found chronicles a story about him—that he takes his public persona very seriously, and his reputation even more so. If someone needs to be 'dealt with'—you know, killed or whatever—he *has* to be the one who does it. Years ago, his second-in-command was supposed to kill someone, and instead he let the person go. That person came after El Toro and poisoned him. He almost died—spent weeks in the hospital. Now he has to do the deed every time, to make sure it's done right."

Carlyle hadn't done a good job of concealing her excitement. Her pace of speech had picked up and she'd forgotten to take breaths. Her family stared at her in horror. She had to admit that she wasn't as excited about the subject matter as she was about her ability to find the information. "Anyway, the good news is, I don't think he has Janine. Or if he does, she's probably still alive—the Miami Herald article said he'd been in Miami for a few days preparing for the event." Her mother's eyes were like glowing round orbs.

"How can you be so cold, Carlyle?" Valerie asked with genuine curiosity.

"It's not that I'm not upset about Janine… I guess I am just having trouble believing any of this is real." She paused. Her family continued to stare, waiting for her to connect the dots for them. "Okay, what I think happened is Janine went to Mexico from Silver Springs and used that refunded money to buy a shit-ton of pot. That's the pot in the trash bags. She used Tom to help her move the product. Now— these cartels don't sell $30,000 worth of pot to just anyone. She's an American, so that was a good start, she could get across the border fairly easily. But she would've had to make friends—connections to keep replenishing her supply. She *knows* these people. That's what I'm saying." Inwardly she was conflicted—what about the blogger? A notice had been posted, El Secreto had been found out. Could Janine be El Secreto? She wasn't sure.

"You don't know that." Tom's voice was crackly—adjusting to being used for the first time since his outburst. "She could've been working for them and then she pissed them off. They found out her family had money and they kidnapped her. Just because she worked with them doesn't mean they wouldn't turn on her."

But something doesn't fit, Carlyle thought to herself. The email, the text, the call… they had all been so vague. They hadn't had direct contact with anyone who claimed to be holding Janine. Except for a brief—possibly hallucinated—echo of Janine's voice over the phone, there was no evidence that she was with these kidnappers. There was the blog, sure, but after rehashing her sister's decline over and over in her head, Carlyle couldn't believe that Janine was the type of person to suddenly pursue a higher purpose.

Carlyle didn't say the last piece of the puzzle she'd been dying to eek out. She hadn't confirmed her suspicion yet, and didn't want to jump to conclusions.

Chapter Ten

Carlyle's family looked just as dumbstruck as they had when this misadventure began. Though she had a strong hunch, there was still nothing to prove Janine wasn't in real danger. There was one way to prove it, but she would need the satellite phone and the ability to swallow her pride.

She excused herself from the breakfast table, vowing to get her mother alone at some point later in the day. There were still so many unanswered questions about what she had seen the night before, but she knew she would get nothing out of Cybil with Valerie and Tom standing by.

Ethan picked up the phone after only one ring. The sounds from the phone were amplified, and she could hear his breath as clearly as if it was on her own neck.

"Hi," he said when he realized who was calling. It was the sweet, relieved greeting he always gave when she called. As if he had been waiting all day for her call, and now that it had come, he could relax.

"Hi, it's good to hear your voice." Their fragile cease-fire seemed to be holding up, and she didn't want to upset its delicate balance by asking a favor. She consigned to let Ethan in on what she had found out from Marius, and see if he would offer his advice. Then maybe she could get the help she needed. She unloaded everything, beginning with her mother's recent dip in income tax brackets and the poker problem. She regaled him with the tale of her sister's whereabouts when they'd all thought she'd gone to get better. Then followed up with the financial information that Marius had so swiftly and effortlessly dug up. By the end of the story, tears were streaming down her face and she had a strong urge to guzzle a beer.

Ethan could hear the fear in her voice. "Wow, it's like you guys have been doing this Private Eye thing for years. Are you an undercover CIA agent?" Ethan joked, but she could tell he was really impressed. "Don't answer that, I don't want to put your identity at risk." She giggled, letting him comfort her.

"Marius is the star here. He has access to all our accounts since he transfers all the money—you know how mom is, she doesn't want to handle the details."

"Looks like that's gotten her into trouble." He sounded smugly self-righteous and she had to stuff down a gut-driven defense.

"I think there's more going on there than any of us know about. I'm going to talk to her later, but right now I'm stuck and I don't know what to do next."

"What do you need?" He was eager to help her for the first time since he'd left home.

"Well, we know Janine took out a withdrawal four days ago from an ATM. If we could just get the footage from the ATM, we would know if she was alone and free, or if she was under duress. Marius talked to the bank and they said they have no ability to view footage from foreign ATMs and some of them don't even have cameras—"

"Do you think my uncle could get it?" he interrupted, excited at the prospect that he could contribute something.

Carlyle almost crumpled under the realization that if she just gave Ethan a chance, he would always come through for her. He had just asked the question she desperately hoped he would ask. "Isn't he retired?" She knew it was a long shot that Eddie would be able to help, but it was her only hope. Eddie Rosen was a retired local sheriff who had seen every spy movie and played out every "good cop bad cop" routine in real life. He'd closed more cases in the Omaha Police Department than any sheriff before or since.

"Well, yeah, but he still has friends in the department. In fact, those guys love him. They'd do anything for a good word from him. What do you think he'd need to get the footage?"

"Well the date—four days ago was September 30th. And a description of her, I think you can handle that much. Blonde. About 5'6". We need to know if she's being forced to take the money out, so look for people behind her, possibly holding her to knife or gunpoint. Look at her expression to see if she looks scared or is looking around a lot." She realized how strange it was for something like this to make them feel closer to each other, but she couldn't help how she felt. She'd been the self-appointed breadwinner, the moneymaker, and the working woman for so long that she forgot what it was like to need someone else—least of all her own husband.

"I'll see what he can do..."

"Ethan, one more thing. This has to be off book. He can't use a warrant or anything to get it. We can't let cops get involved. If they do, and she really is in trouble, they'll..." her voice quavered.

"I know. We'll figure something out. How much time do we have?"

"We should be in Progreso this evening, I think. I know I'm asking a lot." He drew in a deep breath and she could tell he was thinking—maybe writing some notes to himself on a scratch of paper he found. "Oh, uh—I have one more weird request. Just send this in an email when you find out—if you find out."

"What is it?"

"Can you find out who owns the horse track—in Omaha, I mean?" Ethan was quiet and she could almost see the confusion on his face. "I can explain this part later, but I just need to know who it is—if it's owned by a company or something, then I need to know who owns that company. I need a person's—"

"Got it," he was short and his voice was preoccupied. She suddenly felt that she was asking too much, that drawing him into her family's insanity was exactly what he'd fought for so many years to avoid.

"I want you to know that, even if you don't find anything, it really means a lot to me that you offered your help. I know they're crazy—my family—we all are. That's the thing, I am part of this no matter how much I wish I wasn't."

"But you can make choices. You don't have to go along with everything under the pretense that you're a part of it."

"That's what I'm doing. I'm investigating. I'm figuring this out. I'm showing them that they're wrong to believe her." She knew she shouldn't be this defensive; she wanted to keep the white flag intact.

"That's not what you're doing. You're trying to show how different you are. How you would never have gotten yourself into this mess. What does it matter if the kidnapping is fake now, Car? You're almost there. You're going through with it. Do you think if you can figure this out, then they'll see your side of things and suddenly stop dragging you down? You're trying to tell me how you belong with them, while at the same time trying to prove to yourself that you don't."

His voice wasn't angry. He was matter-of-factly weary; weary of the same old conversation. "The truth is you're terrified that you don't belong with them, because if you don't then where do you belong?" She knew that she was crying, but she didn't realize it was loud enough for him to hear. Ethan had always been the only one who could see her down to her bones. She loved him, and hated him, for it. "Hey," he said soothingly. "Hey, I mean, what I'm trying to say is—you belong with me. *I'm* your family now."

Her eyes had been pressed shut so tightly. She wanted to avoid seeing her white flag blown to smithereens. She unclenched her shoulders cautiously and opened her eyes, realizing that instead of a bomb, he'd put forth a white flag of his own—even if it were barbed with truths she was not prepared to hear.

"I'll get to work on these things. Call me when you get there if you haven't heard from me, okay?" He held on the line, waiting to hear her confirmation.

"Okay," she eeked out. "I love you. I know that much," she said finally.

"Love you too," she heard faintly as he ended the call.

CHAPTER ELEVEN

It was midday now and the sun was presiding over the ocean. The blue of the sky bled into the blue of the ocean, distinguishable only by a never-ending horizontal line. Carlyle stood on the deck. The sea air whipped around her, entangling her clothes and her hair, making them dance frantically. She looked up to the crow's nest, where C.J. sat. Valerie was twined around him, a lazy smile across her face. They looked onward, to their destination, though there was no land in sight.

Seeing Valerie and C.J. together made her think of the conversation with Ethan. She realized this was the longest she'd been away from him since they'd first started dating. After that first night playing smoky pool and the subsequent pancake feast, she'd gone to his apartment. They hadn't had sex, but she lay in his bed, his arms around her. She couldn't find sleep that night, though she tried. His breath was uncomfortably hot on her neck and their skin began to sweat, leaving a film wherever they touched. He snored next to her ear. She was physically uncomfortable at the closeness of another human being. Thousands of times she decided to get up, dress and get in her car. She fantasized about driving in one direction for hours with all the windows down, relishing the space. When the needle on the fuel gauge fell below E, she would hitch a ride to anywhere. Anywhere that was away, away, away. Away from sticky, uncomfortable, cover-stealing closeness.

She did not get up. She did not get in her car. She stayed that night and every night after that. She forced closeness on herself as a fat person forces exercise. She knew she needed it. She knew it was the only way. She wanted it to get easier. And eventually, it did—after three months, she was able to sleep again. She would wait for Ethan to fall asleep, his arms clasping her. Then she would untangle herself, leaving just one hand placed in his hand, fingers entwined. She could sleep then, breathe then.

Now, looking out into the sea, she realized the closeness with Ethan she had once tried to reject had become a part of her. She didn't know many people who moved in together after their first date, but things with Ethan just seemed to work. He cleared space in the closet, he emptied drawers for her things, she began to grocery shop for two. Their lives became one as if it had always been that way. A girlfriend once asked her, "How did you know Ethan was the one?" Carlyle had thought for what seemed like one second past too long.

"There was no *thing*. With other boyfriends, I always knew what the *thing* would be, you know? There would be one or two major things about him—he smokes, we fight too much, he's too jealous—and I knew I wouldn't be able to live with those things. With Ethan, there was no thing."

She was never sure if that was enough—did the fact that there was nothing wrong with him automatically mean that everything was right?

Carlyle felt happy for her sister, that she—even in the midst of all the chaos—had found some peace in C.J. She hadn't realized how deep Valerie's sadness had been until it was somewhat alleviated. She thought about how taking the job at Naturebar had affected Valerie. She remembered the closeted conversation that had taken place a few years before, wherein Cybil revealed to Carlyle that she was the family's only hope for a viable successor.

"Think about it," Cybil had said. "Janine is lost to us. She would never be able to handle this job. Valerie is—well, Valerie is weak, to be honest. She can't make a decision to save her life. She's majored in everything under the sun, but can be master of nothing. I guess not all hope is lost for Tom, but he's still so young. It'll be years before he's ready. I want to keep the business in the family—it's very important to me. That leaves you, sweetie. I know you can do it."

At the time she'd felt a mix of honor and resentment. What had her life of reasonable choices and stability gotten her? The brunt of the responsibility with little of the reward of independence. She wanted to make her mother proud. It was the first time Cybil had confided in her the failings of her siblings. It felt good to have her mother's confidence placed in her over the others. Cybil had laid it out as plainly as if they were reviewing applications, only these weren't faceless applicants, they were her family.

She had known it would kill Valerie if she took the job. Valerie had gotten so many degrees in an obsessive pursuit to *be* the perfect successor for Cybil. Yet in this pursuit she had exposed her propensity for fickleness. Carlyle and Ethan needed the money, and she knew she could do a good job—she hadn't, until now, realized what it had done to her sister to be passed up for the job of her life.

Carlyle had taken the job to the chagrin of both Valerie and Ethan, but to the delight of Cybil. She'd managed to assuage Ethan with a long list of promises: it's just a day job, to get us by for now; I don't love it, so I won't get absorbed in it; I'll find what I'm passionate about and then I'll go do that; I can be detached, I won't become like her; I'm just doing it for the money—you want to keep waiting for your dream job, right?

But Valerie had never taken the bait. The rift created between them felt insurmountable. Carlyle had done the one unforgivable thing: she knew she'd hurt Valerie in a way that couldn't be put back together. Looking back now, Carlyle saw that she'd been patching holes between everyone in an attempt to keep the water out, and now it was flooding.

The job had been easy for her—she flew through financial reports and meetings and mergers like she was born for it, which made her think she had been. When something is easy, it's easy to think you're meant to do it. But when she drilled down to the heart of it, Carlyle didn't think that her passion was meant to be easy. It should be hard— sometimes drudging—but she should feel intense reward for having done it. Her job at Naturebar filled time, it filled her bank account, but it didn't fill her need to exist.

She scanned the deck for her mother, hoping she would be easy to find this time. She didn't see any sign of her, and she knew that Cybil didn't want to be found. Her mother, and the things she needed to tell her, had stayed hidden long enough.

CHAPTER TWELVE

Cybil was in the kitchen with Suzanne. They were chattering away about the virtues of Mascarpone cheese and flax seed — not in combination, but rather in the canon of foods, both women felt these were among their favorites.

"You get to travel to so many countries—tell me what's the next trend you see coming to the States?" Cybil leaned on the counter in an enraptured state of captivation. Carlyle wryly tried to remember any time her mother listened that intently to anything she'd ever said.

"The war on sugar and wheat is going to be big. You should try to get ahead of that. Is there a lot of sugar and wheat in your bars?" Suzanne was asking as if she didn't already know the answer.

"They're 90% sugar, but everything's gluten free... Car! I'm so glad you're here. Can you fill Suzanne in on some of our ideations for a gluten-free, sugar-free Naturebar?" Cybil looked to her daughter with pride.

"We're testing a bar with brown rice flour right now. Also, one with nut flour; there's always an option to use something like Stevia, but the tests don't hold up yet. It's going to be a challenge for us, that's for sure," Carlyle said, falling effortlessly into shop-talk. She caught herself. "Mom, can I talk to you about some things?"

"Oh Car, do we have to? I don't think I can take any more deep conversations today." Cybil over-exaggeratedly flopped her head onto the counter in mock exhaustion. Suzanne tried to alleviate the awkwardness with a low whinny.

"Yes. We have to. We're arriving in Progreso in a few hours. I need to clear some things up with you before we get there." She was stern, and frustrated that she had to be the parent in the situation where she desperately needed to be the child.

Cybil followed Carlyle back up to the dining room, the room that had become the makeshift war room in which to air out the family's grievances and misgivings about their situation over the last sixteen hours of sea-travel. Papers and notes were scattered over the table, sliding every time the boat creaked into a high tide.

"What is it, honey?" Cybil asked wearily.

"Well, there are several things. Let's start with something I noticed this morning. When Tom told you the story about Janine leaving rehab and taking the money—you didn't even flinch. Did you know? I mean, I can't believe I even have to ask this, but did you let her out?" Carlyle's eyes flickered with resentment and ire. Was Ethan right? Was she simply on a quest to prove herself different, set apart from these insane, broken people?

Cybil looked down and over her right shoulder. She leaned into the uncomfortable wooden chair back and let out a long breath. She could not meet her daughter's eyes. "Yes, I knew she left. But I didn't let her out." Carlyle began to let loose with a stream of curses.

"Now wait. You brought me here to confront me, at least let me speak."

Carlyle deflated back down and calmed herself.

"Virgil called me," Cybil continued. "He was enraged that I had—how did he put it?—imprisoned her in a place like that. After two days he'd gone to let her out. All she had to do was call him crying a few times and he flew to her rescue. He was still listed as a guardian, so they let him take her. I hadn't seen or heard from him in months. He told me he was like a new man and he sought to right the wrongs he had committed—he even quoted some-such poem about honor and this and that. He said he knew how to cure her. He said he would be the dad she had always needed.

"I had no choice. I was at a customer junket; I was set to speak the next day. There was nothing I could do. I told him fine, just take her—but get me my money back. I'll consider all your debts repaid if you just do that one thing. He told me he would—against all odds!" Cybil made an emphatic gesture, shaking her fist in the air. Her voice became clamped and she resembled Virgil more than Carlyle would've thought possible. It had been years ago—since the divorce—that they'd last spoken of Virgil.

"Then they were gone." Cybil continued with a regretful nag in her voice. "He went off-grid. I assumed he was trying to perform some hippie exorcism on her in the desert or something. I kept waiting for the money to show up, and when I called Silver Springs they said they couldn't give a refund to anyone who didn't complete the program. I assumed that was that—when Janine showed back up in Omaha, I had no idea what had happened. Or where Virgil was. He torched all the numbers I had for him. I decided to do my best with Janine and try to help her find her place in the world again. All along, she was bringing Tom into her disgusting world—" Cybil's mouth twisted into a frown of shame and fury. The corruption of her baby, Tom, was the last straw.

"And you didn't check Janine's account? Or look into where she was?"

"Honey, I'm not proud of myself. She's an adult—and so is your father—I thought they could take care of themselves. I don't know. I'm guessing she got away from him somehow and went on this crazy drug-buying rampage. The one thing I can't figure out is how she got Silver Springs to give *her* the money back..." The two women were quiet for a moment, trying to puzzle out the possibilities. "To be honest, I was going through some things. I'm still going through some things. I know I should have followed up... but I got distracted by my own shit."

"Well, that's also on the list of things to talk about," Carlyle said with a forced chuckle. "What the hell is going on with you?"

"I..." Cybil put her head in her hands. "I don't know what to call it. I guess I'm just... alone. I'm lonely, I think. I must be having some kind of crisis." Carlyle waited for an explanation of what she knew her mother had to be oversimplifying.

"You don't get lonely," Carlyle said finally. "You never have. You just work. You have everything, everything you've worked for…" she stammered, the words felt like chewing flour. "All those years with dad, and then all the years since then. You've been alone for a long time. Why are you lonely now?"

"To be honest, I was alone all the time we were married too. I think I never knew what it felt like to not be alone. That's why it never bothered me. But now, I've met…"

"Todd Novak." Carlyle said his name, and Cybil jumped at the very mention of him.

"Yes," she breathed. "It's different with him. When I'm not with him I feel acutely empty. Not whole. I'm someone who always knew who I was, I knew where my seat at the table was. I knew the next step. Not only did I know the next step, but I took it. I led. I was confident. Now…" she paused. "Now I don't know what I'm doing from one moment to the next. And it scares the shit out of me." Cybil looked into her daughter's eyes, and Carlyle could see for the first time looking back at her stared humility, vulnerability, and love. The hardness she'd come to synonymize with her mother had faded away—had it just happened, or had it been happening for a long while?

"What are you going to do? The poker, the… whale. You can't be this person and run Naturebar. You need to get it together." Carlyle heard herself. She saw her mother breaking down, falling away into a new person: a person capable of feelings previously unborn. But all she could feel was anger. She could not fall into celebration for her mother's reawakening. She saw their lives as a desk toy, marbles swinging to and fro suspended by a fragile wire—as one ball settles into its place, the other goes flying out into the atmosphere. If her mother needed to settle down with Todd Novak, it meant that she would have to run Naturebar and thus lose Ethan. "Get it together, because I am not picking up where you left off."

"What does that mean?" Cybil was suddenly pointed.

Carlyle brought a hand to her face and was surprised when it came away wet. The tears were silent. "Ethan moved out. I can't do this any more. We want to have a family. I can't raise a kid like this—I can't be you, now that you're done being you."

Cybil's color faded, making her look grey in the reflection from the sea outside the windows. "So, I should consider this your notice?" Her tone was flat and unfeeling. "I'm sorry that the prospect of being me terrifies you so much."

"Effective immediately." Carlyle reflected the chill back at her mother. "You should really give Valerie a chance. She wants it. I never did." She stood up, her chair making a loud scraping sound that made them both wince.

"That's the thing, Car. In business you shouldn't want it. You can't *want* it—if you want it too much, you'll never get past that. You've got to stay removed, be able to make decisions, be rational. Wanting it, loving it, needing it, being irrational—that's what you should do at home, with your babies and your husband. You've *got* to love them too much. That's what I never learned. I kept it all at arm's length. You can't do it that way either." Cybil's voice was almost a whisper.

"I want to love it all. I can't take less than that." Carlyle turned and left her mother sitting at the table. Though she couldn't see her, she knew that Cybil wouldn't be crying. She wouldn't break down, her shoulders shaking in a sob. But as she got down the hall, she heard the faint but distinct howl of a woman who, for the first time, saw herself for who she really was.

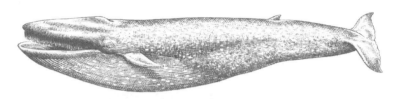

ACT IV

CHAPTER ONE

Each of them stood on the bow of the yacht, watching the tiny port grow from a white speck to a life-sized concrete oasis. Once they were close enough to be seen, C.J. eased the throttle and they slowed to a near stop. They could see two cruise ships docked, nested in the huge concrete barriers that formed a triangle cutout in the dock. If Carlyle squinted, she could see land connected to the port by about three miles of man-made highway. *One way in, one way out,* she thought.

"How do you want to play this, Cyb?" C.J. called down from the cockpit. Since they hadn't left the U.S. legally, their passports weren't stamped and there was no record of them having left. Cybil wanted to keep it that way. She reached into her bag and pulled out a stack of cash. She climbed up a few rungs of the ladder and handed it up to C.J.

"Save some for when we leave, too," she said.

"You got it," he said. Carlyle got the strange feeling the two of them had done this before.

They drew close to the port and C.J. expertly maneuvered the yacht into a parallel position against the heavily barnacled platform. He began casting ropes off to the dock hands, while a few of the crew casted ropes off the back. A man walked out of one of the small round structures perched in the center of the dock. The sign read ¡Bienvenidos a Progreso! Below it, two smaller signs read *Immigración* and *El Centro Touristico.* The man was waving his arms frantically at C.J., yelling and taking pains to organize his face in an expression of "confused."

He held a clipboard and continued to flip the pages back and forth, scanning for something he'd missed.

"Eh?" C.J. yelled. "English?" He exacerbated his southern accent past its normal twang.

The man was standing below them now, just below the bow. "I am sorry. We don't have any yachts scheduled to arrive today," he called up to them in perfect English.

C.J. placed his hand over his face and shook his head. "God dammit, Troy! I thought you radioed ahead to tell them we'd changed course!" He pulled out his phone and began to make frantic calls. "He is going to kill me! His family vacation is going to be ruined and it's all my fault..." C.J. muttered to himself loud enough for the dock agent to hear as he paced the deck. Cybil looked on in demure amusement. The rest of the crew unloaded the ramp and lined it up from the boat to the concrete platform. As they were placing the pins to secure it, C.J. stormed down to the platform, speaking into the phone. "Yes sir, I understand sir. I'll make this right. Please don't say that, I've been with you for ten years, please don't fire me, Mr. Novak." Carlyle was impressed at C.J.'s acting skills. She was sure Todd Novak was not on the other end of the phone—in fact, she was sure no one was there at all.

C.J. pensively hung up the phone, looking terrified. He looked into the dock agent's face, his eyes leaking desperation. "Look, sir. I'm sorry we're not on the schedule. This is Todd Novak's yacht. He's supposed to fly in to meet his family for their vacation. His wife—" he gestured to Cybil, who waved gingerly, "she insisted we stop here to see the ruins. She rearranged the whole itinerary last night." He brought his chin low and his voice to a whisper. "The marriage is on the rocks, you know. This is his last chance," he said. "If I mess this up, I'm toast. Is there anything you can do?" He pulled out the stack of bills Cybil had given him earlier.

The dock agent's eyes grew wide at the sight of so much American money. He looked again at his clipboard, flipping the first page up and down again. "Well, we would be happy to accommodate you. It so happens one of our private yacht slips has just become available."

"One other thing," C.J. said. "Mrs. Novak has a few *habits* she doesn't want to declare to the Mexican government. We're going to need to bypass customs..." he said, taking out a few more of the bills.

"I understand completely." The dock agent looked reverently up at Cybil and nodded to her, as one would to a queen on her first trip away from her kingdom. The agent took the money from C.J. and leaned over to whisper in his ear. He wrote down instructions on a piece of paper from his clipboard and tore it off. C.J. stuffed it in his pocket and hightailed it back up the ramp, then climbed the ladder to the cockpit. The dock crew threw the ropes back onto the boat as the engine flared and once again they were moving. The dock agent waved them goodbye as he began to dial someone on his cell phone.

C.J. drove the yacht a few miles down the coast and dropped anchor. They could just barely see the shore from the deck. He instructed them all to get down to the tender boat garage.

"Are we leaving?" Cybil asked.

"Yep. You've got to get to shore, don't you? I'm taking you in the tender boat to some guy's marina. Elturo—Toron—something. He's letting us drop you there so you aren't seen."

"*El Toro*?" Carlyle, Valerie, and Cybil all said it at once.

"Yeah. Him. The dock agent said all undocumented business goes through El Toro."

"Shit," the women said conclusively.

"What about our stuff, Mom?" Valerie asked.

Cybil's head swiveled, still dealing with the fact that they were headed straight into El Toro's den. "Oh! That's right. We're leaving. Kids, grab enough clothes for a few days. Hopefully we won't be that long, but just in case. C.J., can you take care of the tender boat and the yacht? We may need to leave in a hurry. Is your phone working? If not, turn on roaming, I'll take care of the fees."

"Yes, ma'am. That works for me. I'll stay here with the chef and crew—she can cook for me while ya'll are out." He shot a smug look at Valerie, who seethed with jealousy. "You text me and I can have the boat ready any time."

"Thanks, C.J.," Cybil said. She, Carlyle, Valerie, and Tom went to their rooms to gather their things.

CHAPTER TWO

Carlyle and Valerie were sitting on the bed in the master suite. Their bags were stacked at the open door. They watched as Cybil carefully packed make-up, creams, and serums into her color-coded zippered make-up bags. Each smaller bag was then carefully placed into a larger metal briefcase that clasped closed. Cybil carefully placed the briefcase into the bottom of her roll-top suitcase, where it fit snugly in its place.

"Do you really need all that? You said it would just be a few days," Valerie said, annoyed that they were all waiting on her.

"Don't bother me about it, Val. It's what I need." Cybil was on edge.

"You okay, Mom?" Carlyle asked, trying to be soft.

"I don't know how to answer that question," Cybil replied, shooting a look of regret and anger at Carlyle as she carefully folded each piece of clothing and placed it into the suitcase, forming a perfect, orderly puzzle.

Carlyle remembered her mother's closet at home, rows and rows of shelves filled with shoes, handbags, visors, scarves—each in its own designated place with a label, and organized by color. Her jewelry was arranged similarly in a plastic caddy of drawers that sat at eye level on one of the shelves. All the clothes hung in color blocks down the long wall, a label above each section. In the center of the walk-in closet sat an ab machine.

"We're here now. We actually have to do this. In one moment I'm so mad at Janine I could scream and the next moment I'm so terrified something has happened to her..." Cybil pressed the back of her hand to her mouth and began to breathe deeply, erratically.

"It's okay, Mom," Carlyle said, going to her mother's side. "I'm sure she's relaxing on a beach somewhere."

"Let's get going. See you guys in the boat garage." Tom headed out the door and down the stairs. The others began to amble after him, not as excited to enter the ring with El Toro.

C.J. ran into the open door of the bedroom, out of breath and looking panicked.

"What's wrong, C.J.?" Cybil had never seen her unflappable captain this shaken up before.

"Cyb, I think we should take the boat someplace else," he told her breathlessly.

"What? There's nowhere else. This is where the dock agent sent us. We can't afford being seen again," she said.

"I realized where I've heard that name before: El Toro. He's bad news, man. He runs a big drug ring in Miami. I don't know why he would offer to hide us, but it seems like trouble. A few months ago my—" C.J. cleared his throat, "supplier—for my stuff, he disappeared. I asked the new guy what happened and he said that guy ended up in a barrel of acid for trying to steal money from El Toro. Not the kind of guy you want to pal around with."

Cybil sat down on the floor and brought her knees to her chest. She looked strangely childlike.

"Where the hell is everybody? Don't we have a kidnapper to catch?" Tom busted back into the bedroom, bags in hand, in full-on *To Catch A Predator* mode.

"What if El Toro—or his henchmen, or whatever—have Janine?" Carlyle spoke what she was thinking, not bothering to catch Tom up. "Look, everyone, we knew we were coming into a den of thieves—we may have just gotten there a little sooner than expected. We have to be smart about this. If we leave now it will look suspicious. At least we have a lead. Let's see what this is about. It will be a natural in to meet with El Toro, if we have to. Maybe he can be an asset to us. If he isn't involved we'll just get back on the yacht and send him our deepest gratitude. C.J., you're staying here, so let us know if anything funny happens. Let's move guys, we don't have a lot of time."

Or he'll just keep the yacht and throw us all overboard, she thought. She did not like the idea of her sister being held by someone like El Toro. Part of her had believed—in all the research that she and Marius had done—that El Toro was just a fictional character, someone made up by the DEA to exemplify the dangers of the war on drugs.

Stone-faced, Cybil rose to her knees, gathered her remaining things and crammed them, unfolded, into the roll-top. She flicked the zipper closed and rose, removing her cell phone from her pocket.

Once in the hull of the ship, the family began to don life vests and get ready to go. All of them but Cybil arranged themselves in the speedboat that had been readied to taxi them ashore.

Cybil stood in the boat garage, fiddling with the lights. There were dimmers on every switch and she wanted to get it exactly right. Once the dimness pervaded but did not overwhelm her, she set her phone to camera mode. She approached the whale with more caution this time—as if it might wake up and swim to her, its bristly mouth searching for something more than plankton.

Her children looked on in sheer confusion.

She stood in front of it, trying to look into its eyes. This was difficult, since its eyes were on the sides of its face, separated by its massive snout. It wasn't a snout, was it? No, more like a wide expanse of patchy skin. It just wouldn't do to continue thinking of her as an "it." She was a majestic vessel of the sea. "Doris," she said aloud. "That's your name. At least," she paused, considering that Todd may have already named her, "that's what I'll call you."

She held her phone up at just the right incline and took the photo. When she looked at the results, Doris was smiling at her. "Perfect," she said to herself.

She stowed her phone in her luggage to prevent water damage, and demurely began to put on her life vest.

"Come on, Mom! You are going so slow!" Tom was antsy for his rescue mission to begin. Cybil found her spot and the engine of the tender boat flared to life. C.J. waved his captain signoff to the crew and they were sea-born within seconds. The wind hit Carlyle's face with a spray of salt and the smell of seaweed. She looked over the side of the 20-foot boat to see a school of fish just below them. It felt good to be out of the yacht, and for a moment she let herself enjoy the sea air and the sun on her face.

CHAPTER THREE

They slowed down as they approached the shore, and motored up to a marina just off the beach. The tin roof was rusted almost through and the wood that formed the boat slips was crumbling and covered in algae. There were a few houseboats docked in the slips, and several small sailboats were anchored in the open water off to the side of the docks. A little further down the beach was a massive warehouse that jutted out into the sea.

A little man appeared from the shanty that must have been the marina's office. He ran along the shore with them, leading them to the giant enclosed boat dock a short distance down the shore.

They took a wide turn to curve into the open door of the boat warehouse. A few small boats were tethered up inside, but the tender boat was by far the biggest and most luxurious. C.J. began to cast off the ropes and the little man tied them to the metal castings that were nailed to the wooden dock. Every sound echoed to three times its volume, including the boat's engine. C.J. cut the power, and then engine bubbled to a stop.

C.J. lifted one leg to exit the boat, then the other. He extended a hand to Cybil, Carlyle, and Valerie in turn, helping them to the rickety wooden platform that he'd just tied the tender boat to. C.J. reached to shake the little Mexican man's hand. "God damn, this is quite an operation. Do you get a lot of boats in here?"

"Thank you, sir," he said. "My name is Pepe. And you are C.J.," he said with confidence. C.J. nodded, assuming he must've overheard it somehow. "Just the ones that no one is getting to know about," he laughed, showing a gap-toothed mouth. "This hangar is built by Mr. Malecón for some of his boats. Sometime he need to leave fast."

C.J. wrung his hands at the thought Pepe's boss. "So, does Mr. Malecón know we're here? Is it okay with him?"

"Sí, sí. I talk to him. He in Miami now. All undocumented business go through him. This is how working if you not want to be seen in this part of Mehico." His dark eyes bulged beneath a faded red baseball cap.

"Uh huh. Okay, well be sure to thank him for us." C.J. waited for the last foot to lift off the tender boat before hopping back down into it and firing the engine back up. It was clear he did not want to spend another second in Malecón's secret boat lair.

"You need car? My cousin own car service. It is bit of a drive to see the ruins..." Pepe called over the burbling engine. C.J. could tell he was being tested on his story.

"No," C.J. yelled, the Pierce family looking on. "I think they'll check into the hotel and get settled first before they see the ruins. Mr. Novak is supposed to be here tomorrow morning." With that, C.J. gestured to Pepe to unhook the ropes from the dock slip, and he roared away back to the waiting yacht.

Pepe asked for each of their passports, and produced an identical stamp to the one Carlyle had seen the customs agent using. He stamped their little blue pages.

"Why do we need to go through all this?" Tom asked.

"Si... you get arrested—*la policia*, no?—they not like if you here without stamp. This stamp save you from twenty years in Mexican jail. Si, no persons around to hear your cries," Pepe let out a loud belly laugh, and the Pierces stared at him, their expressions wide-eyed and their mouths clamped shut.

Carlyle got her stamp and moved toward the door. She thought for a moment that there would be a catch—that Pepe would grab her and throw her in some secret marine dungeon. But she walked out into the Mexican sunlight as if she had just passed through a traditional customs line. The rest of the family followed, exhaling large amounts of air and tension.

The family hailed a cab outside the marina on the Calle 19—the street that ran parallel to the beach. From what she could see, Carlyle was not impressed with Progreso. Short, stubby buildings lined the streets. The storefronts were painted in yellows, teals, and oranges, most of which had chipped off with age and a constant battering of sea salt. The windows of the buildings were adorned with ornate, rusted bars.

Valerie told the cab driver to take them to Galleta De Mar, the hotel she found on the internet on her phone, now that she was in range of working cell towers again. She was working hard to find her role in this play, and found the research and execution to be a satisfying answer. By the time Cybil came out of the boat hangar, Valerie had already booked three rooms.

"So, Valerie, we're roomies. And Mom will get her own room," Carlyle reasoned. "And Tom will get his own."

"Good," Valerie snipped, in a hurry.

Cybil appeared next to them, engrossed in her cell phone. "Let's go," she said, not looking up from it. In fact, everyone but Carlyle stared at their phones; one day at sea without cell tower reception had made them all hungry for the connectivity they usually took for granted. It didn't seem strange that Cybil was distracted, since Carlyle knew there was pressing granola bar business that needed to be handled—faux-kidnapping or not. Carlyle looked down at her phone purposefully. A glance at the screen revealed nothing from Ethan or his uncle. She wondered what was taking so long. *I'll call them from the hotel*, she thought. She didn't want to give away her ace in the hole.

They loaded their bags into the trunk of the dingy yellow cab. Cybil took the front seat, her three children piled into the back.

Cybil opened her text messages and started to type. *Doris says hello. And I miss you terribly. Can't wait 'til we're together again.* She attached the picture of the smiling whale and pressed *send*. The reception was poor, but she hoped Todd would at least crack his stoic smile at the message when he got it.

"Who are you texting?" Valerie asked, seeing a glimpse of the screen.

"Todd. I just wanted to tell him thanks for letting us use the yacht, and let him know we got here safely," she said. She kept her eyes forward, but she could feel Valerie's surprised skepticism burrowing through her.

Cybil's phone buzzed.

Glad to see you made it. My stock price went up six percent the day I caught Doris. She's good luck.

CHAPTER FOUR

Galleta De Mar was a three-storey white stucco building embedded between two abandoned buildings. The white stucco shone bright against the dingy grey of the concrete structures on either side. One of the neighboring buildings bore a For Sale sign, and was set so closely to the hotel that it seemed the only thing that could pass between would have been a rat. The hotel itself would have looked nice if it weren't for its surroundings. Royal blue paint cascaded down the columns that stretched from the upper balcony to the ground floor. They framed a small sign that hung between them—*Galleta De Mar: Una Joya En La Playa.* Below it in English, a translation: "The Sand-Dollar: A Jewel on the Beach." Stone steps led up to the main lobby from the street. A few patches of grass had been planted for the express purpose of supporting short, stubby palm trees.

Cybil paid the cabby after their bags were removed from the trunk and sat on the sidewalk. The driver made no qualms about being paid in American dollars. Carlyle began to pick up the bags but her mother stopped her—"Carlyle, the bellman?"—and gestured to the front door of the hotel, where no one stood. "You have to learn to let people do their jobs. Even if you don't want to do yours," Cybil spat. The barb seemed harsh to her siblings, but Carlyle did not stop to explain.

She grabbed her bag. "I'll be in my room," she said, staring daggers at her mother.

A low growl escaped Cybil as she drew up the handle on her roll-top and began to drag it up the stone steps behind her daughter. *Thonk,*

thonk, thonk—the bag made a thick thud with every new step. Cybil refused to pick up the bag, instead letting it drag across the stairs like a popped balloon at the end of its string.

"Pierce," Valerie said pointedly to the check-in clerk. "There should be three rooms." Carlyle kept walking, not stopping to learn which floor her room was on, or which number. She waited impatiently at the foot of the stairs for more information, frustrated that her attempt to storm off was poorly timed.

Valerie reached for her wallet, but Cybil plunked down her credit card. "I may not have $500,000, but I'm not broke," Cybil said, knowing and taking comfort in the fact that her cue came when payment was due.

The Pierces headed up to their rooms, which, as Valerie had requested, were next door to each other. The only three rooms the hotel had together were on the third floor, and since the hotel had no elevator, the family reluctantly hauled their bags up three more flights of stairs. Cybil looked around helplessly for hotel staff who would offer to help ease the climb, but there was no one other than the woman who checked them in. The thud of Cybil's bag echoed through the open-air lobby.

In their room, Valerie unloaded the stash she'd brought from the yacht. She packed the tiny and somewhat unreliable-looking refrigerator with fruits and veggies, hiding the candy and chips that stood at the ready in a basket on top of the mini-bar.

"I thought C.J.—" Carlyle started to say, gesturing to the clearly manic display of dieting.

"What he doesn't know won't hurt him," Valerie snapped. She did care about C.J. and she wanted to make him happy, but what about what she wanted? She wasn't ready to give up on her new body just for an out-of-town fling.

Carlyle couldn't stand to be in the room alone with Valerie. After her conversation with her mother, it took everything not to tell Valerie about quitting. She wanted to offer her the job, to ease the tension between them, to feel like sisters again. But it wasn't her place anymore; if Cybil wanted Valerie for the job, she would have to ask her herself.

Unable to face her sister, she went next door to Tom's room. Tom was shirtless when he opened the door, pulling wrinkled t-shirts and sweatpants from his bag. One by one he laid them across the ironing board he'd unfolded from the wall and sprayed them thoroughly with Flex Body Spray. Carlyle could not turn away from this train wreck, observing as he smoothed the fabric, shook it out and then hung it up in the closet. She coughed at the smell of burnt firewood and musk.

"Looking to make it with some Mexican honeys?" Carlyle teased, barely able to speak since the scent had seeped into her vocal chords.

"You never know," Tom said.

A few minutes later, a knock came at the door. Carlyle found her mother and sister in the hallway. As they came in, a seriousness overtook the room. Cybil sat on the edge of the bed while Valerie sat towards the center with her legs crossed in front of her. She looked around.

"So, now what do we do?" Valerie asked. Each pair of eyes met. One day at sea, another day of air travel before that, and none of them had thought about what they would do—how they would contact Janine or her kidnappers—once they'd arrived.

"Well, the note just said to come to Progreso with the money, no cops," Tom said. "We're here. I guess we wait for them to contact us."

"Yes, but Tom, you forget, dear—we don't have the money." Cybil's preference for Tom over her other children had always been obvious. Where Janine had been their father's pet, Tom was Cybil's. The only boy and the youngest, he was the prized pig. Cybil would never admit Tom's below-average intelligence, and when Janine got him into trouble she became the perfect scapegoat. The reality was that Tom's grades were so bad he wouldn't have been able to graduate anyway. But Cybil excused away any rational evidence when it came to Tom's shortcomings.

"Oh, yeah," he said simply.

"Are we supposed to just wait around? Should we email them or text them to the number they called from?" Valerie offered, unable to withstand Tom's lack of comprehension.

"If they're professionals at all, that would have been a burner phone," Carlyle answered. She spoke with surety about things she had only seen on TV.

"You are so full of shit," Valerie said succinctly. Carlyle felt a rosy, patchy flush surge up her neck—the kind of rage only a sibling can provoke. "You think you're like, a detective, or something? Why, because you can call up Marius and ask him to google something for you? Can you think of any more asinine ways to waste the company's money? Mom went out on a limb giving you that job and you get more excited about disposable cell phones and mythical drug lords than you ever have about Naturebar." The venom was fast and vicious, even though it had taken years to produce.

"Actually, she didn't *go out on a limb*—she hired the most qualified applicant in this sub-par gene pool. And I'm quitting, so you can shove it, Valerie. Now you'll actually have to look Mom in the face and ask her why. Why not you? Why are you never good enough?"

"Whoa, whoa, guys—let's chill out," Tom tried to quiet them, but Carlyle had already gained momentum.

"You want this life? This job? You can have it. In the time since I took the job everything I cared about has collapsed. Ethan left me. I can't get pregnant. But since you're already alone and you don't care about anything except Mom's approval, you'll be great for it!" Her voice was hoarse, but everyone heard what she said. Her family stared. She clutched at her clothes, suddenly wanting to pile on more—anything to put more layers between her and them.

Hot tears streamed down her face and she stomped noisily out of the room, not daring to make eye contact with anyone she passed.

Finally alone in her room, the hot water from the shower could not slow her rapidly beating heart, or the feeling of anxiety blooming in her chest. As the steam rose, she expected to feel lighter, but instead she sank down, lying in the tub as the spray pummeled her from above. She let the water beat on her skin until it turned a bright cherry red and her fingertips loosened. She closed her eyes, not bothering to turn her face away from the uncomfortably hot beads of water hitting her eyelids and cheeks. Her mind raced. She was happy she'd said all the things she'd always wanted to say and yet terrified of what it meant to actually say them.

She was struck by the full force of how much she'd wanted a baby just a few days before. That yearning had dissipated to a quiet whisper now. In an abstract way, the idea still appealed to her, but after spending this much time with Cybil, she wondered why anyone had children at all. Her mother seemed so burdened by them—and at the same time, they seemed invisible to her. The paradox weighed heavy as an anchor around her neck. But if it wasn't the baby she'd wanted, what was it? What was she going to do now that Naturebar wasn't a tether?

She folded her hands over her chest for a moment before realizing she must resemble a corpse. She jumped awake—had she closed her eyes for only a moment or had it been hours? The water ran cool across her body.

She burst from the tub, spraying water across the bathroom floor. The steam that had taken over the air in the room was gone, leaving its mark only on the bathroom mirror, which dripped with condensation. The stiff towel was a few inches too short and a few inches too narrow. She opened the bathroom door and peeked around the corner into the bedroom. Empty. Valerie's bed was still made. How long had she been in the shower? She looked at the clock, trying to remember the time it had been when she'd come back to her room. It was now 9:27 p.m.

Once dressed for bed, she lay down. The mattress was lumpy, mountains and valleys covered by a cloud of sheets and cottony pillows. She picked up her phone and enabled roaming. She watched as the tiny bars grew to mean she had a cell phone signal. She opened her text messages and began composing a note to Ethan.

Hi. We made it to Mexico. Just wanted to say that I love you. I've been thinking a lot about the baby thing and all. I think I want to be us for awhile, just us. I feel lost, like I don't know what I'm good at or what I want anymore. I do know I can be a partner to you, like we used to be. I know how to be your wife, and I can be good at that again. And don't worry about the stuff with your uncle... you were right, it doesn't matter anyway. She read the message to herself again and again. Slowly, deliberately, she pushed *Send*.

Suddenly, a loud knock pounded the door. She quickly rose out of bed and donned the thin, wispy robe provided by the hotel.

CHAPTER FIVE

She flung the door open and Valerie stood, her face pale white. "Tom's gone."

"What? Where is he?" Carlyle asked, panicked.

"We think he went up to the roof deck earlier for a smoke. It's been forty-five minutes and no one has seen him."

"You let him go out there alone without checking on him?" she shouted, but she was already moving towards the rickety staircase that led out into the night.

Valerie and Carlyle clattered up the stairs and burst out onto the deck. Two chairs reclined facing where the sunset would have been. Now the moon draped a glow over the deck, illuminating the two chairs and an ashtray that hadn't been emptied. One single cigarette butt stood crookedly atop the mountain of ash. The sea breeze blew, picking up some old ash and projecting it into the moonlight. Tom was not there. The deck was empty.

"What were you thinking, you fucking idiot? Why didn't you come up here to check on him?"

"He can't have gone far. We'll find him. We'll find him, he probably went to a bar or something," Valerie said, already heading back down the stairs.

Carlyle bent over the edge of the balcony but could see nothing except the tops of more buildings, crammed so close together it seemed there was no need to separate them. *Maybe he's just gone to the corner store. Maybe he just wanted some more cigarettes.* A rational voice in her brain interrupted the panic. She scanned the streets she could see but didn't notice any bodegas, gas stations, or supermercados. The panic set in again. *This is more than being a failure. This is more than disappointing yourself and everyone around you. This is a your baby brother's life and he's gone.*

"Carlyle," her mother called from the landing. "Get down here. Get into my room, now." Cybil had managed to regain her authoritative tone. Carlyle's heart was in her throat as she padded back down the stairs.

The tears, which seemed to never stop flowing, were hot on her cheeks. She did not wipe them but let them fall onto the thin robe. She sat on the bed—her mother's, a full, which was equally as lumpy as the one in her room. "Where the fuck is he?" she kept repeating, sometimes quiet, sometimes a violent, low war chant.

"You're overreacting, Car," her mother said, now trying to soothe her. "He'll be right back. Right back." The edge in her voice seemed to know otherwise.

"Bullshit, Mom. He's been taken. By them. You know it," she spat. Her fear translated to anger.

"Car—why would they take him? He has nothing to do with this. It makes no sense. I'm sure he went out for some air. You know he doesn't like conflict. He'll be back any minute and you'll feel silly," Valerie said. She actually sounded convincing.

Cybil stood and began to pace the room, her hands interlaced behind her head, elbows splayed out like wings. "Fuck, fuck, fuck, my Tommy, my baby," she whispered.

"What the hell are we going to do? We're not even citizens here and we're not here legally. We can't even report him missing," Carlyle's tears streamed faster. Her voice was a thicker, less intelligible version of itself.

"No, Carlyle, no cops," Cybil said.

"Oh, you know what? Fuck you." She felt like a torn stuffed animal with its stuffing strewn out. "You would sacrifice your own daughter and now your son to keep Naturebar out of the news. You are complete bullshit," Carlyle could not stop even more vitriol from escaping her mouth. Her mother, wounded, looked down at the floor. In the silence that followed, they heard a soft knock, low enough to be imagined.

"See? There he is. Everything is fine," she heard Valerie say.

Cybil was suddenly at the door, unable to remember the steps she'd taken to get there. She opened it.

Tom's face was sickly pale and covered in a glaze of sweat. Snot came oozing out of one nostril and his lips were dry to the point of cracking. A red welt was beginning to rise above his right eye. The moment of elation at his return was quickly quelled when Carlyle saw the blood. Her eyes fell to his arm, his hand… a dingy, paper towel was wrapped around it, a red spot deepening almost to black in a perfect circle where his pinky finger had been. She screamed. Cybil reached for him, his eyes blank, expressionless. Sweat beaded above his lip and he took a step into the room. Carefully, his mother hugged him to her, looking back down the short distance into the room to see her daughters' horrified faces. She shook her head at them, telling them everything they needed to know.

Gently, step-by-step, she guided Tom back into the room. He was in a daze, and she smelled tequila on his breath. They must've given it to him to make it easier. Carlyle felt a cold chill go down her back and the saliva began to pool in her mouth. She gestured to Valerie to take Tom to the bed, and barely made it to the bathroom before getting sick in the toilet. Placing a wet towel around her neck, she came back to find Valerie and Cybil carefully holding out Tom's arm. There was a message written on it in permanent marker. He still sat expressionless, his extremities limp.

"Be careful!" she shrieked at them, running to Tom's side. Cybil's hands were shaking and her lower jaw was a cymbal quaking, vibrating from the blow. Carlyle took the towel from around her neck and began to splay Tom's hand out so that they could get a better look. He winced and bit down on the knuckle of his other hand. He seemed to be coming out of the daze brought on by shock and liquor.

Carlyle put her hand to his face. "Tom," she said gently. "Tom, who did this?" As she spoke, Valerie began to unwrap the dirty paper towel that had haphazardly been wrapped around the now-stump.

Cybil brought her hand to her mouth, stifling a gag. Tom looked at his mother, and she tried to disguise how bad the injury was.

"Don't look, son. Let Valerie clean it and we'll figure out what we're dealing with. I'm sure it's not that bad." Even as she said it her eyes grew wide. The paper was tearing away from a ruby tree stump: the rings inside resembling skin, bone and marrow.

"Tom, don't look!" Carlyle tried to keep her brother's focus on her, on anything but his incomplete appendage. "Who did this? Can you remember anything?"

"I... I..." Tom stuttered. "I went up to the roof. I just needed some air from all ya'lls bullshit. I needed to think. I don't know what happened next. They took me down to the basement or somewhere. I don't think we left the hotel." Carlyle's eyes came back into focus on a black scribbled message on Tom's forearm.

"What's this?"

Cybil's face was white and ghostly, each aged line and crease visible in the lamplight. Valerie, one step ahead, held a pen that hovered over the hotel's monogrammed notepad. Below the ball point, she'd transcribed the words on Tom's arm.

Casa San Benito Calle 56 Nu. 43 $$$ Noon Tomorrow.

Valerie slammed down the notepad and began to pace, looking askance at Tom and mumbling under her breath. "Fucking bastards. Fucking animals. He's a kid. A fucking kid."

"You're alright now, you're safe here with us," Carlyle managed to eek out, but the lie stood large in the cramped hotel room. Not one of them felt safe anymore. All shreds of doubt about the legitimacy of the kidnapping were gone in an instant. These were cold, hardened professionals with no regard for human life. "Do you remember anything they said? Anything at all?"

"There were two. Mexicans. A short ripped one and a tall one. The tall one wasn't as ripped. They came out onto the roof too, I thought they were guests. They offered me weed, said they had a source. After we got talking I figured they were good dudes. I followed them back down into the hallway and then I can't remember anything until... until I came to, tied to a chair. The little muscle-man said, 'No one is protected,' or something like that. Then they strapped my arm down and started to write on it. I guess I thought that was all they were going to do. Then they started giving me shots of tequila. I kind of thought it was some weird Mexican drinking game. Then... it happened so fast, I don't even know what they used or—"

"Tom, stop! Please, I can't imagine what you've gone through. Please, you don't have to relive it for us." Cybil had no tolerance for the gore, now that it was so real. She believed it would do Tom no good to rehash the details.

"You rest now," Carlyle insisted, glaring at her mother. "He's in shock, he's been tortured, and for what? What are we even doing here?" Anger boiled out of her.

"Carlyle. Get a hold of yourself for one second. You're hysterical. Think of Tom. Yes, it's awful what they did to him, but they've had Janine for a week. That's if..." Valerie stopped herself, then continued in a steely low tone, "if she's still alive."

Carlyle felt her mother's macabre habit seeping into her brain. She could not stop the thoughts from turning to the darkest place possible. The four of them had been in the country less than 24 hours and they'd taken Tom's finger; what of Janine's still remained? Was she being raped, tortured, brutalized? They'd taken their sweet time getting here, and now she might be dead—taken as punishment for their slow response. She drew her legs into herself—momentarily thankful she still had legs.

The room went silent. Tom whimpered, his adrenaline now fully wearing off. The pain was becoming tangible, instead of the faraway flicker of someone else's nightmare.

"Mom, should we take him to the hospital? We could ask the front desk where the nearest med center is that will accept cash and not ask a lot of questions," Carlyle said.

"Tom, honey," Cybil said gingerly. "I have some pain meds, we'll be back to Big Pine by 2 p.m. tomorrow at the latest. Do you think you can hold out 'til then? Or would you like to see a doctor now?" To Carlyle, this seemed like asking a toddler if he was ready for another round of lollipops and cartoons. "I just never have trusted

Mexican doctors," Cybil said, more to herself than to the surrounding audience.

"I can take some pills and be fine. I just..." he waivered, looking down as his hand for the first time. "I can't believe it's gone."

A plan began to form, a wisp of smoke from a spark of firelight in Carlyle's mind. The smoke began to billow, rolling black and heavy. "I'll stay in his room tonight. Make sure he's all right. I assume we won't be needed much tomorrow since you're handling the exchange and all," Carlyle looked at her mother with an expression that provoked Cybil to stand up and check her phone.

"Yes, I'm formulating a plan. Tom, sweetie, get some sleep. Carlyle, watch him. If he gets a fever or starts tremoring or anything like that, you wake me up. I'm serious." Cybil dug to the bottom of her bag for a prescription bottle. The label read Lor-Tab, and Carlyle wasn't about to ask her mother what it had been prescribed for.

CHAPTER SIX

"You're being watched — we all are." Carlyle reminded her mother and sister as they left the room. "They know we're here. Be extra careful. Go to sleep, act as if we know nothing. *Do not* get out of each other's sight. They won't expect us to do anything until tomorrow. Go!" Carlyle was surprised that they obeyed without protestation.

"Don't. Go. Anywhere." Cybil said finally to Carlyle and Tom. The emphatic pauses were accompanied by a fierce finger point, and they actually made Carlyle think twice about what she was about to do.

Without another word, Valerie and Cybil left Tom's room. Carlyle stood at the door until she heard the heavy metal thunk of the hotel room door in the hallway.

As soon as the door clicked shut, sealing her sister and mother in their room for the night, Carlyle turned to Tom. "Still have that ski mask?" she asked. There was no sarcasm in her voice, only ice.

"I packed it just in case. What's going on? She just said we're not supposed to leave."

"Get it. Put it on. These fuckers are going down."

"Oh, hell yes!" His words slurred. He formed a fist and plunged it into his other hand. The impact proved to be painful enough to bring him to his knees. Carlyle ran to his side.

"Did you forget? You just had a finger hacked off—excuse me for being blunt. Are you really up for this?" she was asking herself more than considering him.

"I mean, yeah. I want to get these guys. It hurts and all, but once the

Tab kicks in I'll be golden. It's nothing, just a scratch." He winced as he made a fist again. "Still think she kidnapped herself?" Tom asked, his first attempt at sarcasm since becoming the nine-fingered man.

"We're going there," Carlyle ignored his question and gestured to the pad of paper with the transcribed address. "We're going to stake them out. Maybe this is where they're keeping Janine. We could help her escape and be back at sea before the sun comes up." She looked around the room. "Bring anything you can think of that would double as a weapon. Clearly these assholes aren't afraid to play dirty." The person speaking sounded sure, confident, and prepared. It was the opposite of how she felt.

"Hey," he said, "I'm proud of you for quitting." His doe eyes looked at her earnestly and she realized he might be the only one who knew how hard it had been to give up her cushy seat at the Naturebar boardroom table. "That took guts."

"Thanks," she said as she turned to leave the room. "But not as much guts as it takes to lose a finger and then go after the guys an hour later. Tom Pierce, an American Bad Ass." She lowered her voice to reflect a movie trailer's voiceover. He smiled and began his patented "returned hero wave."

She left him, his expression expectant, to find the courage—and the proper attire—for the errand at hand.

Carlyle hadn't brought much luggage on the trip, and she'd taken even less from the boat. She plucked the soft, charcoal gray v-neck t-shirt from her bag, along with a sports bra. Her skinny, slightly stretchy black jeans came too; if she needed to run, she wanted to be prepared. When she looked at the shoes she'd brought—a pair of worn brown flip-flops and her lace-up Chuck Taylor sneakers—she chose the latter. She wasn't sure exactly what they were going to do, but when she pictured a daring revenge-rescue scenario, it seemed to involve a lot of hiding, running, whispering and peering through windows. Leather soles rhythmically slapping against the pavement didn't seem to fit into her vision of stealth.

She watched her hands pick up the clothes and put them on; they seemed to be operating independently of her mind, like they knew she couldn't be trusted in her present state. Did her hands know that in her imagination, Carlyle was punching and stabbing everything within arm's reach?

Her dark curls fell in front of one eye. Her hair never obeyed reason, so in the last few years she'd stopped trying to tame it. It was too short for a ponytail, but she didn't want to be messing with it all night. She remembered an old field-hockey trick that had served her well during two-hour practices in the blazing sun. She reached her left arm up to her opposite shoulder and grabbed the short sleeve of her t-shirt. She yanked as hard as she could. The thread let out a sharp blade of sound as the sleeve tore at the seam. She followed it around her rotator cuff, ripping as she went. Once it was separated, she slid the sleeve down her arm, over her head and around her neck. Then, pulling it over her face and across her hair line, it worked as a makeshift headband. The left sleeve remained. She looked in the mirror for a split second and decided she liked the imbalance.

She knocked on Tom's door. It opened after one knock, and she thought he must've been standing there admiring himself in the full-length mirror just inside the threshold. Tom also wore all black—a long-sleeved t-shirt and sweatpants. He had placed a few bandages over his non-finger, which made an X. The bleeding had stopped and his color had begun to return, although she could tell there was a wall of pain just beyond the surface. As soon as he opened the door, she was blasted with the burly scent of his body spray. Over his face was the mask, just as she'd requested. Around the waist of his pants he'd fastened a belt and into it he'd crammed a pen, the coffee pot from the in-room coffee maker and a Swiss army knife, which hung from a chain. "Should I take down the shower curtain rod too?" he asked, his voice muffled. "It would make a kick-ass sword."

She could not stop her hand from flying up over her mouth, stifling the laughter that felt foreign to her. Laughter felt like a betrayal of everything they had gone through so far, so she pushed it down, drawing her hand away to reveal a frozen glare. "Too bulky. We need to keep it light. Want to explain the coffee pot?"

Tom removed the coffee pot from where it hung by its handle on the belt. He mimed swinging it over someone's head, then bashing a few faces on the upswing. He polished it with the arm of his sweat-shirt and slung it back into position. Carlyle could see the coffee pot was not up for debate.

"Let's go," she said.

Carlyle handed the address to the cabby who picked them up out-side the hotel. She kept checking the clock on the dashboard of the cab as they drove. It was 10:03 p.m. She hoped she and Tom would be back to the room before her mother and sister awoke.

The brakes screeched as they pulled up to the corner lot of a res-idential intersection. The other houses on the block were one storey. Some of them resembled old shops with boxy roofs and large front glass windows. She couldn't tell if they'd been remodeled into homes or if they were just abandoned. The house on the corner had no ad-dress, but above the iron gates an arched sign read *Casa San Benito*. Stretching out from the gates, a black iron fence carried on to seques-ter the house away from the surrounding neighborhood. It seemed there was good reason to be fenced in; the house seemed a transplant from another place. Lush greenery surrounded the modern, two-storey structure. She was sure that in Progreso, this was considered a mansion. It reminded her of a house she'd seen that had been de-signed by Frank Lloyd Wright—there were only right angles. The tra-ditional A-line roof was replaced by a flat-top gray rectangle. Like a stack of books, the building seemed at once random but perfectly sensible. What didn't make sense was what this particular house was doing in this particular location.

After the initial surprise of the house sunk in, she was able to take in the human activity that surrounded it. From the back of the cab, she watched as a group of young Mexicans walked up to the gate, opened it and walked onto the grounds. They were hooting loudly and one of them was carrying a case of what looked like beer. One girl stumbled and another of the boys with her bent low to place his neck between her thighs. He lifted her up so that she was riding on his shoulders like a toddler at a carnival. She squealed and rubbed her hands through his hair. Carlyle saw another group of teens headed for the house from a few yards away. They called to the group in front of them and they all acknowledged each other with loud hollers and calls.

"It's a party," Tom said.

"You think so? What could they be celebrating?" Carlyle asked.

"They think they're going to be making $500,000 tomorrow. Wouldn't you be celebrating?" Tom's eyes were locked on the windows of the house. He watched as figures passed each other, dolling out fraternal welcomes.

"I would celebrate *after* I got the money," Carlyle said frankly.

"Not everyone is as smart as you," Tom replied, his eyes not leaving the festivities.

"Would you have a party at a house where you're holding someone for ransom?"

He didn't answer. He just kept watching. After a few minutes the cabby swiveled around to face them. "You want I leave you here? Or stay?" Carlyle reached into her sports bra and pulled out some bills she'd stashed there. She handed him one. "Stay," she said.

"I'll go in. I'll get a feel for the place. I'll try to find Janine," Tom said.

"No way. They'll recognize you."

He began to slip off his makeshift utility belt. "Me? I'll blend in. You and Mom and Valerie can sit around and strategize all night, but this is what I can do. I'm going in!" He slipped out of the ski mask and used the palms of his hands to flatten his hair. He checked his reflection in the rearview mirror of the cab, which was adhered to the windshield with duct tape and rubber bands.

Before she could stop him, he'd slipped out the door. She watched him amble up the yard and through the gate. "This is bad. Shit," Carlyle muttered under her breath.

CHAPTER SEVEN

"**Y**ou no want go party?" the cabby asked her with a twinkle in his eye.

"No, we're staying here. Earn your money." Her eyes stayed with Tom as he stumbled up to the front door. Her guilt almost over-ran her. She'd conned him, under the influence of drugs, to come here to avenge his pinky finger and his favorite sister. He high-fived and fist-bumped every guy he passed and she thought she even saw him wink at a few girls. The music from the house grew louder, a horrible interplay of horns and electronic bass beats. No one would've known he was injured, except maybe those who had done the injuring.

We didn't make a plan. There's no signal. How will I know if he's okay? Her thoughts were running in frantic loops. She decided she would wait twenty minutes. That was plenty of time to get a lay of the land and come back to the cab. If he didn't, she would have to go in after him. It was 10:12 p.m.; at 10:32, she was going in, no matter what.

She took a moment to breathe. For the first time since she'd seen Tom's pale face in the doorway of the hotel room, she was able to feel the air enter and leave her lungs. She felt it rush down her throat and watched her chest rise. She was so full of air, even her stomach felt full. When she exhaled, she realized how empty her stomach actually was. It burbled with expectations.

"Got any food?" she asked the cabby.

"Si, candy and peanuts. Puedo, will cost you," he said slyly.

She handed over a five-dollar bill and he passed her a cylindrical plastic package of peanuts and a sleeve of Starburst. She alternated up-turning the peanut bag into her mouth and unwrapping a Starburst—slowly, intentionally.

More and more people staggered into the party. They were all young, some of them maybe in their teens but most of them in their early twenties. She just couldn't wrap her mind around who would throw a party under these circumstances. Sure, they were a drug cartel, but they were also businessmen. They must know when the appropriate time to celebrate would be. Could this be a trap? She thought about Tom's finger and the kind of people it would take to commit such a vile act. Certainly such monsters would understand the gravity of the situation.

The whole thing didn't add up. This party reeked of Janine. Only she would insist on a get-together at such an inopportune time. "I've been good all week," she could hear Janine pleading to her captors, "can't we have a little fun?" A kidnapper with even a modicum of mercy—or a weakness for pretty American blondes—would allow something like that. Unless Janine was in on it. The truth was, Carlyle couldn't rule out that possibility despite the gruesomeness of Tom's amputation.

She realized that maybe Ethan had learned something from his uncle, but hadn't sent it because of her previous message. She reached for her phone, but after patting down her pockets came up empty. "Shit, I must've left it at the hotel." That did in any hopes of calling Ethan—or the police, if anything went awry.

A startling thought invaded her anxiety. If Janine *was* in on it, that meant she condoned—perhaps even ordered—the assault on Tom, her baby brother. She could not imagine her sister having fallen that far. Janine was her beautiful, ethereal sister. Sure, she was the one who had made bad choices, dated the wrong guys and gotten mixed up in drugs, but she wasn't a bad person, she wasn't a torturer. Or was she? Carlyle did not know what to think anymore, and she felt exhausted from playing out all the angles in her mind.

Time was a turtle—it crept slowly along without regard for any-one else's agenda. Every crunch and slosh of her snacks grew louder in her mouth. The smell of the cab—sweat and sea salt—grew rank in her nose. The clock read 10:25. Tom had long since disappeared through the oversized wooden doors on the other side of the gate. She could no longer see anything but the shadows of revelers wading across silky curtains.

"That's it. I'm going in. How much will it take for you to wait here for fifteen minutes?"

"*Veinte*," he said. She handed him a twenty knowing he would probably floor the gas as soon as she disappeared from sight.

"I'll be right back, I just have to find my brother," she paused. "And sister," she added, but the cabby had already put his headphones in.

She walked up the path and through the unlocked gate. Once inside the house, she was swept up by the sheer magnitude of people. The party was shoulder-to-shoulder and every person held a cup full of something. The house was as uncomfortable inside as it looked from the outside. She searched the faces going by for her brother or sister, but saw no sign of either of them. *Most of the action at a party happens in the kitchen,* she thought. *I'll start there.*

She made her way to the gleaming stainless steel mecca, only to find more faces she didn't recognize. Propelling forward, she went through the sliding door into the back yard. There was a commotion on the other side of the pool. From where she stood she could make out a keg. Someone's legs hung above the crowd, feet to the sky. A chant began to rise from the onlookers. "Gringo, gringo, gringo," they panted.

Oh, no, she thought. *This is my scene,* she mimicked Tom in her head, *this is what I can do.* She couldn't stifle an eye-roll. She made her way towards the keg stand, her hand already in position to grab him by the arm and yank him out to the cab. Tom finished his fraternal feat and was lowered back to the ground, a rock star riding a wave of his adoring fans. Carlyle neared the cluster of onlookers. Tom stumbled and brought his forearm to his mouth and wiped, just as he used to do as a little boy. Only then he was wiping milk or jelly from his face rather than beer foam. She zeroed in on him, but something tugged her vision away from her brother.

Standing just behind the keg was Janine. Her face was as clear and glowing as if she had been basking in the sun all afternoon. Carlyle felt overcome with joy to see her, but the warmth was quickly doused by a sharp, icy doubt. She stopped dead in her tracks and looked at her sister. Janine stared back, her gaze unwavering. She was not bound; there was no evidence of hardship or torture. Carlyle counted her fingers—all ten of them were accounted for. She was simply enjoying a party while on vacation. Her air was light and casual.

"Car! I found Janine! She's here, isn't that—" A blow came down swiftly across the back of Tom's head and he fell limp. His body hit the rough concrete silently. The man standing over him was not tall, but his muscles bulged beneath twisting tattoos.

Carlyle wanted to go to Tom to make sure he was alright, but she never broke her sister's gaze. She began to back slowly away, her fight-or-flight knob finely tuned to "flight." She whipped around and broke into a run, but suddenly every party guest was an accomplice to keeping her there. Their arms flailed at her, nails scratching and hands grabbing at her clothes. She made it through the obstacle course to the sliding door but was met by a large Mexican man holding a revolver. She shot a look back to Janine that was meant to deliver a mix of *How could you? This isn't the sister I knew,* and *Mom is going to be so pissed.* Her sister smiled.

CHAPTER EIGHT

"**T**ake them to the pool house," Janine said. The man in the doorway grabbed Carlyle's arm just above the elbow. He shuffled her past the pool and towards a small, square structure with a satellite dish looming atop the flat roof. She looked back to see the tattooed man scooping her brother up like a baby. He jogged toward the squat poolside structure, trying to close the distance. Janine fell in behind him, the plastic, satisfied smile still stamped across her face.

Carlyle felt in her pocket for her cell phone again before remembering that she'd forgotten it.

Her large chaperone seemed to read her mind and patted her down, enjoying every moment of his search. He found nothing, but continued to search her just outside the door of the poolhouse. "Stop feeling her up, Jaime," Janine said as she walked past them through the door. "You perv."

Carlyle knew their mother would sense something had gone wrong. She would feel her first maternal instinct in her life at this moment. She would realize they were gone. She would know what had happened. She would come after them.

Inside the pool house, the tattooed man laid Tom down gently on the floor, taking undue care not to bump his head. This struck Carlyle as strange and gave her some hope that maybe they weren't going to be hurt. Her escort, seeing the care his accomplice was taking with Tom, loosened his grip on Carlyle's arm.

"Better make sure she's not bruised," Janine said. "You know he won't like that." She sat down on the bed, a mess of cushions and pillows. Magazines were strewn across the room, open to the pages of models smiling and running down empty streets. On the bedside table, Carlyle noticed a matrix of pill bottles, all in perfect rows.

The tattooed man busied himself duct-taping Tom's hands and feet together. Tom lay completely still, and Carlyle wondered if he was knocked out, passed out or both. The effects of the pain pills and the alcohol combined with the smack on the head were enough to worry her about her brother's future mental faculties—even though he'd woken up to worse hangovers. The big man took the duct tape when the tattooed man was done and began binding Carlyle's hands. As soon as the loud rip of the tape sounded, she forced herself to stare at Janine.

"Tino," Janine said lovingly. Tino must've been the name of the tattooed one. "Did you have to hit him? He probably would've passed out anyway." She looked down tenderly at Tom. Tino said nothing, but walked over to where Janine sat on the bed. His mouth met hers before the rest of his body plunged down on top of her, pushing her from a sitting position to laying down. He kissed her hard for a few awkward moments, and she made no move to stop him. Carlyle's cheeks burned.

Tino stood up, his hand pulling Janine's arm toward him. She sat back up but did not rise. "He's not going to like that you hit him," she said simply, pouting up at him. Tino shrugged. "Or that you..." she looked fearfully at Tom's incomplete hand. He motioned to the larger man, who also stood watching them. Tino jerked his head towards the door and the two left the pool house. Carlyle could hear a key sliding into a lock behind them and a heavy bolt moving into place.

"He's a man of few words," Janine said, staring lustily at the door.

For a moment, it seemed they were two sisters sitting on a patio. Maybe they were sipping mimosas and eating salads. One sister told the other about her new boyfriend. Perhaps Carlyle had a dog tied to the table. She would slip him bits of food as she listened intently to her sister describe the man of her dreams. "He has tattoos, like, *lots* of tattoos," imagined-Janine would say. "You know what Mom will say about that," imagined-Carlyle would reply. They'd giggle.

Instead, Carlyle sat on the floor of a dim room. The duct tape itched where it stuck to the skin of her wrists and ankles. She stared so hard at her sister's eyes that they turned into black pools, reflecting light rather than emitting it. She searched and searched within those depths for an explanation.

Janine avoided her gaze.

"What the fuck happened to you?" Years of silence had passed in the dim bedroom that was, Carlyle assumed, where Janine had been staying for the past week, maybe longer. "I mean, seriously, what could happen to a person to make them as fucked up as you?"

Janine looked at her sister for the first time since they'd crossed the threshold of the pool house. The saucy, prim demeanor that Janine carried around like a miniature poodle in a purse seemed to evaporate. Her shoulders dropped, she uncrossed her legs, and she placed a perfectly manicured nail in her mouth and began chewing. With her other hand—her trembling hand, Carlyle noticed—she reached for the grid of pill bottles. There must've been twenty orange-brown cylinders to choose from. She picked one up from the center, examined the label and set it back down. She did this with three more bottles before finding the one she was looking for. She popped three of whatever-it-was into her mouth and tried to set the bottle back in its exact place. It was as though she was constructing a puzzle, and the pieces had to be exactly right. Her hand was shaking so hard now that the inhabitants of the bottle rattled lightly. She slowly tried to place the bottle back on its XY coordinate, but the trembling caused it to bump one of the others. The transparent tubes began to fall like dominoes across the table, some scattering to the floor. They looked like a little orange army of men in white helmets who'd fallen at the hands of their enemies.

Janine fell to her knees chasing each bottle, grasping at them as they rolled past her reach. She let out a frustrated and infinitely sad groan. Carlyle looked on, still waiting for an answer to her question. The army of pill bottles remained fallen. Janine sat up, her back against the bed now, and drew her knees to her chest. She was in the same position that Carlyle was in, but for her it was by choice instead of by duct-tape-force. Janine stared at the pill bottles still clumsily rolling at her feet.

Janine raised her eyebrows and smirked as she brought her hand to her left ear. From behind it she drew a joint—it must've been one she'd rolled earlier and forgotten about. She pulled a silver lighter from her pocket and lit up, inhaling deeply and holding it in. The sounds of the party grew louder. It seemed like the vibrations from the speakers would break down the walls.

"Too bad Tom's passed out," Janine said, smoke escaping from her mouth. "I know he'd hit this with me. Not like your prissy ass, too good for everything." The smell of the smoke brought Carlyle back to the night on the boat with Tom. And then the nausea of the morning after.

"You cut off his finger," Carlyle said, almost a whisper.

"*I* didn't cut it off. Besides, what do you care? It wasn't *your* **finger.**" She took another drag, the joint half-smoked now. The dim light in the room began to fill with fog. Carlyle tried not to breathe, not wanting the smoke that had been inside Janine to be inside her, too. Something was obviously wrong with her, and Carlyle didn't want to catch it.

"We came here to save you, for Christ's sake. And now someone's lost a finger and we're being held captive." She waved away the smoke from her face, but could feel some of it get into her mouth. Janine looked over and ashed onto the carpet. "So what are we doing here? You got lonely?" Carlyle asked cynically, knowing her sister could find company at the bottom of any barrel.

"Three times the victims, three times the ransom. What does that get us to, 1.5 mil?"

"So it was you? You were behind this whole thing? For money, really? Is it that hard for you to just get a job?" Even in the back of her mind, the dots began to connect. Janine had not acted alone. Carlyle didn't want to let on to her sister that she knew who was behind this.

Janine rested her elbows on her knees, the nub of the joint hanging between her fingers. "It wasn't just me. Didn't you hear the door lock? Do you think I would lock myself in here? There's also… him." She looked at the floor where the ash still sat. She licked her thumb and tried to rub out the spot, as if she'd suddenly realized the error of soiling the floor.

"Who's *him*?"

"You asked me before—how did you say it?—*what could happen to a person to make them as fucked up as me*?"

"Yes, that's what I really want to know," Carlyle said sincerely.

"Did you ever think I'm this way so you don't have to be? Maybe I jumped in front of the bullet for you. Ever think of that?" She set the roach on a plate near the bedside lamp.

"Just spare me your martyr bullshit, okay? We all have a choice about who we become." She heard the words come out, and though she knew they were true, they held new meaning for her now. Carlyle had a choice in losing her marriage; she chose to let her job and her fertility crusade define who she was to the detriment of all other qualities or defining characteristics. She'd authored the destiny of her marriage to Ethan when she'd let her fear of becoming her mother—no, she scolded herself—the very *idea* of it subsume all they had grown to mean to one another over the years. If it was true that she had choices, she'd been making some bad ones.

"Well, maybe that's true, but what about what happens before *we* choose? Some of us have a lot more shit to sift through because of the choices that were made for us."

"Are you talking about Mom? Yeah, maybe she wasn't there a lot, but we had a good life. She loves the way she knows how." Had Carlyle forecasted this scene one thousand times, she would never have seen herself coming to her mother's defense. But here she was—and it felt strangely good.

"You don't know what you're talking about. Things happened that you know nothing about," Janine's hands were shaking again, but she didn't search for another joint or start looking for a pill.

"Well, we've got time and I've got nothing else to do but listen," Carlyle said, raising her bound hands in surrender.

"I haven't thought about it in years," Janine said, but it was clear that wasn't the truth.

"You haven't thought about *anything* in years. You've been too wrapped up in this stuff to think about anything. I don't even know who you are anymore." Carlyle meant to gesture to the scattered pill bottles, but because she couldn't move her hands, it looked like she was gesturing to the whole room, the whole house, the whole situation.

"It was him... Dad."

"Dad? He left all of us, not just you! Don't tell me you staged this whole kidnapping because you have Daddy issues—that's too pathetic for words." Carlyle had snapped, unable to stomach that they had come from the same Petri dish of dysfunction, and while she chose to grin and bear it, her sister had thrust them all into mortal danger.

CHAPTER NINE

"**N**o, no" Janine continued, breathing through the dig. "I was seventeen. We were studying Romantic poetry in school. I was never good in school—you know I'd rather experience things than have someone talk at me. Anyway, I needed his help with some of the interpretations—you know how he was always into poets and philosophers and shit." Carlyle nodded, exasperated by the thought of her father reciting Romantic poetry. "Well, I would meet him at the track after school. Disgusting place. He would play his regular games of pool while the horses raced, but then one day a new guy came in. He was hot. Young-ish, maybe twenty-five. He wore a suit. I tried to tell Dad I needed his help and that we should just go to the pancake house—that he didn't need to play this guy. But he insisted."

Carlyle could picture the scene perfectly. She knew the track well, knew that her father had liked to play on the back pool table near the jukebox. When he was on a hot streak he would play The Doors, because Jim Morrison was "a poet in rock star's clothing," he would always say. The track had been the first thing to tip her off.

"Dad won the first game. And the second. He was up something like two thousand bucks, which was a lot for him since he usually played for a tenner, y'know? The guy nudged him into one more game. He couldn't resist. I pretended to be reading my book, but I was watching this guy. He was smooth. '$5000, winner takes all,' he said. They played and suddenly this guy was sinking them, running the table on dear old Dad. He didn't know what hit him. He lost, of course." She paused, lost in memories of the pool hall.

"So what happened?" Carlyle prodded.

"Well, Dad didn't have the money. I saw him talking to the guy and things looked pretty tense for a minute. Then Dad pointed to me. They said a few more words and the guy nodded. He walked out the back door real slow, and as he went he lowered his sunglasses at me—his eyes peering over the frames. I didn't know what that was supposed to mean. Dad came over with a Shirley Temple—I was seventeen but I guess he thought that was still my favorite drink. He called me 'Pumpkin' and told me he needed a favor. I told him I wanted to help him, I loved doing favors for him. Wash the car, clean out the fridge, maybe keep my mouth shut about his late hours around Mom. This was a different kind of favor."

"No." Carlyle was suddenly incredulous. For all Janine's seeming sincerity in this moment, wasn't she the ultimate bullshitter? Weren't they all down in Mexico—hadn't Tom just lost a finger—because Janine was such a stupendous liar? "Dad wouldn't do that. Are you saying what I think you're saying?"

"He told me he owed that guy a lot of money and that I could help. I told him I didn't have any money, but he said that was okay. I just needed to go out to the back parking lot and sit in the man's car. If I did that, everything would be okay," Janine was talking fast now, spewing the words out as fast as she could.

"Why didn't he just ask Mom for the money?" Carlyle could not believe what she was hearing. Seeing her sister come home late all those nights, wondering what she was getting up to, who she was seeing… was this really the answer?

"Too proud. In fact, he told me he couldn't ask Mom for the money because then she would want a divorce. That if I wanted to keep them together, I would have to just do this one favor for him…" Janine's voice trailed off and she stared at the carpet.

Carlyle could remember when she was very young, Virgil would ask Cybil to pay a gambling debt for him and she would do it grudgingly. By the time Janine was seventeen, Cybil must've drawn the line.

"So I went out to the parking lot and sat in his car. That first guy, he was cute and sweet actually. He didn't push me. I wanted to do it. I liked him. I gave him my number and we actually went out a few times after that…"

"Wait, that *first* guy? There were more?" Carlyle felt cold and clammy. The sweat between her wrists began to drip down the inside of her arm.

"Not that many—it happened a few more times after that before I moved away. Most of the other guys weren't as nice as Vick. A little while after, I heard guys were lining up to play Dad. They heard if they won they would get a shot at his hot daughter. That's when I decided to leave."

The question burned inside Carlyle. She didn't want to know the details of Janine's time with the men, but she had to know one thing. "Did Mom know?"

"It came out after my first stint in rehab. I guess I was twenty-one. They both came to Family Week and I spilled it all to her. Dad just sat in the metal fold-out chair, twiddling his thumbs. When the counselor asked him how he felt, he quoted Rilke. 'Don't be too quick to **draw conclusions from what happens to you; simply let it happen.** Otherwise it will be too easy for you to look with blame . . .' That was when she divorced him." Janine paused and looked around the room, a sudden paranoia overcoming her. "I don't want it to sound like I'm blaming him for everything, y'know. I liked it that first time. I liked helping him and I liked having the attention. I liked being the prize. The next few times, I told him I wanted to. I wanted to help him. I wanted to keep them together, for you and Tom.

"I've been with a lot of guys since then, since I moved away. I've done a lot of stupid shit. None of that was his fault. I don't think any of it is his fault." She hugged her knees, placing her chin in the small divot between her legs. Carlyle had buried her eyes in her kneecaps. The pressure felt good against her eyelids, forcing them closed—keeping them from opening and looking at her sister. But there was nothing to stop the information from pouring into her ears, like they were being submerged in a pool of cool water.

Carlyle and her father had never been close. He'd showed the first inkling of paternal interest when she was finally old enough to be considered literate; he made her read Shakespeare's plays to him at bedtime. He would turn off all the bedroom lamps and light a candle so she could read "more authentically." While she struggled to pronounce the antiquated English, he would sit back in the chair in her bedroom and stare blankly into the center of the candle's flame. Her mother had supplier dinners and bulk orders to manage, so she was rarely there to put any of them to bed.

As soon as Carlyle began to show an interest in the visual arts, her father stopped trying to mold her. It was as if he'd been attempting to produce the next great poet, and when she didn't share that ambition, she became invisible. Drawings, paintings, and photographs brought home from school would be placed in a drawer where they stacked until the drawer wouldn't close. One day, the drawer was empty.

"Daddy, where's all my art?" she'd asked. Virgil had told her it had to be moved because the drawer got too full. He could never produce any of the missing pages, however. Carlyle wondered about them for a long time, until the wondering stopped and realization dawned.

Virgil was a late-night fixture at Roxy's, the tiny bar housed inside the racetrack. The only times he came home early were when their mother had charity events to attend. Virgil would don his tuxedo and escort their mother to every community function. On weekend nights the nanny would let Carlyle, and sometimes Tom, stay up late to see their parents when they got home. On the rare occasion she didn't fall asleep on the couch waiting for them, Carlyle would see her parents flounce through the door, laughing, their limbs draped around each other. They would nuzzle her nose and scoot her off to bed, then paw at each other on the way to their bedroom.

She'd known her parents' relationship hadn't been great—or even good—despite their bi-monthly game of dress-up. As she grew older, a darkness filled her father that she was afraid to broach. Eventually, he stopped going to charity balls and dinners. Her mother would wait at the kitchen table dressed in something covered in sequins. She would stare towards the back of the house, where their bedroom door remained closed. Eventually she would gather her matching clutch and head out the door alone. Virgil would leave the house twenty minutes later, bound for the track.

"I remember them going to Family Week," Carlyle said after a long time. "She came in from the airport and Tom had made a little sign that he drew with crayon. It said 'Welcome Home Mommy and Daddy.' He was like, eight I guess. Only Mom showed up. When Tom asked where Dad was she just said, 'Your father isn't going to live here anymore.' And just like that, it was over. She never explained why. You were already gone, so was Valerie."

Carlyle had to admit to herself that she wasn't surprised about what her father had done. What did surprise her was the idea that Janine had done it to protect her. Would it really have protected her if her parents had stayed together? She thought the lie of protection was just something Janine told herself when reality became too heavy. "So why all this? What has anyone done to deserve this?" Carlyle asked, hoping to get a straight answer now that her sister was opening up.

"I never thought you guys would come," Janine said plainly. "Now everything's gotten so out of hand, we can't go back. Once we have the money, it'll all be over. I won't bother any of you again," she said, tears rolling down her cheeks. Carlyle was wary of the victim role Janine so easily adopted. For a moment, she wondered if any of the story was true.

"You can still call it off. Just let us go and forget about the whole thing," Carlyle pleaded.

She heard a key in the door and the bolt slip from the lock. Someone was coming in.

CHAPTER TEN

The room stank of stale marijuana smoke, and Tom was still passed out next to her. Carlyle's eyes burned from exhaustion and adrenaline. She looked up into the doorway to see the two thugs from earlier followed by another man. He flicked on the overhead light, and it took a moment for her eyes to adjust from the darkness. She tried to bring her hand to her eyes to shade them, but her bulky bonds stunted the gesture's efficacy. She wondered if this was the *him* she'd heard about, the *him* she instinctually knew. The ringleader. Finally the brightness of the light became bearable and she looked into his face.

"Hello, Bunny," he said.

All at once, Carlyle knew that everything Janine had told her had been true, and her own amateur detective's intuition had been right on the money.

A partially-smoked cigar poked out of the pocket of his Hawaiian shirt. "Get over there and wake him up." Virgil pointed to Tom but spoke to Tino.

"Dad," Carlyle said out loud so she herself could believe what she had suspected to be true. "Why would you do this?"

"Now, Bunny, we wanted to make sure no one got hurt. We are still family after all. Tino is going to apologize to Tom—as I've told him, only a knave hits a man when he's not looking," he glared at Tino, who gingerly bent down and prodded Tom to wake up.

Tom began to rouse from his slumber and grabbed Tino's hand in an attempt to use it as a pillow.

"What about the finger? Your son is minus a finger, you call that not hurting anyone?" Carlyle erupted.

Virgil walked over and examined his unconscious son, and as his eyes lay on the bandaged hand, his shock was unadulterated. He glowered at Tino, disgust and anger changing his face from that of a lifelong tourist to a hardened psychopath. "You fucking meathead. S'wounds! What is it with you thugs? Don't you understand that there is a time and a place for this kind of behavior? Torture was unnecessary! You didn't need any information from him, you just needed to scare him and give them the address. Is that so hard to do without maiming my only son? This is a major fuck up, Tino. This makes me want to reconsider your promotion."

Tino did not turn away or hang his head in shame. He looked Virgil in the eyes and said, "You don't have the balls to be the Capo. Things need to be done, I do them. You don't like it, go back to your books." His accent was thick, yet he knew what he was saying. Virgil flinched for a moment before removing his cigar from his pocket and slowly puffing on the end as he put a lighter to the already-burned tip. He seemed to be considering Tino's words. In a flash, Virgil had Tino pressed against the wall, a forearm pressed into the short man's throat. Virgil took the cigar and placed the burning end squarely in front of Tino's left eye. "I understand the job. This is my son, and it's because of him we're now commanding a $1.5 million ransom, so show some respect." Virgil lowered the cigar and stamped it out on Tino's cheek. Tino made no motion at all, and the only sound was the faint hiss of his skin smoldering under the ash.

Virgil pulled away from Tino and threw his cigar on the floor. The circular red burn on Tino's face was smudged by graphite colored soot. If he was in pain, he made no show of it. "That's more like it," Tino said to Virgil, who suddenly perked up as if he'd scored a perfect score on a final exam.

"You'll excuse us. It's been awhile since we've all been together." Virgil made a show of gingerly waking Tom up out of his stupor as Tino and his accomplice moved to stand in front of the door. It became clear that they weren't going to leave Virgil alone with the hostages for fear his compassion might come into play again.

"Son, wake up. I'm sorry about the finger. The ladies will love a mystery like that, trust me. Even your mother—especially your mother—will tell you that you have to crack a few eggs to make an omelet." Tom was awake but still drowsy. He groaned and grabbed his head, rubbing where the blow had come down.

"Uh, what the fuck is going on? Dad, what are you doing here?" Tom was bewildered and shrank away from Virgil as his nose wrinkled from the smell of burning flesh.

"This is my little operation. My home. What do you think, pretty nice, huh?" He looked around the pool house and the surrounding property as if seeing it for the first time. "Unfortunately, an operation like this can be expensive to maintain. I want to grow; I want more. We're going global. That's where you all come in, right Janine?" He looked at her with a manipulative tenderness, and she nodded.

"But we're going to let them go. You said we would let them go," Janine said, avoiding eye contact.

"Yes, darling, but we need the money first. Remember? We have an empire to build. I've texted Cybil. She's aware of the situation. We're still set to do the exchange at noon. Then everyone will go home happy."

"Dad, what the hell are you talking about?" Tom was still struggling to understand.

"Tom, try to keep up." Nothing annoyed Virgil more than lack of comprehension, even if his son was drugged, drunk, and concussed. "This is my cartel. I'm the one who kidnapped Janine, although it wasn't a true kidnapping, was it, dear? Since it was your idea and all."

Carlyle looked scathingly at her sister, who stared at the wall. "All those years your mother said I had no ambition, no drive—well, I just hadn't found my niche," Virgil said.

Tom looked at Carlyle, dumbfounded.

"'You've got to find your passion,' she would always say, as if a passion for life wasn't enough. After the divorce, none of you seemed to care whether I was around or not. I had nothing to offer. I was penniless—all I had was what I got in the settlement. But most great artists are destitute when they make their greatest work, so I examined my life—as my old friend Socrates suggests one should do. I had accomplished nothing. Your mother had been like a muffler on my true self. I was too comfortable to see who I really was. I was... dampened. Dreary. To be frank, I was castrated." Carlyle could tell her father had been thinking about this moment for a long time.

"As for the illegality of it all, I've never felt much allegiance to laws—they are only social constructs representative of our time and customs. There was money, heaps of money, to be made and that's what I was after. I came down here and started my business after watching a documentary on Pablo Escobar. Been at it a few years now. We started in Juarez, but it was a very messy business. Janine helped me move a lot of the product—she can be very industrious—as well as you, Tom. Sorry to hear you couldn't finish school, though. School isn't for everyone, my boy." He patted Tom's shoulder condescendingly. "We decided on Progreso as our hub—it's a perfect access point to Florida, as well as the other Gulf states, and it's much easier to breech them by water. A lot less bloody, as you can imagine."

"Using the track to launder your money, that was smart." Carlyle's uninterested voice piped up from the floor, and Virgil's chest puffed up at the compliment.

"Oh Car, I always forget about you. You are smarter than you look. Yes, the track, my old haunt. I bought it through a few shell corporations and we run about a million through there every six months. Janine was the main punter—that means better—when she was in Omaha, but since she's departed I've had some of my old pals go in with some money and place it on a horse we know will lose. They take a cut, of course."

"The one thing I can't figure out was how you got Silver Springs to give you the refund. And put it into your account. That was impressive." Carlyle feigned reverence.

"Yes, well... we needed an influx of capital to get the business going. No chance of a legitimate Venture Capitalist taking interest in our operation, and borrowing money from these types," he gestured to the thugs by the door, "is ill-advised. Your mother proved the perfect angel investor. As for getting the refund, I give all the credit to my esteemed co-conspirator." He held a theatrical hand out to the leading lady of the show. Janine did not look proud, but rather ashamed.

"One of the doctors there. He liked me. He snuck into my room the first night. I told them my lawyer would light the place up if they didn't get me a refund into *my* account. I showed them the doctor's nametag as proof—he'd forgotten it. We didn't have to wait the standard three to five business days for approval on that one." Although her words were bragging, she stared at the floor.

"Trojans! Thieves! Crooks!" Virgil spouted. "They deserved it. If only we could've taken them for more… But Janine, you're forgetting your shining moment. You're not taking credit for your own true gift." Virgil looked at Janine expectantly. Just as she opened her mouth to speak, he butted in again. "Oh okay, I'll tell them. The blog. The *blog*. It was a perfect mixture of poetry and technology, and casting El Toro— my competition and most notable Capo in the area—as the villain. It was just pristine work."

Carlyle lost her cool. "People admired you!" Her wrath fixed on Janine. "They said you were a hero! Every watch-dog group and tabloid magazine would've lined up to interview El Secreto. You… you could've gotten away from him. Gotten out free and had a whole new life. Instead, you chose this? The writing was actually *good*. God dammit Janine, no one knows how to squander opportunity like you do." She seethed. Her powerlessness overcame her like a lion on a gazelle.

"I knew you'd fall for it." Janine's voice was a barely audible whisper. "That one line. It gets you every time. How is Ethan, anyway?" Her sisterly meanness overtook any sense of shame or regret she might feel.

Carlyle let out an animalistic groan, burying her face in her knees.

The larger thug leaned over and whispered something to Virgil. He waved his hand as if he was swatting at a fly. "Yes, yes, always something to do… anyway, where was I before you interrupted me Carlyle?" he stammered, wanting to complete his perfect soliloquy. "Um, Gulf states, bloody, yes… oh, yes, I would like to say that woman—your mother," he kept reminding them, as if they had forgotten who she was, "never gave me anything, but even so, I learned a lot from her. I learned how to build an empire. After this infusion of cash—*capital*, I should say—we'll be able to take down our competitors and become the number-one supplier in this area." Virgil smiled and nodded his head in what Carlyle determined was a slight bow. Though it was buried far beneath the anger and shock at who her father had become, she felt a small flicker of pride that he had finally been able to find something he was good at.

"What if you don't get the money?" Carlyle asked.

"Let's not think about that, okay, Bunny?" He'd lost the theatrical air and his face hung gaunt against the too-bright overhead lights.

CHAPTER ELEVEN

They had just settled into bed when Cybil's phone dinged with a text message notification. It was 11:35 p.m., and they had heard nothing from the room next door except the incessant ringing of Carlyle's cell phone. The tissue-paper walls should have belied a few sounds, but no human sounds, not even a snore, came from Tom and Carlyle's room.

"I am sure they're both just sleeping," Cybil had said to Valerie as they lay down.

"Don't you think it's strange she's not answering her phone? She barely even lets it ring once, normally." They both felt unsettled as they listened to the electronic notes repeat again and again through the wall.

Cybil was checking her phone as Valerie settled into her bed. Valerie's feet had been pacing since leaving her brother's room. She was physically exhausted, although her mind felt like a full house on a wintry night—all the lights were on. "Shit," Cybil said. The word hung starched in the air.

"What is it?" Valerie asked.

"Get the hotel manager. We need to open their room," Cybil said, suddenly moving fast as lightning. "Give me your room key," she was breathless. She was out of her room and into the hallway before Valerie had heaved her thousand pound body into a sitting position. Cybil was pounding on the door to Carlyle and Tom's room. Valerie knew not to ask questions. She passed the thin plastic card to her mother, then ran down to the desk and asked the night clerk to open the room next door. He lazily handed her the skeleton key and put his feet back up on the counter.

Valerie raced back up to open the room and found her mother sitting on the floor, her back against wall made by their now-locked hotel room door. She was weeping. Tears streamed freely down her face as she looked up at her oldest daughter. "They have them. Tom and Carlyle," she eeked out.

"What? How do you know?" Valerie replied, fumbling with the key.

"The text. *Three out of four ain't bad. 1.5 mil, noon tomorrow.*"

"Shit." Valerie busted through Tom's hotel room door to find it empty. "What are we going to do? We don't—you don't have the money. What the hell are we going to do?" She was speaking to the empty hotel rooms, yet her mother could hear her from the hallway. Cybil buried her face in her hands.

"I never thought it was real. I just thought it was a cry for help. If I had known…" The tears leaked out from between her fingers.

"Mom, none of us knew. You couldn't have known." Valerie went to the bedside table and saw that Ethan was calling. She picked up the phone and answered it. "Ethan, it's Valerie."

"Valerie, what the hell is going on? I've been calling for twenty minutes. Where's Car?"

Cybil frantically mimed instructions for Valerie to avoid telling Ethan that Carlyle was missing. She knew he would go to the police if he knew the truth.

"Uh, she's in the bathroom. Mexican water and all that. Can I tell her something for you?" Cybil nodded her approval of the lie.

"She asked me to talk to my uncle about some stuff to do with Janine. He found out something weird. I should probably wait and tell her. Is she okay? Is she really sick?"

"No, she's fine. We're all just tired. You can tell me and I'll tell her, it's no big deal. I think she'll go to sleep as soon as she comes out." Valerie thought the new information might help them formulate a plan.

"O-Okay." He was unsure but went on. "Well, there's no way we're getting that ATM footage without a warrant, but my uncle did find out who owns the racetrack here in Omaha. Are you ready for this?

It's owned by two investment companies headquartered in Latvia. When you trace the chain of command through all the legal council and foreign board members, the two companies are owned by the same person: your dad."

Valerie put her hand to her forehead, trying to comprehend why the racetrack in Omaha had anything to do with a drug ring in Progreso. "Okay. Weird. I'll let Car know. Hope you're doing well." As Valerie was putting down the phone she heard Ethan say something.

"Is it okay if I meet you back in Big Pine? I can get a flight out in the morning?"

"Mom, Ethan wants to meet us at Valha—er, your house in Big Pine, is that okay?"

"If we make it back to Big Pine," Cybil muttered.

Valerie took this as an affirmative. "Sure. See you there." She put the phone down and turned with wide eyes toward her mother.

"What did he say?"

"Dad owns the racetrack. It's sheltered by two corporations in Latvia. Why did Carlyle send Ethan's uncle on a wild goose chase to find out who owns the racetrack in Omaha?"

"Hmm. I don't know, but we need a plan here." Cybil wiped at her face with the sleeve of her sweater. She looked again at her phone, then at Valerie. She considered Valerie's face for a long time. Then looking up and down the hallway, she began to gather herself. She stood up, straightened her clothing and turned to her daughter. "I have an idea," she said. "Come back into this room."

Once inside, Cybil began to check the phone and peer behind pictures. "They must still be watching us, otherwise how would they know where to find them?" Heeding her own words, she lowered her voice to a whisper. "We're going to call El Toro."

"Toro?! The lunatic drug king of Miami whose boat slip we're borrowing?"

"Yes, I've been thinking," Cybil peeked out the curtains. "If he isn't the one who has the kids, then he's competing with the person who does, right?" Valerie started searching for bugs too, but realized she didn't know what one looked like. "He could be an ally here," her mother continued.

"But what can we give him to help us? Guys like that don't work for free. And how are you so sure he's not the one behind all this? He might have just trapped us, him being the only one who knows we're here, and us here with no way out unless we pay up."

"Yes, it may be him. We've got a line to him and I'm going to use it. Assuming it's not him, I'm hoping that the opportunity to clean out a major player would be enough, but if it's not, I have a backup plan." Cybil had gone into fierce mama bear mode; it was one thing to kidnap one of her children, but quite another to kidnap three of them. "I need you to call C.J. and get him to find El Toro's man."

"Pepe?" Valerie clarified. She was scrawling notes on the hotel notepad.

"Yes, Pepe. Tell him we need to speak with El Toro tonight, as soon as possible. I know he isn't here in Progreso, so we can talk on the phone if he finds that agreeable," Cybil began to put her jewelry on, as if she was getting ready for a big meeting. She clasped the opal stone that hung from a gold chain—which was said to channel the power of the inner-goddess—around her neck. "You should make the arrangements, I'm going to prepare myself," she whispered. "Text me when you know something, I'll just be in their room. I need to be alone."

Fifteen minutes later, Valerie's text chirped its arrival on Cybil's phone. *He's calling you in 10 minutes.* Cybil had been staring down at the device, her back leaned against the bathroom counter, flipping between the pages of applications. She'd taken her sweater off, the heat of her fear rendering it unnecessary. She emerged from the bathroom and sat on the bed, looking around. She could see Tom's disheveled suitcase sitting open on the luggage rack. Next to it on the floor was Carlyle's duffel bag, the clothing scattered carelessly in and around it. The bathroom had been much the same scene: things left adrift—as soon as their usefulness expired, the toothbrushes, deodorant, and other odds and ends were left in the exact spot in which they became obsolete. Carlyle's area was littered with lip balm and uncapped eye-liner, toothpaste squeezed from the middle and moisturizer sealed with what looked like a push-on pencil eraser. Lids remained off, or nonexistent until Cybil felt them dig into the ball of her bare foot. She resisted the urge to straighten and tidy, reminding herself that there may not be anyone returning to these belongings.

Cybil marveled at how two people so different from herself could come from her, and she realized it had been a long time since she'd considered Carlyle. She thought of her often—she was counted among the guests for family dinners—but she hadn't considered her. She hadn't given much thought to Carlyle's feelings, what she might be going through, how she felt about Janine. Those two had always been close, but Carlyle was an island unto herself—or so she'd have Cybil believe. Cybil had long since abandoned trying to take care of her because it seemed she did such a good job of it herself. She wondered how her daughter was doing now.

The phone rang with a sharpness that pierced the air and she looked down to see the black box that sometimes felt attached to her hand. Unknown number.

"Hello, Cybil Pierce," she said in her CEO voice. It was the easiest to slip on and she found it hid the shaking in her throat best.

"Hola, Ms. Pierce. I don't get out of bed after midnight, even for my wife. This better be good." Diego Malecón sounded just as she expected he would. His voice was heavy with sleep.

"That's interesting, Mister—" she struggled with what to call him, "Toro. One would think in your business, you'd get a lot of late night wake-up calls," Cybil said, testing his boundary for banter.

"That is only in the movies, I am afraid. And please, to you, I am Malecón. El Toro is only a nickname. Do you lose a lot of sleep in the granola bar business?" he asked, a hint of humor flavoring his tone.

"Malecón, of course. There are good days and bad days. But I'm calling more about your business than mine," she said, knowing they both wanted to get to the point.

"Please, go on."

"Someone kidnapped my kids. I know whoever's behind this is the

leader of a cartel based in Progreso. I know you fit that description...
You were generous enough to help us gain access to this country un-
noticed, and I was able to assume the rest. Your reputation precedes
you. So, Mr. Malecón—was it you?" She was calm, and her tone took
on the authority she was used to. It did not give way to the flood of
terror she felt below the surface.

Chapter Twelve

"**A**y, your kids? Why would I do something like this? I was simply offering you a port in the storm. I knew you were coming to Progreso for reasons that may be... unsavory. But I have no beef with you, Cybil. I know who has done this—a very amateur move if you ask me."

"Who is it?" Her urgency was seeping in.

"El Poeta. What does he want from you?" Diego asked intently.

"One-point-five million by noon tomorrow. What did you call him?"

"El Poeta. The Poet. That is his nickname." A sick, bottomless pit began to form in Cybil's stomach. "He is the only other capo who works from Progreso. He has been infringing on my territory for the last few years. Very sloppy work. Do you have the money?" It seemed Malecón wanted to know for his own curiosity more than for the promise of a deal.

Cybil cleared her throat and felt a blush creep up her cheeks. "Unfortunately, no—I'm cash poor at the moment."

"Ah—granola bars, for the dogs, no? We could use more women like you on our side, and the pay is better." He laughed loudly at his own joke, then continued. "So Ms. Pierce. What do you want to do?"

"I thought we might have a mutual interest in getting rid of this guy. He's your competition, after all, and of course my interests are self-explanatory. Can we come to an agreement? We have an address where we think this person is headquartered." Cybil wasn't ready to give up her ace in the hole.

"Normally this would be agreeable to me since you would then be in my debt. But you see, Ms. Pierce… you already owe me. I helped you enter Mexico illegally. I did not ask questions. I was very generous. Now you come asking for another favor, with nothing to offer? I am afraid this is not how it works."

Cybil sighed. She could not believe what she was about to do, but she would simply have to figure it out later. "I thought you might say that. Has Pepe told you about the yacht?"

"All he said was that it was very big. And expensive. He mentioned the name, *Stuffed to the Gills*. It is yours?"

"That yacht is easily worth $50 million. Would you take it on layaway until I can come up with the money?"

Malecón was silent. Cybil knew intimately the power of a long pause—she used them universally, and almost always got people to say more than they wanted to. She wasn't falling into that trap. She stayed silent too, waiting for an answer.

"I hate to play hardball, Ms. Pierce, but there's no layaway in my world. It's the yacht for the rescue—a clean trade."

"The ransom is 3% of what that boat is worth. I'll call a spade a spade, even with you Malecón—you're taking me over a barrel, here."

"And I am supposed to risk the lives of my men, my reputation, and possibly being caught by the police to get involved in some white woman's problems? And for what? To save some children I do not know because you were stupid enough to bring them into the den of a dangerous man? I think you have called the wrong person, Ms. Pierce. It's time to say goodnight."

"Wait!" The desperation leaked out of her voice, and her hard-nosed negotiation was lost. He was calling her bluff. As soon as Malecón heard her anguish, he would know she would do anything to save her children. Could she gamble Todd's yacht away? Could he ever forgive her? And what about Doris? Maybe there was a hidden play she could employ. "Okay, Diego. You know what a mother will do for her children. My only condition is that you provide safe passage back into the U.S. for me, my family, and my captain. You will let the crew disembark and return to America, if they choose."

"I'll double their pay, I'm sure they won't mind staying. My helicopter will be waiting at the helipad two blocks east of the yacht slip. Be there at 12:30 sharp tomorrow. I will deliver your kids."

Shit! She forgot to say alive, deliver them alive, all in one piece, unhurt. "Malecón! Alive, deliver them alive—unharmed. Do you hear me? Hello? Hello?" The line was dead. She put her hand to her chest and pressed hard, sure that if it was there at all, her heart had stopped. What had she done? She went to the bathroom counter and leaned down low, then turned on the cold water and let it run over the back of her neck and hair. She watched as water beaded in her eyelashes and dripped into the drain. What the hell was she going to do? She'd gone from being in the grips of one drug dealer to the next, and now she'd given away a $50 million yacht that didn't even belong to her. It belonged to Todd. Sweet Todd. He could've been the love of her life. He would never forgive her for letting Doris go. He could never forgive her for any of it.

"It's okay, Cybil," she said, raising her head to face herself in the mirror. "You've been in worse situations. You can get through this. You did what you had to do to save your kids. It was your only choice." She looked deeply into her own eyes, waiting for an idea to leap forth. She thought of Todd's breath on her skin and the sureness of his touch. She was sure she could not go the rest of her life without it.

Then she thought of Virgil. Her ex-husband had finally found something he was good at. And Carlyle had figured it out days before any of the rest of them. *Why hadn't she told them?* "Feel the fear. Recognize it. Let it go," she recited the old mantra she used to use before big speeches. "Give the fear the space it is requesting. What is it trying to tell you?" She looked again, hard, into her frightened eyes.

She quickly turned away from the mirror, the water from her hair now dripping down her back and soaking her clothes.

Cybil peered into her hotel room. She found Valerie asleep on the full bed closest to the window. Technically it was Cybil's bed, but she didn't mind. She set her alarm for 5:00 a.m. and laid down in the double bed closest to the door. She worried for a moment that she would

not be able to sleep, but exhaustion and necessity took over. She fell
into the kind of sleep that feels like wakefulness until true wakefulness arrives. She could steer her dreams, but only with the bitter cave-
at of knowing they were figments of her imagination.

The gentle buzzing sounded but Cybil's eyes were already open.
She woke when she heard Valerie rise from bed, use the bathroom,
and go to sit at the window. She could hear gentle sniffles escaping
her and a wave of guilt so potent overcame her that she was frozen,
unable to move. Malecón's words echoed in her mind: *You were stupid
enough to bring them into the den of a dangerous man.* What had happened
to Tom was her fault, and ultimately, what had happened to all her
children, Janine included, was her fault. She lay silently listening to
Valerie cry until 5:00 a.m., when her alarm went off and her daughter
turned to meet her eyes.

"Can I get you anything, honey? How about some water?" Cybil
rose, still wearing her clothes from the night before. Her hair felt wiry
and frantic from where it had dried on her pillow.

"How are you feeling?" she asked, not wanting to let Valerie know
she had heard the crying.

"I just want this to be over." Valerie sipped the water and looked
hard at her mother. "What are you going to do about Carlyle? Are you
promoting from within or is the job posting open," she wavered for a
moment, "to anyone?"

"Let's talk about it when we get home, okay?" Cybil was not one to
criticize Valerie for talking about work at inappropriate times, but this
was too much even for her.

"These beds suck," Valerie exclaimed, sensing her faux pas and trying to change the subject. "Why the hell are we up so early?"

"Well, because I need to tell you the plan."

"Plan?" Valerie asked.

"Well, I'm going over there. Malecón told me he would deliver the
kids to the helipad near the yacht slip, but I forgot to tell him that they
had to be alive. I don't want him bringing three bodies to the helicopter and getting off on some technicality. I've seen Scarface."

"So it wasn't him? He's not the kidnapper?" Valerie struggled to fill holes in the story she'd missed by falling asleep.

"No, it's someone called El Poeta."

"Hmm. Are you sure you should get involved?"

"I'll only step in if something goes wrong. Otherwise I'm going to stay hidden. I need you to pack up everyone's things and check us out of here. Meet C.J. and get to the helipad."

"What about the yacht?" Valerie drew her lips back to reveal a face that said *uh oh*.

Cybil shook her head. "The Pierces are land-lubbers through and through," she tried to smile but her face felt paralyzed.

Cybil reached into her purse and pulled out an American fifty and laid it on the foot of the bed where it balanced, one half in the air. "Use this for anything you might need." She slipped into the bathroom with her clothes and got dressed in a hurry.

Chapter Thirteen

She sat in a cab at the residential corner facing the house that read *Casa San Benito* above the gate. It seemed like a nice place, though it wasn't her taste. She preferred classic over modern, and the more lavish the better. This house was interesting, but on the whole it was plain. Lots of whites and grays, very boxy. In the breaking sunlight she could just catch a glimpse of the sun sparking on the ocean a few streets away. It reminded her of her favorite place—her home in Big Pine Key.

"This must be some fiesta," she heard the cabby mumble.

"What was that?" she asked him.

"Oh, nada. There was a party here last night. I drop off lots of people. Even two people from your hotel. And now you going—it almost 6 a.m. That's a good fiesta that's still going at 6 a.m."

"You said two people from my hotel? What did they look like?"

"Young kid, a boy. He really wanted to party. A girl too—older. She not want to so much, but he went in and she go in after. Eh..." he wanted to continue but wasn't sure if he should. Cybil stayed silent, expectant. "She pay me to wait awhile. For her to come back. I wait twenty minute! She never come back. That is the thing with tequila, no? You can't just have one."

"Fucking kids," she said, unable to hide her maternal rage.

"They is your kids? They good looking."

"Yes, they are mine. I'm here to get them. Thank you for your time and for the information." She threw money across the invisible barrier between the backseat and the front. She opened the door to the cab to step out when she heard him say one last thing.

"If they been here all night you probably have to carry them out," he said with a jovial laugh.

You don't know how right you may be, Cybil thought as she turned to walk into the house.

After Malecón cut the line the night before, Cybil was unable to let go of the idea that he might not stay true to his word. After all, what is a verbal contract to a blood-thirsty drug lord? Now she was standing outside El Poeta's home, trying to figure out her next move.

She wanted to get close, get eyes on the situation, though she promised herself she would not step in unless absolutely necessary. She walked up the neatly manicured path and through the open gate. There were tequila bottles strewn across the yard and one upturned in a flower bed. As she got closer to the house she began to stoop towards the ground, looking into windows. Through the gap in the curtains of the front window she saw pairs of feet, some intertwined, lazing across the floor. Her heart filled with dread as she tried to surmise if the feet belonged to people who were passed out or dead.

Cybil continued creeping along the front of the house, then slipped beneath the minimalistic carport, held up by a roughly sanded raw wood beam. She tried not to let the true danger of the situation press down on her. Hidden from the view of the street, she put her back up against the wall and moved sideways along it, feeling cold plaster scrape across her back. She was simply following the playbook laid out by every episode of *Miami Vice* she had ever seen. She peeked around the corner into the back yard. The pool rippled with the light breeze that was now feeding in from the ocean. She felt the sun's glow growing hotter as it rose. On the surface of the pool, red cups floated like buoys. Pool noodles and floaties congregated at one turquoise-watered corner where the filter must have been. She saw a few more pairs of feet, this time attached to bodies. Young girls in bikinis, men in khakis and vacation wear, their flip-flops dangling about the necks of their toes.

Cybil's gaze wandered to the pool house—at least that's what she would call it. It was about the size of her own pool house, and she shuddered to think how many times her own back yard and pool must've resembled this scene after one of Tom's blowout parties.

She tiptoed through the maze of body parts, trash, bottles and cups, trying to be as silent as possible. She needed to see inside that pool house. A hollow *thonk* echoed out across the silence and she looked down to see a red cup rolling at her feet. One of the arms attached to a body began to stir. She elaborately chose each step to the back of the pool house, hurrying noiselessly out of sight.

Carlyle creaked her eyes open to see the sunlight streaming in from high in the sky. Her hands and ankles were still taped together, and the skin felt moist and pruney. She thought there might be enough moisture, both from the humidity and her own sweat, that she could slide the tape up over her fists. She tried to push it with her knees but there wasn't enough give. She flattened her hands, mimicking a prayer. Still the silver tape could not fit over them.

She pointed her toes and straightened her knees, nudging her brother. "Hey, wake up."

He groaned, again raising his linked hands to his head and rubbing the place where he'd been hit. She nudged again. "What?" he grumbled.

"Let's try to get out of here," she whispered. She scooted over to Tom and put her hands in his face. "Can you find the end of the tape? Can you start to unravel it?" He sat up slowly and began to feel blindly for a seam.

"I can't find it," he said drowsily.

"Tom, we have to get out of here. Find the end," she said firmly, looking to the bed where her sister still slept. He found a spot that felt rough and attempted to peel. The glue had set more strongly than he'd expected after so much time and such dense humidity. It was difficult to maneuver with both his hands stuck together, but he made some headway after a few moments. Each time he pulled a strip, a loud ripping sound spilled from around Carlyle's wrists. Janine was beginning to stir when they heard a key in the lock.

"Good morning, darlings. It's a very big day. You've slept late. It's time to get up and move into the living room. She'll want to see that you're well." He beamed a look of anticipation and pride into their faces. When Virgil looked at Janine for her approval, he saw that she was still sleeping. His face turned sour. "Janine. Get up. This is it, the big day. You cannot stay in bed. Get yourself together," he said the words as if he'd been saying them every day for the past thirty years. Everyone in the room knew that he hadn't.

Janine lurched out of bed and gathered her clothing, taking it to the bathroom. Carlyle heard the shower spray stutter to life.

"You two. Let's go." He waited for Carlyle and Tom to get to their feet—a challenge, given their restraints. Once they found their feet, he gestured for them to exit the room ahead of him. Awkwardly, Carlyle hopped on the balls of her feet out the door. Tom followed her form until they got out into the yard. There were still a few people sleeping on the lawn even though Carlyle could tell by the position of the sun that it had to be almost noon.

Carlyle saw a rustle in the indigo bushes lining the house. "Eyes forward!" Tino commanded.

An awkward mix of half-stepping and hopping got them across the textured concrete and into the main house. Virgil watched, amused. Once inside, he instructed them to sit on the overstuffed couch, flanked on either side by six men—two of whom were the thugs she already knew, Tino and the large man who'd stopped her the previous night. The other four she hadn't seen, but they looked like they were all still drunk from the night before. The room stank of alcohol and old limes.

Chapter Fourteen

Minutes later Janine breezed in, looking as if she'd just walked off a Paris runway. She wore a printed maxi dress and smelled of fresh-cut lilies. Carlyle couldn't stifle her jealousy even in this moment. Janine whisked over to Tino and threw her arms around his neck.

"Good morning, mi amor," she said seductively.

"I missed you last night," he said, eyeing Tom and Carlyle as if they had gotten in the way of his amorous activity.

"Tino," Virgil said stiffly. "What's that old story about dating the boss' daughter?" Tino glared at him, silent. "Let's just say it doesn't work out," Virgil said, a threat hanging loosely in the air. "Janine, you're much too good for a common thug. You've got to have higher standards for yourself." To Carlyle, Virgil's hypocrisy was dizzying. Tino glared at Virgil and Janine left her arms around his neck in her own private protest.

"Well, it's noon on the dot. She always was tardy. I can't stand tardiness." Virgil took a deep breath and his crew rolled their eyes as if they knew what was about to happen. "I think it was Horace Mann who said, 'Unfaithfulness in the keeping of an appointment is an act of clear dishonesty. You may as well borrow a person's money as his time.'"

"True to form, Poet. I hear from the gutters that you are always rambling on about some old quote or another. I am glad I got to hear you do it this one last time." The voice had started in the entryway and was making its way to the living room. Virgil's face grew pale as he searched his waistband, patting at his stomach and hips until he found the butt of the gun jutting out behind his spine. He pulled it out and pointed it at the archway that led in from the front door.

"Who's there?" he called out, the lyricism gone from his tone. In its wake was coldness and precision.

"Don't you recognize me?" Diego Malecón entered through the archway. He wore a tailored charcoal gray suit and his black shoes gleamed like glass. His manicured mustache stood above his upper lip like the eyebrows on a frightened cartoon. Tied around his shoulders was a black cape, though it must've been eighty degrees outside. Each of his fingers sported a gold ring, some with glowing emeralds and others crusted with diamonds and rubies. A diamond stud perched in his ear. Glowing triumphantly on his lapel was a jewel-encrusted brooch fashioned to look like a bull. It reminded Carlyle of her mother's hummingbird.

Virgil's crew whispered amongst themselves, clearly in awe of the figure before them. *El Toro,* Carlyle heard them utter down the line to each other. From behind the well-appointed stranger, eight men boasting varying states of physicality from toned to ripped began to file in. All of them wore tailored suits too. Suddenly the room was very hot and crowded. The stark contrast between the two organizations before her was surprising; the closest approximation Carlyle could make for Virgil's crew was gas-station-chic. Khaki cargo shorts seemed to be the prevailing statement piece among them.

Virgil took in the scene, keeping his gun trained on Malecón's head. "El Toro. I don't remember inviting you here."

"I was invited by someone else. I want you to meet someone—this is my associate, Dave." Malecón raised his hand and a tall black man took a step forward from the lineup of henchmen. "He's a world class martial artist, and he can take that gun from your hand before your nerves tell your finger to pull the trigger. I suggest you put it down, otherwise we won't be able to talk." Malecón's voice was smooth as marble.

Virgil reluctantly sat the gun down on the coffee table. "What are you doing here? Where's Cybil?" he demanded.

"Cybil won't be joining us. I'm here to take the children—Tom, Carlyle," he looked at them as he said their names. Then he leaned sideways to look at Janine, who still stood next to Tino. "Janine. You are all going home, and we are going to forget this ever happened. I am still deciding what is going to happen to you, Poet. I definitely want to kill you." Virgil eyed the gun again and Dave took another step forward. "You've been invading my territory. Recruiting my men," he paused meaningfully after each of Virgil's transgressions. "You take my business. To me that is stealing. And nothing is worse than stealing. Not only that, you have kidnapped these children. You harmed an innocent boy. And you have caused me to have to come down here and clean up your mess. Now, doesn't it sound like I should kill you?"

Virgil stayed silent. He showed no feeling. His hands were steady. "I'll just take the ransom, then," he said.

Malecón let out a laugh that made Carlyle jump. It was loud and jovial—the kind of laugh one would overhear at a park on a Saturday. "Every fiber in my being tells me to kill you. Instead, I am going to take the kids and go. You are going to sit here thinking about the fact that you owe me your life. When I come calling for a favor, you should answer." Dave took the remaining steps toward Virgil, putting the two men inches from each other. Malecón gestured to Tom and Carlyle, who stood from the couch and hopped as quickly as they could toward the door. He held out a hand to Janine, beckoning her to follow them. She stood, her feet firmly planted, unmoving. Malecón shrugged and walked back toward the front door as silently as he had come in.

One of Malecón's men removed a pocket knife from his suit jacket and began cutting the duct tape to free Carlyle. She looked back to Janine, begging her with her eyes. *Please do the right thing for once,* she thought. For the cavernous opening Janine had left in their lives, Carlyle saw now how small her sister was, and how unsure. Janine returned her sister's gaze and seemed to waiver a little, but still her feet were stones.

Carlyle gave up her silent pleading and turned to walk out the door, her limbs still a little unsure now that they were fully mobile again.

A shot rang out; the sound pierced her brain and instinctively she threw her hands up to the back of her head. She wasn't hit. Nothing hurt except her ears. She turned around to see her father slump to the ground, Tino still holding the gun extended at a right angle.

Tom, just having his hands freed, cried out. "No! Dad, no!" He struggled to free himself of the tape and ran to Virgil's body. No one else made a move to help. Blood was beginning to cover the floor and the body lay limp. Tino stuffed the gun into his waistband and grabbed Janine by the shoulders. He kissed her quickly and said, "It was for you. For us. Now I am boss. And you will be my wife." Janine's face was pale, frightened. She said nothing, and could not take her eyes off the cooling pile of flesh that had been her father. Tom rolled Virgil over and, sobbing, tried to do CPR.

"Why am I the only one trying to save him? Someone call an ambulance!" he shouted.

Suddenly Cybil was there, twigs and leaves decorating her hair and clothing, hovering over Tom.

"Honey, he's gone. He's gone. You have to let him go." She reached down and pulled her son's bloody hands from his father's chest. She was cool, collected, and relieved. She looked at Janine as if she were a stranger, a vagrant for whom she felt pity but was not willing to reach into her pocket as she'd done so many times before. Malecón's men moved to assemble around Cybil and Tom, ushering them towards the door. Cybil looked back one more time to see her ex-husband; it would be the last time. A thousand micro-calculations ran through her mind. To an observer, it would appear that the truth had just reached her, but the realization took a half-second too long.

"Wait," Cybil said hysterically. "He's my husband. He's their father. We have to take him. Pack him up, we have to give him a service, something!" She was sobbing now, trying to squeeze out tears, but none arrived. "Pack him up, I saw a cooler in the garage. Fill it with ice. He's coming with us." She went back over to Virgil and bowed over his body, mumbling some version of last rites half-remembered from a movie.

"Lady, we're not packing up this body. We've got to go." One of Malecón's henchman gingerly took her by the shoulders and tried to talk sense into her.

"Malecón said my family has safe passage and he was my family, goddamnit. He's coming."

Tino rounded up the men who were now his crew and moved them out into the back yard. Janine still stood in the same spot, her feet growing roots. Carlyle was surprised to see her mother so distraught over Virgil. Was it possible she still loved him after all these years, even after all he had done?

Chapter Fifteen

"**R**un it up the chain! We're not leaving without him," Cybil cried. Tom left the room and returned a few minutes later with the large cooler. One of Malecón's men walked out the front door, exasperated.

"El Toro had other business to attend to," he called back down the hallway as he left. "Pack up the body and let's go." With the order hanging in the air, the men began to mobilize. It was clear stowing a body was something they had done before. Each of them was careful not to bloody his suit. One returned from the kitchen with bags of ice. The sound of the ice pouring into the cooler was like an avalanche in Carlyle's ears. Cybil stayed close as two of the men picked Virgil up and crumpled him so that he would fit into the plastic coffin. They lay him on his side, his knees bent, blood still oozing—albeit more slowly now—onto the clear, pristine ice cubes. Cybil closed the lid and snapped the floppy plastic clasp. Two men hefted the cooler and carried it down the hall.

Carlyle looked back to Janine, who was still staring at the blood slick on the hardwood floor. It pooled but trickled into tributaries near where Virgil had been laying.

"Now will you come with us? We're your family. You could get better..." she trailed off. She had not even convinced herself.

Janine crossed her arms slowly, considering the prospect—or seeming to. Her eyes remained on the blood. Breaking her stare, she looked outside at Tino. He was busy reassigning roles to each of the members in his new organization. "He's my family now," she said quietly, her voice breaking. She walked out the sliding glass door and joined him.

Carlyle didn't have time to mourn. She ran to the driveway where the two black town cars already had their motors running. She jumped in the back seat and the caravan launched forward. The car had two rows of back seats that faced each other. Her mother faced her, and Cybil was startled to see her face when she looked up.

"Are you okay, honey?" she asked.

"I just can't believe she didn't come." She paused. "She told me about what Dad did to her. Back then. And now, he's gone…" She wasn't making sense. Her thoughts weren't tying together in a linear string but rather coming loose from each other.

Cybil looked out the window. Tom sat next to her with his head in his hands. He didn't ask questions about what Carlyle meant, or even look up at her as she spoke. He just sat quietly slumped over. "I'm just glad you're both safe," Cybil said finally, reaching to pat his back. The car stopped suddenly, straining her in her seatbelt and leaving her hand fixed in the air. The car lurched again and she tucked her hand back by her side. Gravel came under the wheels and the car stopped again. The driver popped the trunk. He and the man in the passenger seat hauled the cooler toward the massive helicopter that sat casting a shadow onto the water. The helipad was just a concrete square in the middle of a gravel lot. Carlyle could see the boat hangar just down the shore.

"What about the yacht? We're not taking it back?"

"It's gone," Cybil said woefully. "Everything has a price," she said, looking into her daughter's eyes. "But it was well worth it to get you two back home." Cybil put her arm around Carlyle. "Are you really okay?"

"I think I will be. It's just a lot to take in," she said.

"Well, there's a surprise waiting for you back at the house in Big Pine. I think you'll like it." Carlyle smiled. The physical contact felt strange, but she was too tired to shrug it off. It seemed strange to her that her mother was not upset about essentially seeing one of her daughters for the last time.

Valerie came down the steps of the helicopter, beckoning the rest of the party. Tom, Carlyle, and Cybil made their way to the door as the propeller began to spin. They had just gotten inside and buckled their seatbelts when they felt the ground beneath them float away.

C.J. was strapped in, his knuckles white, fingers clutching the arm-rests of the seat.

"What's wrong, el Capitan?" Cybil asked, settling in.

Valerie laughed. "This is his first flight ever," she answered for him.

"I'm a sailor, a sea dog. If man was made to fly, God would've given him wings or some shit." C.J.'s voice was full of terror, and with every gentle fall of the aircraft he jumped in his seat.

"Well, there's no nicer bird than this for a first flight," Cybil said, looking around at the leather seats and the gold-trimmed windows.

"This is the helicopter the Marine Corps was going to buy to replace Air Force One. They backed off—you know, recession and all," the captain called back to them. Carlyle looked around. There were sixteen seats in all, and the interior looked more like a private jet than a helicopter. She pressed a small golden button on the armrest and a tray popped out. Private TV screens folded out from the walls in each row. The window ledge had a hinge, and when she raised the compartment she found two champagne flutes and a bottle of Brut buried in ice. She raised her eyebrows and nodded at her mother, who was visibly impressed.

C.J. opened his eyes and gathered the courage to peer out the window. Valerie reached over and gently squeezed his arm. He took her hand, his eyes never leaving the sea outside the airplane window.

Carlyle watched the two of them. Turning her head away to give them a private moment, her eyes fell to Tom's hand, still bandaged. She wanted to reach for him, to offer to change his bandage and clean his wound—anything that would serve as penance for the pain he had suffered. She wanted to hug him, to comfort him, but most of all she wanted more for him than the loss of a sister, a father, and his finger. She wondered if Janine would ever fully comprehend the loss each of them had suffered—visible or not.

She thought back to the years when she and Janine were children. They had been close; Janine was her primary caregiver during those years when their mother was growing the company. They'd had babysitters and nannies, but Janine had taken it upon herself to raise Carlyle.

One time Carlyle had begged and begged Cybil for a pet, a cat or a dog or something. They were at the pet store picking up fish food when Carlyle saw the frogs. They were bright green African tree frogs with beautiful bulbous orange toes. They hopped from branch to branch in their terrariums. Carlyle loved them instantly and pleaded with her mother—"Please Mom, they're in a cage just like your fish. They won't make a mess. I love them!" She got the frogs, a male and a female, and she named them Jemima and Louie. She got everything that one needs to take care of frogs, including a month's supply of frozen worms.

To prove that she was worthy and capable of taking care of her own pets, Carlyle dutifully fed the frogs a tiny packet of frozen worms every morning before school. When she got home from school she would dote on them and watch them from outside the cage. She would stick her finger inside the cage and pet them. She noticed after a few days that the frozen worms she'd left for them were still there on the bottom of the cage and had melted into a slimy, watery pile of goo. "What's wrong, Jemima, you don't like your worms?" The frogs blinked their big eyes back at her and hopped about. They seemed happy enough, maybe they just weren't that hungry. She cleaned the cage and refreshed their water, constantly trying to think of ways to improve their lives.

As more days went by, the frogs still weren't eating. After a full two weeks, the frogs began to turn from green to white. Carlyle was distressed and wanted to stay home from school to make sure they would be all right. "We can figure out what to do with them when we get home, ok?" Janine told her.

That afternoon the frogs were looking worse, the color almost completely drained from them as they limply hopped around. Their skin looked almost transparent and the beautiful orange bulbs at their toes were now a dull beige. Carlyle cried. She knew that she would never be trusted with a pet again, and why should she? She'd let Jemima and Louie down. She tried a few more times with the worms—she tried heating them up, she even tried digging in the flower beds for live worms—but to no avail. Janine looked on as Carlyle came undone over the frogs. "I bet they've turned white because they miss the outside. They want to be in the real trees and grass. They would love you so much if you let them go to live in the back yard. They could hunt worms and I bet they'd turn green again in no time," Janine said. The girls carried the terrarium outside and opened the lid.

Carlyle laid the terrarium on its side and called to Jemima and Louie, "You're free now! You can come out. This whole yard is yours to live in. You can find all the worms you want." She was shattered to let them go, but knew it was their only chance for survival. Janine patted her on the back and stroked her hair as they watched the frogs find their way out of the cage. Once they'd made it out, Janine picked them up and placed them in a nearby tree. They sat side by side, and both girls knew that the frogs would probably not last the night. "But," Carlyle thought, "at least they'll spend their last night free."

She cried for a few minutes more, and her sister hugged her in the twilight. When they turned around Jemima and Louie were gone.

"You were a good mom to them, they'll remember that," Janine said. Carlyle had never been so grateful to have her sister there than at that moment. She wondered now if she would ever see Janine again.

Chapter Sixteen

The helicopter landed in an empty field off to the side of Overseas Highway. There were few areas that weren't sinkable, so this would have to do if they were to be undetected. Within seconds of landing, two more black town cars were there to meet them. The drivers filled the cars with their luggage and thunked the cooler down in the trunk. The car sank with its weight. They could hear the ice getting slushy inside and Carlyle hated to think what this heat and water would do to a decaying body.

The drivers took them straight to the doorstep of Cybil's house and helped them unload their bags. They then disappeared as quickly as they had arrived.

"Say what you will about psychotic drug lords, that guy's got class," Carlyle said. Her mother exaggerated her nod comically, and the family laughed. They were happy to be alive and back in their own homeland. "Hey, Valerie... I'm sorry." She finally managed to get the words out. "About what I said, I mean... at the hotel." Carlyle stumbled through, hoping her sister could discern her sincerity. A brush with death—and the confirmation that although life often seems permanently fixed, anything and everything can change in an instant—made her wish she hadn't been so awful to her sister. That bile could've been the last thing she'd said to Valerie.

"It's okay. You were just playing the hand you were dealt." Valerie's smile was smug, and she was already adopting the jargon required of Cybil's second-in-command. Carlyle could tell their argument had truly wounded her sister, and it would take more than a half-baked apology to make amends.

The door of the house opened and Ethan emerged. He ran down the steps and took Carlyle in his arms. He squeezed her tight and she glued herself to him, cursing herself for all the times she'd held back, all the times she'd been too distracted, when she'd halfheartedly kissed him goodbye. She wished every hug and every kiss could be like this one. It felt like ages since she had seen him. "What are you doing here?" she asked excitedly.

"I talked to Valerie last night. Didn't you get my message? About your dad and the racetrack? I told her I'd meet you guys back here," he said, still holding on. Carlyle shot her sister a look and Cybil bowed her head a bit.

"Oh, I got the message alright," she said, looking sideways at her family.

"I knew you'd like the surprise," Cybil said sheepishly as she carried her things inside. The rest of the family followed and left Carlyle and Ethan alone.

"Did you get my text?" she asked.

"Yes. Did you not see my response?"

"The last twenty-four hours have been... crazy." She looked at the ground, momentarily remembering the dim room, her sister's confession, and what followed. "My phone battery died, so Valerie packed it in my luggage."

"Hey," Ethan said, lifting her chin so that her eyes could meet his. "Your text was all I wanted. I just want you. I want us."

Carlyle looked into his eyes and remembered what she'd told her sister. *We all have a choice in who we become.*

"I'm tired of being inside my head. I want live out here, with you. I *do* want to have a baby with you someday, but only because I want to meet that person—I want to give that person to the world. I don't want a baby because it's the next step, or because it will keep you with me, or because *then* I can be the person I was meant to be. I want one because the best of you and the best of me will make one amazing person." This confession made her realize that there just might be a minute but distinct part of herself that was happy with who she'd become. "But I want him or her to come of their own free will, in their own sweet time. Because I've got to figure out what I want to be when I grow up. And I've got things to do, places to see and a husband to love in the meantime." She felt clear and calm and radiant. The voice in her mind rose up, full of predilections, judgments and fears about the future, but for the first time she was able to quell it, tame it. To turn it down to a whisper.

Ethan smiled at her, the smile she'd forgotten to check for. It was here, and she knew she had never really lost it. "You got it," he said.

He held her again, the sun warm on the back of her neck. A slight breeze ruffled the long thin leaves of the palm trees and she had the feeling of coming home, though she knew the place she called home was three thousand miles away.

"Valerie, can you really do this? You really think you can handle the stress?" Cybil was debating with Valerie when Ethan and Carlyle walked inside the house.

"I've been through law school and I have a food science degree. I am the most overqualified applicant ever, I have lived my life for this job. It means everything to me." Valerie, never one to hold back, was earnest.

"There are no tests. No assigned reading. No points for participation. This is a real job. Your grade is measured in stock points, your final exam—"

"Stop, Mom! I get it!"

"Your final exam is firing someone with three kids to support," Cybil rambled on, knowing that she'd become a walking joke.

"Your dorm room is a cubicle!" Carlyle preached on. "Your roommate is an over-emotional gay man who is scarily good at googling things!" The family laughed harder, picturing Marius hunched over the keyboard typing furiously. "Oh, that reminds me. We'll have to tell Marius. Oh, that makes me sad." She looked at Ethan.

"You can always go by and visit," he said.

"What are you going to do now, Carlyle?" Tom interjected the one obvious question that no one was supposed to ask. Her face burned red as the room's attention landed on her and waited for an answer. She had to have an answer, as a Pierce. Pierces always have a plan. But, just as she was about to say, "I don't know," a plan actually did begin to materialize.

"You guys will laugh," she said sheepishly.

"No, tell us!" they clamored.

"I think I actually want to try to become a detective. And if Mom wouldn't kill me for taking him, I'd like Marius to come with me and be my crime-fighting assistant." She realized how ridiculous it sounded. A childhood dream, a silly, romanticized, nonsensical notion. A notion that she was sure she had to pursue.

"Isn't that dangerous?" Ethan knitted his eyebrows.

"Well, actually, there is some intel I would love to get from some of our competitors..." Cybil remarked.

"Corporate espionage is highly illegal, Mom," Carlyle's face turned serious, but she knew striking out on her own would be easier if she already had one big client.

"You've got to crack a few eggs to make an omelet!" Cybil chirped. Carlyle shot Tom a dubious look.

"So she really didn't want to come back with you?" Ethan asked.

"I don't know. She just looked... empty. She walked out to join Tino—the boyfriend—on the patio to become Mrs. Cartel. It was like someone getting shot and people being kidnapped was everyday life for her. My Dad said the whole thing was her idea." Carlyle thought about Janine, still not sure how to feel about who her sister had become. Should she mourn her as dead? Did she still even have a sister? Should she live in fear that Janine would show up at her house in the middle of the night, running from something?

"I have to say, I never saw this coming," he said. "I knew she was trouble, but it all escalated so fast."

There was really no more to say about the subject, and Carlyle resigned herself to give Janine a funeral in her mind, take the time to grieve for the Janine she'd known and loved: the girl who had helped her release her pet frogs, the girl who had born the brunt of their father. That girl was surely never to return. She felt a sick pit of grief but knew not where to place it.

"Why don't you and I take some time down here? We could explore, take some time to, uh, I—we could… reconnect." He said the word tentatively, not wanting to assume there was something lacking, but bold enough to suggest it.

"Are you sure?" Carlyle asked Ethan. "What about work?"

"Well, I kind of left in a hurry, and I told them that it would be great if they could hold my job for me until I got back, but I had a marriage to save and I didn't know how long that would take," he said. Ethan had never quit a job without leaving the proper two weeks' notice. "Charlie understood, and Simone—his wife—thought it was romantic as hell. She told me they would have a place for me whenever I wanted to come back."

"Wow. That's amazing," Carlyle said. She couldn't remember the last time the two of them spent a whole day together, let alone several days with no distractions. Her fear began to sing again, like a canary—or a stool pigeon. *What if they weren't the same people anymore? What if he'd fallen out of love with her, and the idea of rescuing her was the only thing that brought him here? What if too much bad shit had happened? How can you come back from that?*

"Hey," he said in that same soothing voice. It was tuned to her frequency. "I'm scared, too. This is all new. You actually quit Naturebar—I never thought you would. I thought you would choose it over me, and then it would be easy to walk away. But you're here, and I'm here—it's the end of the date, and I want to eat pancakes."

She looked at him, her eyes full of something like hope. This was the man she'd wanted. The man she threw it all away for once before— the poor musician bartender who had no connection to her mother, her mother's friends or her mother's company. The man she threw it all away for a second time—renouncing the corner office and the black trousers and the certain future. She had to thank Janine for that. She saw an alternate path—a path in which Janine had not sent a text message—and in that reality, she saw herself staying later and later at the office, pushing Ethan away until one or both of them spoke the D word: divorce. And they each would've been relieved they hadn't had children, they each would've carried on. And again Carlyle saw her slack face drooling on top of a whale while Ethan met a light, bouncy server at the bar.

Tears began to pool in her eyes, both for the man before her—that he was in fact before her—and for her sister. That she would never be able to thank Janine for changing the course of her life.

"So, let's make pancakes," she said, placing her fingers in his hair and pulling him to her, their mouths forming the perfect overlapping-movie-scene-kiss.

Ethan jerked his head back suddenly, looking at her with intensity. "But, I really am hungry. Can we *actually*—and metaphorically—make pancakes?" He smiled.

After a filling breakfast-for-midnight-snack, Carlyle and Ethan trotted off to bed together, and she was giddy to be sharing this sacred space with him again, though they almost felt like strangers. They lay together in the guest room of her mother's house, the window open and the tropical breeze blowing through. She pressed herself against him, relishing the heat and stickiness brought on by the humidity. She tried to hold her eyes open. She wanted her homecoming to be romantic and sexy. She had visions of pulling off lingerie and making pouty faces for him. Instead, she lay limp on his chest, fighting to stay awake. She groggily moved her hands on his chest and he raised his hand to clasp her fingers.

"There's plenty of time for that," he said. "Is it okay if we just do this?"

"Yes. Let's just do this. Strange but—" Carlyle interrupted herself with a yawn, "—this is one of the things I missed the most." Her head settled onto his chest and his arms encircled her shoulders. She noted to herself as she fell asleep that no part of her wanted to run away; she craved no space between them. She was happy as they were, and she was able to remain there.

EPILOGUE

A few weeks had passed since they'd returned. Cybil had been calling and texting Todd, but since he'd found out about the yacht, he'd gone cold. Though he was well practiced in the Buddhist art of letting go, he was struggling with letting his prized trophy, Doris, go to the wind. She checked with his assistant to make sure he was in Big Pine Key before calling the delivery driver to meet her there. The Fedex truck pulled up just as she was getting out of the car, and she watched as the delivery driver opened the back of the truck and wheeled out a tall light-colored wooden box on a dolly. He lowered the lift to the concrete driveway. When he'd reached it, he tilted the box back onto the dolly and began bringing it up the front steps to the front door.

She rushed forward to stop him before he rang the doorbell. "I can take it from here, thank you so much," she said to him.

"But what about my dolly?" he said, still holding its handles.

"I'll buy it. How much do you want for it?"

"I don't know, like twenty-five?" he said. She paid him and he got back into his truck and pulled away. Cybil smoothed her hair and checked her makeup in the shiny windows that framed the door.

She pushed the button and listened to the monks chanting. Her heart flickered and she hoped like hell he was home.

The door clicked open and there he stood in white linen pants and bare feet. When her eyes made their way to his face, she saw that he was not happy to see her.

"Hear me out, please don't slam the door," she said, putting a hand out. "I am so sorry about your yacht. And about Doris." All the air left her as she said the whale's name. "Please understand, it was really the only way I could get my children back." He looked into her eyes, and she could see that he was truly grief-stricken for his loss.

He spoke in a quiet voice. "For years I've been embracing the unknown. I've known cognitively that nothing is permanent. But my heart aches nonetheless. I have given up killing, but the thing I have not been able to give up is the revelry—revelry in my past, revelry in my successes. Doris was the crowning moment of my past life. And you just gave her away, without consulting me, without so much as a wave goodbye. We could've talked through other options—we could've..." he choked. "I just don't know if I'm ready to forgive you." His voice was full to the brim, and he knew if he moved or blinked the tears would come spilling out. "I'm looking into putting a team together to get the yacht back—high level investigators, former Seal Team Six guys—"

"Ooh," she broke in. "I know someone who can help with that. Carlyle quit Naturebar to become a detective. She owes you, I'm sure she would help." He looked at her as if she had a screw loose. "And, about Doris, I know all that. She was beautiful, and nothing can replicate that moment, the moment you took God and nature in your hands—and you won. There's nothing that compares to it. And I truly am sorry." She paused, waiting to see if he would turn away. He stayed facing her. "If you'll allow it, I've brought you a peace offering. If you still want me to leave after you see it, then I will leave and you will never hear from me again," Cybil said.

"Alright," he said. "What's in the box?" His curiosity was getting the better of his bitter exterior.

"You'll need to take me to the trophy room. We can open it in there," she said, looking side to side for any evidence that they were being watched. He let out a sigh and began to walk down the hall. She leaned the heavy box back against the dolly and rolled it after him. The secret door opened and the two of them went through it.

"Okay. So what's the big secret?" A smile began to crack through, and for the first time she felt that her scheme might work to win him back.

She removed the dolly from beneath the box and began to gently shimmy the lid off. Beige strips of crinkled paper fluffed out as soon as the lid was removed. She began to clear away the paper and the object started to take shape. Todd raised his hand to his face in disbelief. Once the paper was cleared away, she began to shimmy the figure out of the box. Standing at 5'7" with his arms crossed, a smug look on his face, was her ex-husband Virgil. Stuffed.

"How did you… ?" Todd was shocked, and she couldn't tell if he was disturbed or giddy.

"I found Gil's mark on Doris when I was… examining her. It was like, his seal. His signature. I knew you must have a pretty unique and… discreet taxidermist, and at the time I thought it would be good to save the name in my phone just in case I ever needed it."

"What did Gil say when you brought him this?" Todd asked in wonder.

"He said, 'At least it's not a whale,'" she couldn't stifle her intense laughter, and he joined her, the two of them laughing until their sides hurt.

"Well, who is he?" Todd asked, gesturing to the figure once he'd recovered.

"He's… my ex-husband. Also known as El Poeta, the Mexican drug lord. He was killed by one of his own men, a mutiny." Todd was rapt at the story of the catch. He took a step toward her, and reached for her earlobe, giving it the gentle tug she'd come to crave. "He was the one who was behind it all. The whole kidnapping. I had no idea—until I heard his name—'El Poeta.'" Todd drew himself into her, and she could feel his hardness against her. He began to kiss her neck. She tingled from head to toe.

"Tell me the tale of your biggest catch," he whispered.

"He'd ruined Janine's life and had my other two kids in restraints. Malécon—the guy who has the yacht…" she stumbled through the story, unable to think with him so close. "He'd walked away and El Poeta was going to live. I couldn't believe he was going to get away with it—with all of it. But then his second-in-command, tired of taking orders from such an old windbag, grabbed the gun off the table and shot him. He shot him right in the head. He was dead instantly." She stared into the eyes of the figure as Todd wrapped himself around her. The weight of the story fell on her. "I wanted you to have it—him. He's a token from me. You'll know that I trust you with my darkest secrets now. What other gift could have made up for Doris?"

"I understand this gift," he breathed. "I understand you. You took a risk giving it to me, and I respect that. But this tells me a lot about you, Cybil—a lot about us." He moved from her, taking her in with his whole vision. He took her hand and warmth oozed across her chest.

"There's an us?" she asked, her head bowed so that her irises rested just below her lashes when she looked up at him.

"There is an us, just as there is a sky and an ocean. Let's go for a drink, and you can tell me the story again, tell me of the rescue, tell me of the great heroine, Cybil Pierce." He seemed to have regained his composure, but his hand gripped hers in a gesture that said he was not going to let her go—ever. Thus entwined, they left the trophy room, where the lights went out on all the creatures there, and all the secrets they kept.

AUTHOR'S NOTE

It is important to recognize and talk about the fact that there is darkness inside of all of us. It comes out in different forms for different people, and we don't always know what to do when someone we love is struggling with issues that are beyond our control. That being said, there are organizations to help us deal with these realities.

If you know someone struggling with addiction issues, you can learn how to best support them at http://www.projectknow.com.

Additionally, this book in no way endorses or idealizes the killing of big game animals for sport. Trophy hunting is a real and present danger for many animals, most of whom are endangered. Unfortunately, the world we live in allows for so many forms of animal cruelty that this and many other atrocities fall to the bottom of the list for organizations like PETA (People for the Ethical Treatment of Animals). A British organization called The League Against Cruel Sports (www.league.co.uk) seems to be the only resource available for people who want to get involved in stopping this kind of hunting. If you feel strongly about this issue, I encourage you to do some research, and start a movement to protect these animals.

ACKNOWLEDGEMENTS

Although you wouldn't know it, it takes a lot of people to write a book. The popular picture of a writer working on a book is someone huddled over a computer screen, haggard and surrounded by coffee cups, wine glasses and junk food wrappers. While I'll be the first to admit, there is a fair amount of that, there is also a lot of collaboration, support and love that happens too. First I have to thank my understanding, dreamy husband Rusty who always knows to head for the bunker anytime I say, "I have an idea." He's a soundboard, a co-conspirator, a warm shoulder and a devil's advocate and I thank him for every bit of it. Thank you to my baby, Eva, who inspires me to be the best version of myself every day. I want you to be proud to say, "That's my mommy!" Thanks to Sharí Alexander for recognizing my love of writing and encouraging me to pursue it. Thanks to Becca Heyman, who I found in a very fortuitous turn of events many years ago, and who has become a cradle for all my crazy. Without her, this book would have never happened. To Nils Parker, I appreciate your honesty and expertise—it takes courage to tell authors what they definitely don't want to hear. To my early readers, Jim Stovall, Kelly Morrison, Rick Thompson, Greg Augsburger, Kristin Valentine, Avery Skalla, Adam Hetherington, and Janet Mobbs—thank you for taking a chance and many hours of your time to offer your opinions, thoughts and kind words. You encouraged me more than you know. To Courtney Stubbert, thank you for the amazing cover design, and for seeing art in something I was far too close to. To Peter Barlow, thank you for your ever-seeing eye for detail and your creative spirit—the interior design is perfect because of you.

Most of all, thank you to my family—Dad, Mom, Cristi, Jen and Jacob—without whom I wouldn't have humor, inspiration, or creativity. I know that it takes grace and grit to see parts of yourself (however miniscule) in print and I appreciate that all of you are overflowing with both.